The BONSAI

The BONSAI

CARROLL HOFELING MORRIS

Shadow Mountain
Salt Lake City, Utah

Shadow Mountain is a registered trademark of
Deseret Book Company, Inc.,
P.O. Box 30178, Salt Lake City, Utah 84130

First printing August 1986
Second printing September 1986

Library of Congress Cataloging-in-Publication Data

Morris, Carroll Hofeling.
     The bonsai.

     I. Title.
PS3563.O87398B6   1986   813'.54   86-10121
ISBN 0-87579-038-0

To my parents,
Bill and Dola Hofeling,
for their examples of
courage and dignity

Acknowledgments

Special thanks to Peggy Martinson, Cancer Care Coordinator at Methodist Hospital, who read the manuscript and made valuable suggestions, and to bonsai expert Kevin Oshima, who explained the art of bonsai, gave me a tour of his garden, and also graciously agreed to let me include him in the book.

Mae Thomlinson's Family

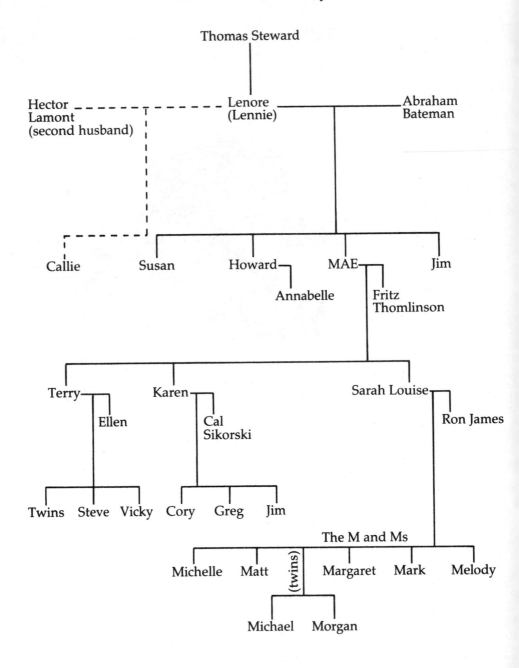

1

She laughed when the doctor told her.

The sound that filled the hospital room was not an inane whinny, nor was it a voiced exhalation of fear; it was, rather, a sound of genuine amusement.

"I'm not sure you understand," said Dr. Melton, his frown extending to its accustomed place between his eyebrows.

"Oh, I understand, all right," replied Mae Thomlinson, patting his hand in a motherly fashion. "It's just that God has done it again, the old sneak. Oh, don't be shocked that I talk about him that way. We've known each other for a long time."

She lay back in her hospital bed, an enigmatic smile on her lips. "He's got this little trick he pulls on me: every time I think there's something I couldn't possibly stand, he gives me the chance to find out that I can after all."

"Mrs. Thomlinson—"

"You know what I'm talking about, don't you? If someone says, 'I'm glad it's Diana's daughter in that situation; I don't know what I'd do if it were mine,' your first response is, 'Don't say that out loud, or you'll get a chance to find out!' Isn't it?"

Dr. Lee Melton smiled slightly. "I guess I know what you mean."

"When I nursed Callie—did you know my half sister?— through those awful last months, I made sure I never once said, 'Anything but cancer.' I was practically paranoid about it: I didn't write it in my journal; I even tried not to think it, much good did it do me." She paused and an amusing thought gave her mouth an oddly humorous slant. "You know that little gnome I have in the corner of my flower garden? He's been sitting there so long, I sometimes forget he's even there. Well, God sits in my mind like that gnome in my garden, and he knew all along."

The doctor almost laughed out loud. Instead, he twisted his mouth against the inappropriate sound, and when he could trust himself, he asked, "You don't mean to say God's to blame for this?"

"Not exactly. I guess I feel like Job: 'The thing which I greatly feared has come upon me.'"

"Is that in the Book of Job? I don't remember it."

"It's not an exact quote, but close enough. So. Have you told my daughter yet? She won't take it very well. She doesn't like me to be sick, you know."

"No, of course not. You did say you wanted me to tell you first. But I've called Sarah Louise. She and her husband will be coming at eleven."

"I'm glad you're going to break the news—she would probably tell me not to imagine things."

"I wish this were a matter of imagination," said Dr. Melton soberly. "Now you get a little rest before they come, okay?"

Mae nodded and leaned back against the pillows he arranged behind her.

Well, I knew it all along, she thought, remembering that odd moment when she had been suspended in the air above her hard bathroom floor. She had stepped out of the shower, expecting her feet to rest safely upon the bath mat with the special nonskid back. Instead, the strange, unbacked mat—which she hadn't noticed before stepping into the shower—slid out from under her. It seemed to her that she fell in slow motion. In the moment before she hit the floor, the thought came to her clearly: this is the end.

At first, she was sure she had broken her hip, for she knew that happened often enough to be a cliché and was the beginning of the end for some older people. But the X rays revealed no breaks—the pain she was suffering was due to deep bone bruises on her hip and a sprained ankle.

Still, the emergency room doctor had admitted her "So you can get a head start on healing," as he put it.

Because her own doctor had recently sold his practice and retired, "young" Dr. Melton took her case. She was surprised when he spent more time asking her about the frequent, severe gallbladder attacks that she had been plagued with recently than the injuries caused by her fall.

"How long has this been going on?" he had asked, frowning.

"A few weeks, I guess."

"And have you had any other problems?"

"Nothing except the flu."

He raised his eyebrows.

"I couldn't seem to shake it this spring. I would just get over one bout, and I'd get hit again."

"What makes you think it was the flu?"

"What else would it be? I was so nauseated, I couldn't eat a thing." Then she added with a smile, "This slim figure you see is not my usual condition. Normally, I'm pleasingly plump."

But Dr. Melton had not been convinced. "Now, I don't want you to worry, but I have a feeling there's more to it than the flu, Mae. I'd like to give you some tests."

"What tests?" asked Mae, the strange certainty strong in her again.

"Oh, X rays, a gallbladder series, things like that."

He had ordered the tests to be done immediately, in spite of the pain that moving caused Mae. The results he had just explained in cool, clinical terms had not surprised her.

So this is what it's like to know that you're going to die, she thought. Strange, but it doesn't seem so awful. It seems rather inevitable. I don't suppose that Sarah Louise will think of it that way, though. She'll probably take it personally.

But Mae had never been one to take things sitting down, much less lying down, so she eased out of bed and went into the bathroom to fix herself up. After all, Sarah Louise would be coming soon, and later on, afternoon visitors.

Mae washed herself, changed gowns, then brushed her

hair and put on her makeup. She did it quickly, because she didn't like looking in the mirror. In fact, she had avoided mirrors as often as possible since her thirties. Her husband, Fritz (God rest his soul), had teased her about it, accusing her of being oversensitive about the lines that were beginning to fan out from the corners of her eyes. She hadn't told him the real reason for fear he would laugh. How could she tell him that she often didn't recognize the face she saw in the mirror as being her own, that it sometimes surprised her? Is that what I really look like? she would ask herself then. It didn't seem to match her strong inner feeling of self.

She felt much better when she eased back into the hospital bed. With her hair combed, her makeup on, and a splash of cologne behind her ears, she knew—at least for now—that she didn't look spectral, despite her recent weight loss.

Her short grey hair was clean and, thanks to a permanent, curly. She had pulled a few strands down on her forehead and in on her temples. She had worn her hair that way for years because she thought the curls made less of her forehead, which was so much broader than her once-pointed chin. The rosy blush on her cheeks had been applied carefully so as not to look clownish, and her still-full lips were colored lightly in the same shade.

I'm ready, she thought. But she was taken entirely by surprise when, an hour later, Sarah Louise opened the door to her room. "Oh, Mama," she cried and rushed across the room to fling herself, sobbing, into Mae's arms.

"There, there," said the startled Mae. Taking advantage of the rare opportunity to hold her daughter, she stroked Sarah Louise's hair (which gave meaning to the word "mousy") and patted her back. "It's all right," she said.

"Oh, how can you say that?"

"Well, I didn't mean it literally." Mae smiled at her son-in-law over the top of her daughter's head. Ron managed a wink in return as he took her extended hand in his own.

Sarah Louise sat up, wiped her eyes, and blew her nose. In spite of her tears, she looked neat and in control. Her round, blue eyes weren't reddened from crying, nor was her undistinguished nose. Only her small, bow-shaped mouth was less than just right: it lacked the frosted pink lipstick she usually wore. "Mother, Ron's already called Brent," she said, folding her tissue. "He'll be here soon, and they'll give you a blessing."

"Thank you, Ron," said Mae, grateful that the lay priesthood-holders of her church could perform that ordinance.

"And Dr. Melton says that if you start chemotherapy right after the operation—"

"We'll talk about it later, Sarah Louise."

"It sounds perfectly awful, I know, but Dr. Melton says it's necessary, and that there's no time to wait. You can have the first treatment right here in the hospital before you come home."

"Sarah Louise—"

"Remember how you hated seeing Callie after all her beautiful hair fell out? You don't need to worry about losing yours. They've got some sort of hat made of freezeable material that you wear over your head. It's supposed to help."

"I suppose I can survive the loss of my hair, dear, *if* I decide to have the chemotherapy. That's not what I'm concerned about."

"Well, you don't need to be concerned about a thing," said Sarah Louise, ignoring the "if" that her mother had stressed. "You can come home with us when you leave the hospital. We'll move the twins out of their bedroom. That way, you'll have a bath of your own. I'm sure you'll enjoy having the kids around you. It'll keep your mind off of things."

"I don't want to keep my mind off of things."

"Oh, Mother, don't get morbid. Aren't you the one who's always saying it's best not to dwell on negative thoughts?"

Mae was tempted to point out the difference between being unnecessarily negative and being realistic, but she decided not to. Instead, she retreated into herself, even though she knew Sarah Louise would find that equally exasperating. Her hand felt warm and safe in Ron's; the sound of her daughter's voice, by the time it filtered

5

through to her consciousness, was as soothing as the murmur of a distant sea. She had no idea how much time had passed when Ron squeezed her hand and said, "Brent's here."

Mae opened her eyes and smiled at Brent Weinburg, whom she had known since childhood.

"How are you doing, my dear?" he asked, leaning over to kiss her cheek.

"Not too well, the doctor says."

"So what do doctors know?" he joked, but Mae noted the unnatural glitter in his eyes. He pulled out his handkerchief and wiped his eyes and nose. "Hay fever already, imagine that," he said as he finished.

Mae pushed herself up in her bed so that the men could give her a blessing. She closed her eyes in anticipation of the cool oil on her scalp and the pressure of the men's hands upon her head. Ron James did the anointing, and Brent sealed the anointing and pronounced the blessing. Mae felt the strong inner presence of the Spirit as the ordinance was administered and words of comfort spoken. But they were words of comfort only: no promise of healing was pronounced upon her. It was a fact that escaped no one but Sarah Louise.

"I feel so much better, don't you?" she asked Mae in the soft, childish voice Mae thought of as Sarah Louise's Sunday School voice. "We'll get you through surgery and then get started with the chemotherapy, and everything will be fine. Of course, you might not even need it now."

The expression on Sarah Louise's face was easily readable; to Mae it was as if her daughter had spoken aloud, so clear was the thought visible there: Well, that's all taken care of.

The rest of the day Mae was kept busy by a string of visitors and calls. Mae's brother, Howard, and his wife came to see her, as did her long-time friend Edith, her bishop, and her visiting teachers. Her sister, Susan, called from Billings, and her two other children, Terry and Karen, got in touch with her after hearing the news from Sarah Louise. It was only much later, after the indifferent hospital food had been brought and then taken away, after the evening visiting hours were past and the uneasy, watchful quiet of hospital nights had descended, that Mae had time to consider what Dr. Melton had told her. But she didn't—exhausted, she slept.

It wasn't a refreshing sleep, however. Mae slept and dreamed, jerked awake, slept again and dreamed again, and finally woke fully, only to become aware of an ominous pressure behind her left eye. A migraine! That's all I need, she thought, and she began the exercise that in most cases relieved her of such pain. Although she felt better after a while, she couldn't go back to sleep, so she floated in the uneasiness of the hospital night, waiting for the dawn.

As it began to grow lighter, she busied her mind by noting the gradual sharpening of outlines that could only be identified because she already knew what they were: table, chairs, TV. Except for its spotless condition, the room occupied by Mae in the small hospital of Shelton, Wyoming, had nothing to recommend it. It was cold and graceless by thin morning light and had no cheering spots of color save those provided by the many cut flowers that had been sent to Mae after her fall. The linoleum was a shade of tan that could have been either dirty or simply ugly. As the light grew stronger, Mae, who by then had been awake for hours, decided it was not dirty.

It's probably the same ugly stuff that was on the floor when I came here to have the kids, she thought, although that hardly seems likely, seeing as how Terry will be thirty-eight this year.

But it was the same room she had lain in after Terry had been born, of that she was absolutely certain. It had the same north-facing window beyond which a box elder grew. The tree had been young then; now it was so large that the branches almost touched the glass.

She found it interesting that during her childbearing years, and for some years after, the section of the hospital demanding the greatest space had been the obstetrics ward. It was not so now. The social changes that had taken place during the intervening years had affected Shelton (population 4300) as well.

What's that new word everybody's using nowadays?

7

she asked herself. *Demographics*, that's it. The way space is divided in this hospital now is a lesson in demographics. Sarah Louise had her last baby in that new, tiny addition, and I'm lying here with a whole ward full of old folks.

The large ward, which had once been the scene of life's beginning for whole generations, had become the place of endings for another. But Mae refused to think of it that way. Her memories of what it had been were stronger than the knowledge of what it had become; they made it possible for her to keep other less pleasant facts at bay. The ghosts that haunted her room on the ward were benevolent spirits, puckish sprites of great individuality.

There was Sarah Louise, whose determination had been cloaked from the very first in a body round and soft. Just thinking about the sweet flesh aroused such a hunger in Mae that she could hardly bear it. She could almost feel the contours of a downy head in that special spot on her shoulder. Not that Sarah Louise had ever let it rest there for very long.

Then there was Mae's second-born, Karen, mouth opened in a squall, skinny arms and legs jerking in undirected motion as she sought her mother's breast. From the first, Karen had cried incessantly unless in her mother's arms. The raw, husky quality of her cry was so distinctive, Mae had been able to recognize it from far down the hall.

And Terry. Even as a newborn, he had been alert and full of energy and charm—he instinctively knew how to get everyone to gladly give him what he wanted. He was the child most like Mae's father, Abe. Although both the girls' reddish-blond birth hair had been replaced by white tresses that eventually turned an unremarkable blond, Mae knew the moment she saw him that Terry's coarse, carrot-red hair, so like his grandfather's, would not change. She knew that the milky skin that comes in tandem with such hair would be covered by freckles the moment he exposed it to the sun.

Such thoughts made her smile in spite of the headache, which had reasserted itself. She tried to forestall it again, to no avail. The pressure was spreading from behind her eye around her head, and she was beginning to feel nauseous.

8

She knew she would have to ask for something before long, and she didn't want to. As a matter of principle, she avoided taking medication unless absolutely necessary. It was an idiosyncrasy that had annoyed her husband, who couldn't understand why she wouldn't just take a pill and "get it over with." And indeed, the headache was now so severe that a "quick fix," as she called it, seemed desirable. She was almost ready to push the call button when the door opened.

An enormous male figure filled the doorway but didn't advance into the room until Mae said, "Come on in. I'm awake."

"If this is room 207, you must be Mrs. Thomlinson."

"If you've come for blood, I gave yesterday," she said, glad for a diversion.

He laughed. "Nope. Guess again."

"Ah. I know who you are. You're the infamous new nurse."

"Keith Sullivan, at your service. So my fame has preceded me, has it?"

"You have to admit, male nurses are rare around here."

"So it seems," he replied, picking up her wrist to take her pulse.

"Hardly anybody new ever moves to Shelton. What brings you here?"

"Let's say a desire to get as far west from Chicago as I could without running into California."

"There're lots of places between Chicago and California besides this little stop in the road. There must be some other reason."

"I know your doctor. Melty was my buddy in 'Nam. He found this job for me."

"Melty?"

"Dr. Melton to you."

"He's a friend of yours?"

"Hey, babe, war makes strange bedfellows, as they say."

Mae chuckled. They were strange bedfellows indeed, she thought. Everything about the trim Dr. Melton was neat and contained, from his hair, which was trimmed around his ears, to his well-defined features, to his ever-crisp white coat. In contrast, Keith Sullivan seemed blurred and out of control. His longish brown hair was very curly, and Mae knew it would seem unkempt within minutes after being combed. His eyebrows grew in a line across his forehead—they were curly too, as was the hair Mae could see above the neck of his white T-shirt. It stopped abruptly in a straight line at his collarbone, and above that line his neck and chin and cheeks were shadowed with stubble.

Not only was he hairy, he was huge. Mae imagined that if he stopped shaving, he would look rather like a big bear getting ready for hibernation; his body was replete with enough stored fat to last many months. But his odd, amber eyes didn't look ferocious; they were warm and liquid—and Mae thought, I like him.

"Yeah, Melty and I were medics in the same unit. When we got out, Melty went on to get his M.D."

"And you?"

"I dropped out."

"So what happened, then? How come you decided to rejoin the rat race?" asked Mae, trying to ignore the insistent pressure behind her eye. "Religion or a woman?"

"It wasn't a woman," he said enigmatically. "Hey, do you feel all right? You don't look so hot."

"I just have an awful headache."

"Migraine?"

She nodded.

"Do you want something for it?"

"I usually don't take pills."

"None? Zero? Zippo? *Null comma nichts?*"

She had closed her eyes; she only nodded in reply.

"So how come? I don't see any virtue in suffering when you don't have to," he said, adding an expression that made Mae crinkle up her nose.

"Ah ah ah! Better watch that."

"Cripes. Melty told me I had to clean up my language. I've given up every colorful word in my vocabulary, scout's honor," he said, holding up three fingers. "I just slip once in a while."

"It's a good idea, you know. Shelton is mostly Mormon,

me included. You'll be better off if you avoid any word that has a remote connection to deity or bodily function."

"It's that bad, is it?"

Again Mae smiled, but there was nothing but pain behind the smile.

"Hey, you look rocky. Are you sure you don't want anything? Some Tylenol 3, maybe?"

"Not if I can help it."

"Why not, for cripe's sake?"

"There are natural ways of healing the body. Taking drugs seems somehow like abdicating, like giving control of myself over to something or someone else. Does that make sense?"

"Oh yeah. I've been clean for a while, but not so long that I've forgotten what the stuff does to you. But a little painkiller now and then just isn't in the same class—"

He stopped abruptly as tears fell roundly, then ran their flattened course down Mae's cheeks.

"Hey, babe, don't do that. The nurse in charge of the floor will take advantage of any excuse to get me off her shift. The way she looks at me, she must think I'm a pervert. But I'm not—I'm just fat. Okay, so don't laugh. Just tell me what you do when it gets this bad."

"Something I read about once in *Prevention*. If I can relax and warm my hands, the headache usually goes away."

"Biofeedback. Your hands get warm because more blood is going through them, and that diverts blood away from the constricted vessels in your head."

"I taught myself to do it, but I have to get started when the headache first comes. I waited too long."

"But you're still determined not to take anything?"

"I'm not sure I can avoid it now."

"Do you trust me?"

"Aren't I a little too old for that kind of line?" she asked with what was meant to be a coquettish smile.

"Actually, I had something else in mind. Are your feet ticklish?"

"They were once, but after sixty-one years, I think I've worn the tickle out."

"Do you mind?" he asked, as he raised the covers, exposing her feet.

"You might; they look pretty awful." She was embarrassed as she thought of her feet, deformed by bunions and the thick, yellow toenails of the aged. "Why do you want to look at my feet, anyway?"

"I can help you get rid of your headache, if you're willing to let me play with your feet."

"What are you going to do?" she asked as he squeezed some lotion onto his hands.

"Give you a massage, that's all. It'll hurt at first, especially your big toes, but afterward you'll think you've died and gone to heaven. Oh, cripes! I'm sorry. I forgot."

"Forgot what?"

"The cancer," he said with surprising frankness. "I read your chart when I came in."

"Well, forget it again. It's not the cancer that's killing me now, it's this headache."

Keith Sullivan began to massage Mae's feet. At first he worked slowly and carefully, every motion progressing upward from her toes toward her ankle. Then he began to concentrate on her big toes, exerting considerable pressure. She grunted with pain but didn't ask him to stop, and soon she realized that not only were her feet feeling wonderful, her headache was gone as well. In fact, her whole body was so relaxed and limp that she could barely raise her hand to his arm as she whispered, "Thank you."

Then she fell into a luxuriously deep sleep.

2

"You're taking it very well. I'm pleased to see how you're keeping your spirits up," said Dr. Melton.

If you only knew, thought Mae. But few knew, or cared to know, how she really felt. Most of those around her gladly (and sometimes willfully) interpreted her steadiness as a reflection of her faith and hope in the future. She had neither: she knew that she was going to die. All her life she had relied on the knowing that sometimes defies logic, and she had learned to trust in it implicitly. In this instance, the facts supported what she had instinctively understood even before they were noted in her chart. She had accepted it from the first. Her steadiness stemmed from the certainty that struggle, denial, or flight would be of no avail.

But even in cases such as hers, it was considered cowardly to abandon hope, Mae knew. Hope, even false hope, relieved those in attendance of experiencing the pain of helplessness and loss; it made the patients' last days easier—for them, not necessarily for the patient.

Mae remembered clearly the attitude of the professionals she had had to deal with when first her mother, then her husband, and finally her half sister, Callie, were drawing their last breaths. She had alternately clung to or despised their unwillingness to deal plainly with her. Their denial of death and insistence on hope, even at the end, had made a difficult situation more so. Their message was clear: To speak of death openly and straightforwardly was gauche.

The only person Mae could really talk to freely was Jungle Boy, as she had begun to call Keith Sullivan. She wondered if this ease of communication didn't have something to do with the fact that he was on the night shift. She thought perhaps that something about the wakeful hours of night, when the unearthly silence was punctuated by cries or desperate coughing, made it easier to drop pretense and speak openly. Then again, perhaps their candidness with one another stemmed from the fact that they had not known each other previously, making it possible for them to meet squarely on the issue that had brought them into one another's lives. Whatever the reason, she hoped that he would not get into trouble for talking to her the way he had—Mae was certain Dr. Melton would be furious if he knew that Keith had answered questions he himself had not been willing to answer.

It was Keith who had told her that her case followed the typical profile for the rare cancer of the gallbladder that she had: she was a woman over fifty years of age; her symptoms had been confused with those of gallbladder attacks; the surgery she was scheduled for would probably include the removal of the organ, after which she would need to restrict fats and other hard-to-digest foods.

It was Keith who told her that since cancer of this type was usually discovered after it had already metastasized, the prognosis was never good.

"Thank you for telling it straight," she said. "Not that it comes as a surprise, but I just wanted to hear someone say it out loud."

"Don't let on to Melty that I did—he'd have a fit."

The surgery took less time than anticipated. When Mae had come out from under the anesthesia enough to ask the inevitable "Did you get it?" the surgeon shook his head.

"There was too much involvement, Mrs. Thomlinson. Surgical removal was impossible."

Still, neither the surgeon nor Dr. Melton was about to give up, and their tone let her know they expected her to put up a good fight. Her unusually quick recovery rate convinced them that she was.

"Good heavens," said Dr. Melton four days after the surgery. "I didn't expect to see healing like this until a week had passed, at least. What are you doing?"

"Not much. I've just been imagining my incision as already healed."

"You must have one vivid imagination. You're going to be in good enough shape to start chemo before we release you."

"Can we talk about that—" Mae began, but Sarah Louise interrupted.

"That sounds fine, Dr. Melton. And thank you for all you've done."

After Dr. Melton had left, Sarah Louise said, "I know you don't want to take the treatments, Mom, but unless something dramatic happens, you have to."

"Such as?"

"You could use that imagination of yours on the cancer, for one thing. If you can think your incision healed, you can think the rest of yourself healed."

Mae shook her head.

"Why not? As long as I can remember, you've preached the same sermon. First you called it positive thinking; now it's visualization—but it's all the same. If you really believed it, you could do it."

"Not this time."

"But why? I don't see the difference."

"The difference is, I know I'm not going to die from this useless operation."

She wasn't sure afterward why she had allowed herself to be talked into having the first infusion of chemicals meant to kill the cancer without killing her, but she knew without a doubt that no matter what pressures were brought to bear, she would never agree to it again. Still vivid in her mind was the agony of the ice hat, and the wracking nausea resulting from the treatment was far more intense than the pain caused by the disease itself thus far.

It was useless pain, as far as Mae could see, for there was no beneficial trade-off. The doctor said it was meant to buy her more days, perhaps even weeks, but Keith had told her it was essentially a palliative measure. He said some experts didn't even bother with chemo for patients in her condition. Most important, however, was Mae's feeling that she had lost too much of herself in the process, for when she could finally think clearly again, she realized that three days had been stolen from her finite store.

That made her think of Callie again. She remembered the sunny day when she and her mother had sat on the lawn of her stepfather's big Victorian house in Cody, watching two baby girls who were lying in the shade on a hand-pieced quilt. The older was her own six-month-old daughter, Sarah Louise; the younger was her newborn half sister.

"I just can't think of Callie as a sister," Mae had complained.

"Then think of her as a niece," suggested Mae's mother, Lenore.

It was a way of relating that was comfortable for Mae, and sufficed for both of them until Lenore's increasingly debilitating diabetes led Mae to make the trip from Shelton to Cody twice a week. During that time, Mae and Callie learned to respect and love one another in a new way.

"I'm so glad you're my sister," said Callie one day, and Mae was surprised that she could answer truthfully, "So am I." When Callie moved to Shelton in her early thirties, their companionship grew, marred only by Sarah Louise's jealousy.

Seven years later, despite her statistical advantage as a Mormon practicing good health habits, Callie discovered a lump in her left breast. Her breast was removed immediately; a year later, the same procedure was performed on her right breast.

When she began chemotherapy after the second operation, Callie pleaded, "Stay with me, Mae."

Sarah Louise protested, "Mom, that's asking too much! Nobody can really expect you to spend all day and half the night in that hospital. You have to think of yourself."

"Sarah, where would you want me to be, if you were in Callie's place?"

"I'm not saying you shouldn't visit, but you don't have to set up camp, for heaven's sake. We can have the Relief Society arrange for someone to sit with her, and Uncle Howard and Aunt Susan can put in their time, too."

"Susan never got to know Callie, Sarah Louise. She got married and moved to Billings when Callie was two. Anyway, you can't expect her to leave her family for who knows how long. As for Howard, he does come several times a week; he just doesn't stay more than fifteen minutes. It's up to me."

Mae continued her vigil at the hospital, then at Callie's home, and finally back at the hospital.

Callie reacted violently to the chemotherapy. The drugs they gave her to counteract the reaction knocked her out for days at a time. When she finally came to, she was always weak and disoriented, a condition that lasted the better part of a month. By the time she was strong enough to enjoy visiting with her husband and children, it was time for another infusion.

It didn't help. When Callie escaped in a sigh after a ghastly death watch, Mae could feel nothing but grateful relief. She had seen something she never wanted to see again.

Remembering those awful hours now, Mae became furious. She had let other people talk her into doing something she had had no intention of doing. She was angry at them for pressuring her and angry at herself for acquiescing. No more of this, she thought. No more.

"Today is the first time I've felt like a human being since chemo," she said to Dr. Melton when he made his rounds.

"I know it's tough," he replied sympathetically.

"And I'm supposed to go through it every week?"

"Until the series of treatments is complete."

"Does anybody ever rebel against this?"

"No. It's not pleasant, but it's necessary."

"Well, Dr. Melton, I rebel. I refuse. I'm not having any more chemotherapy."

"Now, Mae—"

"Don't patronize me," said Mae sharply. "If you're *Dr.* Melton, then I'm *Mrs.* Thomlinson."

"I thought all of this had been decided, Mrs. Thomlinson," he said stiffly, his red face stern.

"Well, it's undecided."

"Maybe I'd better talk to your daughter and son-in-law."

17

"Maybe you'd better talk to me, young man. I know what I'm doing. I went through all of this with my sister, remember. I made some decisions then, Dr. Melton. For the life of me, I don't know why I didn't stick to them, or how I got talked into this, but I'm going to stick to them from now on."

"Not to have chemo was one of them, I take it."

"Yes. That's not exactly what I thought, of course. I said to myself, 'I think Callie should stop having chemotherapy. It's too hard on her when she's too weak to even get out of bed.' But I was really saying, 'I'm not going to go through that, if I am ever as bad off as Callie.' And I am, aren't I. The stuff is everywhere."

"There's still something to be gained by treatment."

"I hear the doctor speaking. I would like the doctor to remember that I am sixty-one years old, and I have a terminal illness. What exactly do I have to gain by your treatment?"

"There's always hope, Mrs. Thomlinson."

"I have my own brand of hope, thank you."

"I don't understand you," said Dr. Melton angrily. "There is an excellent protocol developed for the treatment of cancer, and you are refusing it. That's stupid, and I never thought you were a stupid woman."

"I'm stupid if I don't do what you tell me to do?" Mae demanded, her grey eyes like flint. "I'm old enough to be your mother, and I know a few things myself. The most important is this: follow your instincts. And my instincts tell me that whatever time I have left is going to be more valuable to me if I spend it the way I want to. So you can just keep your protocol!"

Dr. Melton gaped at her for a moment. Then he snapped his jaw shut and left the room, slamming the door angrily behind him.

Once he was gone, Mae pressed the buzzer urgently.

"What do you need?" asked the nurse who answered the call.

"Has Keith left yet? I need to talk to him."

"Can't it wait until he comes on duty tonight?"

"No, I must speak to him now!"

"I haven't seen him this morning."

"Will you please see if he's in the cafeteria? He eats breakfast before he leaves sometimes."

"After I get everything done, perhaps—"

"Please check now."

"If I have time."

Well, I can't wait for you to have time, thought Mae.

The bone bruise on her hip and the sprained ankle that had brought her to the hospital in the first place were much better now, and her incision no longer hurt when she moved, so she was not bound to the bed anymore. I can find him myself, she decided grimly.

Heedless of the stares, she walked into the small cafeteria that was hardly more than a lounge and scanned the tables. Keith was not hard to find—he was the only 260-pound male nurse on the staff. She walked as quickly as the lingering pain in her joints and her unaccustomed legs would allow over to the table where he ate alone.

"Hey, babe, what're you doing here?" he asked when he saw her.

"I need your help."

He got up and pulled out a chair for her. "Here, sit down. What's the story?"

She opened her mouth to speak but instead began to cry.

"Ah, don't do that," he said, taking her slim, still elegant hands in his.

"I'm sick, Keith."

"I know."

"I have cancer."

"Yes."

"They say I'm full of it. Then they turn around and say if I have chemo, there's a chance."

"What do you think?"

She considered the shape of her nails. After a while, she raised her head and looked at him steadily. "I want to go home to my flowers."

"Do you want me to help you go home?"

"Please. And I want to stay there."

He was silent for a moment, then he said, "Listen, babe, you'll have to deal with Melty about getting released. I can't afford to get him mad at me right now, you under-

19

stand? But about the rest, I know what's involved in home care, and I'll do all I can to help you, once you get home. Okay?"

Mae nodded.

"Now let's get you back to your room."

By the time Sarah Louise and Ron arrived late that afternoon, Mae was ready for them. Keith had volunteered to stay with her, but she told him she would be okay; she didn't want him to get into trouble. He was in an awkward position as it was: he was a highly visible stranger in a small town; he was a non-Mormon in a predominantly Mormon community; he had intruded on a profession traditionally reserved for women. Beyond that, he was "into" many strange things, of which foot reflexology was only one. Mae found him truly delightful and authentic and was unwilling to jeopardize his tenuous foothold in Shelton.

Sarah Louise opened the door a short time later and strode in, her face grim. "Well, you sure stirred up a hornet's nest," she said without preamble.

"I guess you've talked to Dr. Melton."

"Yes, indeed. But I won't be talking to him anymore, will I? He doesn't want to have anything more to do with you."

"I know."

"Mother, why in the world won't you do what he's asking you to do?"

"I don't want to."

"With that attitude, I doubt if any doctor will take you on. What are we supposed to do then?"

"Sarah Louise, don't push, okay?" entreated Ron.

"Well, I want to know what Mother thinks she's up to."

"I'm going home tomorrow," said Mae calmly.

"Dr. Melton told us you insisted on it. You didn't have to do that, you know. He said he probably would have released you tomorrow, anyway. And as for the chemo, I know it's not pleasant—"

Mae snorted.

"—but we'll just have to stick it out."

"Ron, Sarah Louise, please sit down," said Mae firmly. "We need to have a family conference."

Sarah Louise shrugged her shoulders. It was an "I don't

know what she's talking about, but let's indulge her" gesture. Mae's mouth tightened into a grim line.

"You've got the floor," said Ron.

"I'm going home, and I'm going to stay there."

"Of course you are, where else would you go, unless you move in with us?" This from Sarah Louise.

"Sarah Louise, please listen for a minute. I made some decisions a long time ago, before I had any idea I was going to get sick. Only I didn't really have a chance to get things straightened out in my head when all of this happened. I have everything clear now, though; I wrote it all down so there wouldn't be any misunderstanding."

She held out a piece of paper. Sarah Louise didn't take it, so Ron did. He read it, then looked up with a solemn expression.

"There's no way to misunderstand this," he said to Mae after clearing his throat.

"What does it say?" asked Sarah Louise.

"Read it for yourself."

"No, you read it for me."

Ron shook his head, exasperated, but still he read the list ,of "Noes" aloud: "No chemotherapy. No radiation. No nursing home or hospital or extended care."

Sarah Louise could only gasp, "But—"

"Are you sure this is what you really want?" Ron asked his mother-in-law.

"Yes. And there's this. It's what they call a living will. It stipulates that no 'heroic treatment' will be taken to keep me alive. I've signed it." She handed that to Ron. "Will you go along with me on this?"

"I'm not sure I agree with you, Mom. But if that's what you really want."

"Well, I won't," said Sarah Louise harshly. "I don't understand why you're doing this. You're just giving up! I never thought you would do that."

"What do you want me to do? 'Rage against the dying of the light'?"

"I want you and Ron to stop talking like that. You've always said people cause half of their problems with negative thinking and talking, now here you are, doing the same

21

thing yourself. You should be thinking about positive things, like getting out of here. That's the first thing."

Mae didn't argue. Going home was indeed the first step; the rest would inevitably follow. That fact was made abundantly clear by the prescription for a painkiller containing codeine that Dr. Melton had written out in his last official act as her doctor. "You'll need to take this for the pain," he had said. "When it doesn't help anymore, let Dr. Donnelly know; he'll increase the dosage, or give you something stronger—Dilaudid, perhaps."

His words simmered in the back of her mind all the time Ron and Sarah Louise were with her, and all through the subsequent visiting hours. They were still there late that night, when Keith looked in on her.

"How is the infamous Mae Thomlinson?"

"Who's that?"

"You've caused quite an uproar, or didn't you know?"

"What are you talking about?"

"Your decision. You're not exactly playing by the rules, you know. Some of those—, uh, some of my colleagues think you're just committing suicide."

"So do Dr. Melton and my daughter. What do you think?"

"You know I'm with you, babe."

"But what do you think, really?"

He sighed heavily and lowered himself into the chair at the side of her bed. "I think I know what you're doing. I've seen it in 'Nam. Guys doing whatever they had to, just to stay human. I don't mean staying alive; that's something else. That's easier, sometimes."

"That's what I'm afraid of," said Mae.

3

The house Mae Thomlinson went home to in Shelton was a two-bedroom frame structure three houses down from her daughter's home on Cook Street. It was one of the oldest houses in the town, dating back to the advent of Mormon pioneers in the early 1900s. In fact, the house, which Mae had bought a year after her husband's death, was across the street from her grandfather's original homestead. Mae often thought of Thomas Steward as she looked at the row of houses on the other side of the street and of the old place she had loved so much.

Her memories of it were vivid, for it had still been in the family when she was a child, and many were the picnics she had attended on the grassy meadow in front of the old house. Now there was nothing left of the homestead built up by her grandfather, who had taken part in the last organized colonization effort by Mormons in the West. The large but undistinguished farmhouse was gone, as were the barn and other outbuildings. Missing also were the huge, silver-leafed poplars that had lent shade and some measure of grace. Forty years had gone by since the land had passed into the hands of a real estate man after World War II, but she still thought of it as the Steward place and mourned its loss.

After weeks in the hospital, Mae was anxious to get back to her little house across from the Steward place. She didn't go straight home, however; she was too glad to be finished with the long confinement to go directly indoors again. "Oh, the air!" was the first thing she said when she was wheeled through the hospital doors. She instructed the nurse who was pushing her to stop while she drew in deep hungry gulps of the air that was as good as any tonic as far as she was concerned. She had visited her son, Terry, only once since he moved to Dallas, primarily because of the heavy moist air that was so different from the dry, pollution-free air of the Basin. "I'm sorry, but I can't stay here any longer," she had told him a few days into her visit. The air outside was too oppressive, and the conditioned air inside was too cold and lifeless.

After the nurse helped her into the waiting car, Mae asked Ron to drive her around a bit before going home. To see the still-snowy peaks of the Big Horns to the east and Pryor Mountain to the north was better for her than any medicine could have been. Although it was still early in the spring, it was warm in the Basin, warmer than usual for that time of year. The grass was greening, and tips of tulips and daffodils could be seen coming up in the beds that lined the walk in front of her house. And there was one other sign of spring: the cottonwood by the ditchbank was dropping long squiggly seed capsules that stained the sidewalk purple where they lay.

"Oh, I'm so glad to be home!" she said as she walked through the door Ron held open for her. "I see you took good care of the plants, Sarah Louise. Thank you."

Sarah Louise joined her mother where she stood before the flower-filled bay window. "Thank your friend Edith. She checked everything while you were away. I wouldn't have even known what to look for, I'm so terrible with plants."

"Look at the ivy. Oh, you're doing so well, you pretty thing. And the violets. How are you, Milly?"

Talking and touching as she went, Mae made the rounds of all her plants. She gave special attention to her indoor bonsai, pausing to admire each separately. Among her favorites were an astonishingly natural-looking forest of myrtle in a shallow, oblong container; a magnificent Kingville box; and a thick-trunked azalea, whose well-developed, horizontally trained branches held a profusion of pink blossoms almost ready to open.

"I was afraid Edith was going to drown your bonsai. For some reason she insisted on watering them every day. The outdoor ones, too," commented Sarah Louise.

Mae cringed at the way her daughter pronounced *bonsai*. She had never been able to get her to hear the difference between the word meaning "tree in tray" and the battle cry *banzai*. Her correction was automatic: "It's pronounced 'bone-sigh,' Sarah Louise. And it's a good thing Edith did water them every day; they need it, they're in such shallow containers. The ones outdoors need water at least twice a day in this dry country."

"Oh."

Having completed her survey, Mae sat down in her rocking chair and her cat jumped up on her lap. "Well, look at me. You'd never think I'd left at all, would you? Me and my plants and my cat. Now all that's missing is a grandchild or two."

"They're not missing," said Ron, motioning toward the door. "They must have seen the car."

Through the open screen door, Mae could see two big, brown eyes and a pug nose.

"Come on in, Mr. Matt," she said.

Five-year-old Matt James walked shyly into his grandmother's living room. He was followed by Michael and his twin Morgan, then Margaret, Melody, and Mark. Melody, who at seventeen was the oldest, held Michelle, the baby.

"Oh, they're all here," said Mae, delighted, as the children crowded around her, welcoming her home. Before long, Mae was regaling them with stories of her stay in the hospital. She was a born storyteller—she could make a grand tale out of any experience. She couldn't resist making the most of Keith Sullivan's foot massage.

"I couldn't believe what he was doing," she told the children, marking with satisfaction the widened eyes of the younger ones. "First, he put lotion on his hands and rubbed his hands together. 'To get the lotion warmed up,' he said. Then he started squeezing my big toe, and before long he was massaging my whole foot. I was a little worried—I wasn't sure how much of me he intended to massage!"

25

Mark, sixteen, sniggered, and Melody laughed as she said, "Oh, Grandma!"

"Who did that?" demanded Sarah Louise, who had the habit of catching onto the ends of conversations.

"Why, my nurse, of course. I had a male nurse. Very innovative."

"A *male* nurse?"

"Why, yes. His name's Keith Sullivan. He's a very nice man."

"That's indecent! You should have objected."

"Come on, Mom. Grandma's just teasing," said Mark.

"No, I'm not," protested Mae. "It's true, every word of it. Truly true."

"Then I'm surprised at you, Mom. Why did you let them assign him to you?" demanded Sarah Louise.

"I liked him."

"Then it's a good thing we got you out of there."

Mae shook her head in disbelief.

"I've got all of your things in the bedroom, now, Mom," said Ron, joining them. "Can we get you anything before we leave?"

"No, thank you. I'm doing just fine."

"Come on, guys, let's give Grandma some peace now," he said. "Give her a kiss, all of you, and then we'll go back home."

"M and Ms—just what I like," commented Mae as she kissed her grandchildren. She gave this one a hug, that one a pat on the cheek as they went by. Although she was physically expressive by nature, she did this consciously; she knew how hard it was for her daughter to give warm, spontaneous hugs and kisses.

"Remember, if you need anything, you just call. We can be here in no time," said Sarah Louise as she herded her children out the door.

"Don't worry, I'll be all right. Anyway, Edith said she would come over later on, and Keith is planning on coming, too."

"Keith?"

"Keith Sullivan, the nurse. It's his night off."

"Don't you think that's a bit much? If he had to do some

things for you while you were in the hospital, well, okay. But I'm not sure it's a good idea for him to be coming here."

"Don't be ridiculous," said Mae shortly. Then her voice softened as she added, "You don't need to worry, dear. He's really very nice."

Sarah Louise paused slightly, then shrugged. "Okay then." She bent down to kiss her mother awkwardly before leaving.

Mae sat in her chair long after they had left, savoring the nest she had built for herself in her years alone. It was a cozy room: priscillas hung at all the windows except the bay, and a large rag rug she had made many years ago covered most of the wooden floor. Sarah Louise had insisted that Mae get wall-to-wall carpet since it was easier to keep clean, but Mae had resisted. She liked the wood floor topped by her rag rug. Sitting on it were the camelback sofa and matching wing chair, which formed a conversation group with her oak rocker. She had bought them second-hand after giving away or selling the spare Danish furniture that had been her husband's choice. The crimson velvet upholstery of the sofa was bare in places and a bit faded, but the springs were still good, and Mae was satisfied with it. "It's like me," she often said. "Well-worn, but still useful."

She wondered if she could be useful now, considering. Of course I can, she thought. Nobody needs to know what's happening. I'll just go on as I always have.

So the very next morning, Mae went out to her flower beds. In spite of her weakened condition, she cleaned the dried stalks and accumulated leaves from around the tender green shoots. It was slow work, and she had little stamina, but she kept at it, doing a little, then resting a little on one of the stump chairs scattered throughout her garden.

Ron had put them there for her one spring after she had complained that what she really needed was a place she could park her bones right in the middle of her flowers. "That way I can rest a bit and work a bit. I guess I'm getting too old to go at it like I used to." She had been delighted when he brought over several 2½-foot sections of a large

27

tree he'd recently cut down. He put one by the peonies, one among the daisies, and one by the hollyhocks.

He's such a dear, thought Mae now, resting by the peonies.

That was where Edith found her.

"I knew you'd be here!" Edith Sidwell said as she marched across the lawn. "Just what do you think you're up to?"

"No good," replied Mae with a smile.

"Don't get smart with me. I want to know why you're not in bed."

"You really didn't expect to find me in bed, did you?"

Edith shook her grey head in exasperation. She was standing with her tiny hands firmly planted on her protruding hipbones. Mae would not have been at all surprised had Edith pursed her lips and said, "Shame, shame!"

"Nothing's going to change until it absolutely has to, Edith. As long as I can, I'm going to do all the things I'd normally do. As a matter of fact, I called the school this morning to find out when they want me to give my 'plant lady' presentation. I'm going next week."

"I'll go with you," said Edith quickly.

"You don't need to. Not yet."

"Will you tell me when—"

"You'll be the first to know. By the way, thank you for watering my bonsai."

"Well, I sure couldn't let them die after risking life and limb to help you find them."

"I can't believe we really did those things, can you?" Mae said, laughing.

The two women had driven many miles into the foothills of the surrounding mountains to scramble over rocks and climb ledges in search of junipers that were naturally dwarfed because of growing conditions. Strangely shaped junipers clinging to clefts with shallow roots were most prized, since they would take to bonsai conditions more readily, and their already picturesque shapes would make training them easier. However, digging them out had often required Mae and Edith to work in precarious positions. At the time, they were both in their twenties; the risks they took then were astonishing to them now.

"Speaking of watering . . . " said Mae pointedly.

"It's that time, is it?"

"Um-hum."

"You might as well have a herd of cows as these things," grumbled Edith, but she was smiling.

Arm in arm, they walked over to the corner of Mae's yard, which was shaded by a large tree most of the day. Underneath the tree were three redwood benches, and on the benches stood Mae's collection of dwarfed trees. Most of them were junipers, but Mae had tried her hand at dwarfing a variety of trees and bushes, even the homely sagebrush whose gnarled trunk and lovely grey-green foliage pleased her.

It was possible to read the development of her expertise in the plants themselves. She had begun with more desire than knowledge. Since very little literature on the subject had been available at the time, she had been forced to rely on her sense of beauty and her love of living things to guide her. The mistakes she had made were visible in trees with shapes that were not as pleasing and in bark scarred by training wires improperly applied or left on too long. But she had kept them all and cared for them equally, knowing that the final judgment of success or failure could only come after many years.

They were almost finished with the watering when the sugar factory blew the noon whistle. "How about a sandwich?" Mae asked her friend.

"If you'll let me fix it."

But Mae didn't feel like eating the sandwich Edith prepared—she was nauseated again. That dreadful, queasy sensation was becoming ever more constant, a drone accompanying all she did. Nevertheless, her body needed the nourishment, and her odd sense of duality had always prompted her to care for what she thought of as her "earthly instrument." So she ate—the act of nourishing herself was a way of nurturing herself.

After Edith left, Mae took a nap and was out again about the time that children started coming home from school.

29

She liked this time of day the best of all, for there were many children who passed by her house on the way home. If they didn't know her as Sister Thomlinson, the Sunday School teacher, they knew her as the plant lady or "the crazy lady in the white house." She could always count on an afternoon of entertainment when the weather was good enough for her to be outside when they passed by.

She had her favorites among them: Samantha, the stutterer; Kim, well-mannered but far too solemn; Lucy, overweight and harassed by the other kids; and Bobby, who was the town punk.

"Used to be we had the town drunk. Now we've got drunks and punks," she had said when she first saw him done up so fancifully. But she remembered Bobby of the now skillfully done, checkered haircut as a quiet, attentive kindergartener and a sweet seven-year-old in her Sunday School class. Sometimes, when he stopped to talk to her on his way home, she thought, He's not so different. Just has himself costumed-up.

Today Bobby's hair was spray-dyed bright green.

"Oh, my," said Mae, shocked.

"D'ya like it?" he asked, grinning.

"Well, I'm not sure I like it, but I'm certainly impressed."

"Here, you missed this." He pulled out a weed and tossed it to one side.

"Thank you."

"Where's your glider?"

"My glider?"

"You know, the swing you used to say you wanted."

"When did I say that?"

"When you were my Sunday School teacher."

"But that was so many years ago!"

"Yeah. So why don't you have it yet?"

"I don't know," replied Mae honestly.

After the children had gone by, Mae went inside to rest. Then, about six, Margaret came to get her grandma, for Mae took supper with her daughter's family.

"Maybe I'd better eat at home now," Mae had suggested to Sarah Louise. "I'm not really much on food these days. I don't want you to go to the trouble of fixing something for me when I might not feel at all like eating."

"But you have to eat; that's what the doctor said. And it's no problem. I have to cook anyway. Just tell me what tempts you, okay?"

So Mae ate a little of the lamb and green beans and potatoes Sarah Louise had prepared. And she actually enjoyed the applesauce they had for dessert, which surprised her. Afterward, she moved to the couch, where she could more comfortably look at this child's books, that child's latest drawing, and listen to Melody practice her violin. After a while, she leaned against the back of the couch and closed her eyes, savoring the lovely sound that reminded her of her father. She almost went to sleep that way.

"Come on, Mom. I'll take you home," said Ron gently.

"Thank you. I guess I overdid it."

Although she had only half a block to walk, Ron drove her and helped her into bed before going home.

"Remember, if you need us, all you have to do is call. We'll be here in a jiffy. And be sure to call us first thing after you wake up in the morning."

She assured him that she would, then turned on her side, which was her favorite sleeping position.

Unaccountably, just before she slept, green-haired Bobby's question came to mind: So why don't you have it yet? It was on her mind again when she woke. Not because she wanted a glider so desperately, but because she knew one day it wouldn't be a matter of *yet*; it would be a matter of *never*. There was only so much time, and she had less of it now.

That was when she decided to get the greenhouse extension she had always wanted. She would have it connected to the south wall of her living room, where the bay window now was. She made her plans as she lay in bed, and by the time she got up, she knew exactly how she was going to proceed. She didn't consult with anyone, nor did she tell anyone. A representative of a building company in Powell specializing in leisure-time additions came to the house, and together they decided what would work best for her.

When Sarah Louise asked who had been by to visit, Mae just said, "Some people I know."

The workmen came within the week, for business had been very slow, and they were more than glad to have the job. Mae was so excited by their arrival, she felt much like her old self again. She watched with great interest as they began digging up the sod on the south side of the house and laying the foundation blocks.

She was less inclined to stay nearby when they put up a sheet of plastic on the inside of her house to keep down the dust and began to rip out the wall. Mae plugged her ears as they began the noisy, dirty job. Thus she didn't hear Sarah Louise pounding on the door—she saw her daughter first, as she grabbed one workman by the arms and shouted, "Hey! What do you think you're doing?"

Mae came to the workman's rescue.

"It's all right. It's for my greenhouse," she said, pulling Sarah Louise by the arm. "You can go ahead," she assured the bemused fellow.

"Your what?" demanded Sarah Louise, as they walked outside for privacy.

"My greenhouse extension. The one I've wanted for so long."

"Why didn't you talk to us before you went ahead and did this?"

"I didn't think it was necessary."

"Mother, this doesn't make sense. It's so extravagant, you'll never get your money out of it when you sell. Besides, it'll make the house look totally out of balance—from the looks of it, that 'extension' will be almost as big as the house itself."

"I'm not worried about getting my money out of it. I've always wanted one, and I thought now would be a good time to get it."

"I suppose this is just a strange reaction to what the doctor told you," Sarah Louise said, her piping, childish voice earnest. "But Mother, if you have to do something, why don't you do what he wants you to instead of this? At least having the treatments would accomplish something."

"You ought to be a lobbyist, Sarah Louise."

32

"Somebody's got to talk some sense into you."

"I'm not going to change my mind."

"If you'd think about me and the kids for a change, you wouldn't be so stubborn about it. We need you. And we'd be right by you, all through it."

"You don't know what you're talking about, Sarah. You hardly have time to do my wash, although you insist upon it. How would you have time to care for me when I'd be so weak from those poisons all I could do was puke?"

"Mother, do you always have to use such blunt language?"

"I'm just being realistic."

"Well, *that* doesn't seem to be a very realistic reaction," said Sarah Louise, pointing at the construction in progress.

"My greenhouse? I think it's very realistic. When I get so I have to stay in bed all the time, I can have the bed set up in my living room, right next to it. That way I'll be able to care for my flowers as long as I can."

"You've got it all planned out, haven't you?"

"Yes. I spent some time on the phone yesterday. I'm going to get a hospital bed when it's necessary, and the kids can climb right up on it."

Sarah Louise's face suddenly contorted. "No way! Not if I can help it. They come over here all the time anyway; they talk to you about things they won't talk to me about. It's always Grandma Mae this and Grandma Mae that. I won't have you using them to make entertainment of this!"

"How else am I supposed to live through it? It's the way I've always handled things. I've made a production out of life."

"This time you'll have to play to an empty house."

4

Mae's flair for the dramatic was evident as she talked to the kindergarten children of Shelton Consolidated Schools. As she spoke, the children could sense the proudness of tulips in their cultivated beds; the mystery of asparagus spears poking up like mythical dragon's teeth all along the ditchbanks; the gallantry of desert flowers blooming beyond the swath of green that followed the Shoshone River and extended into the desert wherever canals built by the pioneers made water available.

"Well, you've got another set of fans," remarked Sally Morgan, the kindergarten teacher.

Mae acknowledged the compliment with a smile, grateful that neither Sally nor the children had been aware of anything odd during her presentation. She had been afraid they might, for she had noticed the signs of subtly encroaching pain and had used the technique she had developed against migraines to hold the pain at bay.

"How many years have you been doing this?" continued Sally.

"Eleven years or more. Ever since Mark boasted to his kindergarten teacher that his Grandma Mae knew more about flowers than anybody."

"Judging by the children's reaction, you could do it another eleven years without anyone getting bored."

"Not likely. I'd be an old lady of seventy-two."

"We'd still take you."

"Thank you," said Mae. She didn't share her knowledge

that she wouldn't be coming until she was seventy-two, that she wouldn't even make it to sixty-two.

Together, she and Sally loaded the books and plants she had brought; then Sally waved a final good-bye before going back into the school.

Mae slid behind the wheel and was about to start the car when suddenly her nostrils filled again with the chalky, sweaty, erasery smell of the room she had just left. Again before her eyes were tangled locks and cowlicks and the sweaty bangs that showed how hard the children had played at recess; staring at her were their eyes, wide with willingness to believe. A sense of loss washed over her, and she leaned her head upon the steering wheel and wept; she would never be 'the plant lady' again.

It's the little good-byes that hurt, she thought as she drove home. How often in the past two weeks had she looked at or touched something with more awareness and found herself thinking, This I may never do again.

This I must do, was the other frequent thought. One of the must-does for Mae was to go through her pictures and set some aside for each of her children. She didn't do it on the same day as she spoke to the kindergarten children; already she knew that she could accept or absorb only so much in one day. In the same way that she was only able to mourn in little increments, she was only able to plan in little increments. She had also found that she was most able to carry out her plans in the early afternoon: morning seemed too hopeful a time to think of death; evening was too frightening a time.

When she finally did get out the many albums and boxes of photographs and negatives, she was astonished at how many there were. Good grief, she thought, where do I start? She ran her fingers along the old, leather-bound book in which photos of her parents were affixed with little triangular corners on black paper. She hesitated before opening it up. Somehow she knew that what she was doing was more than a sorting job (this for Karen, this for Terry, this for Sarah Louise).

On the first page was a photo of her father, Abraham

Bateman. He was five at the time it was taken, only he didn't look at all childlike. He was wearing a cut-down version of a man's dress outfit, and on his face was the solemn expression requisite when having a portrait taken in those days. There was nothing in his eyes of the delight in living that had made him so dear to her. Next to it was a photo of her mother, Lenore, at about the same age. Below her bangs, done for the occasion in the now-forgotten, five-strand braiding, her expression was one of fright. In her hand, she clutched a porcelain doll, whose dress matched her own.

On the two succeeding pages, her father's pictures were on the left-hand page, and her mother's pictures were on the right-hand page. The few photos there traced their youth up to the time of their engagement. Their wedding portrait marked the beginning of their life together; from that point on there was no division.

The portrait taken on their wedding day was stiffly composed in the fashion of the times: Abe was sitting; Lennie (for so she was called by her husband) was standing behind his left shoulder. Her dark eyes were dutifully solemn and matched the straight line of her mouth, but there was a glimmer in Abe's eyes and a turn to his lips that disturbed the effect of the portrait. Looking at it, Mae thought, I wonder if Mama ever questioned marrying a man who couldn't even be serious on his wedding day. I wonder if she knew what life with him would be like.

There followed pictures of their first home, which Abe had laid out on part of Thomas Steward's large homestead on Cook Street. Abe's father-in-law intended that all his children build nearby, and as Abe had no land of his own and little money, he was more than glad to accept the land that was Thomas's wedding gift. Abe had laid out the markers by the light of the Northern Star, helped by Lennie. She had helped him with the building as well—one photo showed her triumphantly nailing shingles to the roof of the one-room structure.

On succeeding pages were pictures of Abe and Lennie's favorite horses Blaze and Molly, one of Abe holding a string of trout caught in a stream on Big Horn Mountain, and another of him turning water into a bean field. Mae's favorite picture of her mother showed her in a broad-brimmed hat, hoeing in her flower garden.

Then came the children. Jim in the 'christening' dress that had been handed down through his mother's family, then Mae in the same dress. Two others followed, Howard and Susan. Their little faces smiled up from the Saturday-night washtub, or down from the back of a wagon. There they all were, dressed for Sunday School.

Those pictures had all been taken on or around their home on the Steward property. The next group of pictures had a different background: the new Bateman homestead west of Shelton. One picture showed Mae and Jim standing barefoot in the yard of the place to which Abe had moved them all, tired of his father-in-law's insistence that he do something more constructive than barter, race, and fiddle. Behind the two children were the red-dirt acres that grew greasewood, sagebrush, and rocks so well.

Lennie Steward Bateman was in few of those pictures, but Mae knew that her mother had always been there. Perhaps she had been taking the pictures herself; perhaps she had been just past the edge of the image caught by the camera. Her constant presence had been one of the joys of Mae's childhood, for she and her mother had been companions. But when Mae turned thirteen, a change took place. It was clearly marked in the family album: here was a picture of Lenore, Lennie no longer, all dressed up for her first day of work as a school teacher.

Mae sat quietly for some moments, surprised that the photos could still call up the feelings of frustration and abandonment she had felt then. Her life had changed substantially when Lenore had begun teaching in order to help the family survive. It had been necessary, Mae knew, but that understanding hadn't softened the effect.

Although she always chided herself for such thoughts, Mae had often wondered how her life might have been different if her father had been more concerned about worldly things. But Abe hadn't been able to take the mundane things of life seriously. Interspersed with photos of Mae and her brother Jim herding cows or working in the fields were photos of Abe playing his fiddle, Abe astride one of his racehorses, Abe leaning against the car Lenore's parents had provided her as he worked out a deal.

He joked about the car. "What's happened to your flair for the romantic, Lennie? How can you replace such a noble animal as the horse with *that*? Everything on this place has its own name, from the horses to the cows to the cats. But you can't even put a name to that creation. And anything a body can't put a name to isn't worth having."

He teased the children, too. Mae remembered the night during the Depression when he prowled outside his children's bedroom window, reproducing with frightening accuracy the howl of a coyote. When they rushed into the kitchen, he listened to their story with mock solemnity, then suggested that they look for tracks in the ground outside their window. "Well, that doesn't look much like coyote to me," he said, "unless it's the two-footed variety." Then he favored them with a howl that would have sent them under the covers had they not heard it come from his own mouth.

Oh, Daddy! Mae thought, touching a photo of the face that had almost never fallen in solemn lines, except when bearing his testimony of the gospel. At those times, his expression was not simply solemn, it was grand. For when speaking of the things of the Lord, his face had always been lit by an exultation that captured the attention.

Abe Bateman had been truly subdued only when there was a death in the family or in the small community of Shelton. Even then, he could not maintain such solemnity for long. Right in the middle of the funeral dinner for the family (which in Shelton meant almost the whole town, related or not), he would suddenly start singing in his clear, sweet tenor or play the deceased's favorite fiddling tune. After a while, this performance became mandatory. He even fiddled after the funeral of his oldest son, Jim.

Mae found it hard even now to reconcile his engaging personality with his incompetence as a farmer, dairyman, and sheepman, despite the fact that it had shaped her life.

Because of his incompetence, she was captured on one page as a gawky, shy fourteen-year-old wearing a plain print dress and heavy, masculine work shoes. They were her only pair of shoes that year: she had worn them in the bean and beet fields whenever it was too cold or wet to go barefoot, and to church and school as well. She never went to any of the young people's gatherings, for she was too ashamed of the enormous, clunky appendages her feet became when she put the shoes on. She went barefoot as often as she could.

Because of his incompetence, her rich, naturally placed alto voice that carried to the end of the beet fields was never formally trained; her love of learning was never furthered beyond high school.

Because of his incompetence, she did all her traveling through the pages of the magazines Abe unashamedly brought home after they had been read by those well enough off to subscribe. She devoured those magazines and lost herself in the full-color plates of exotic places. She was filled with wonder at all the world contained. Although she felt herself to be part of the greater world, she never set foot outside of the Basin until she drove to Salt Lake with her beloved Fritz to be married in the temple.

None of that changed her love for Abe. She was inconsolable at her father's death. She never got over the absence of his wit, his sparkling eyes, his tenor voice lingering on the tones of "Mother McCree," his fiddle calling every able-bodied person from his chair.

She loved him still, and as she sat gazing at the last picture ever taken of Abe Bateman, she could almost hear him speaking to her. She looked up, startled, but it was only Mark, calling through her screen door, "Can I come in, Grandma Mae?"

Mae wiped the unshed tears from the corners of her eyes, not sure whether the dull persistence of pain or memories of the past had evoked them. "What's the magic word?" she asked with determined cheerfulness.

Mark's smile was accommodating. It was a game his grandmother liked to play, and he didn't mind indulging her. "Scintillating?" he asked.

"No, that was last week. We're on the Ts now."

"What was it? Come on, Grandma, help me out."

"Truculence."

"Hah! You can't get me on that one—we had it in vocabulary. It means gruffness or fierceness."

"Correct. Come in, Wordmaster!"

"You're weird, Grandma," said Mark, as he gave her a hug.

"Oh, thanks."

"Weird in a nice way, though. Whatcha looking at?"

"Pictures of your great-grandmother and great-grandfather. You've seen them before."

Mark flipped through some of the pages. The pictures more often than not showed Mae and her siblings working in the sugarbeet fields, stacking hay, or herding cows or sheep on horseback.

"You sure had to work hard, didn't you? I bet it made you mad that your sister Callie didn't have to. I mean, she grew up in that big house in Cody and went to college. You didn't get a chance to do any of those things."

In the pause before Mae responded, she smoothed Mark's remarkably thick red-red hair tenderly. He had much of Abe Bateman in him, as did her son Terry, but Mark was not like Terry at all. Her son had never been sensitive to her feelings; he would never have asked the question Mark had asked, the question Mae now answered. "There were times that I resented it, yes."

"That Hector Lamont who married Great-grandma wasn't too bad, but his sister must have been a snob. Mom says that she didn't even act like you were part of Great-grandma's family and that she was always trying to run things. I'm surprised she let you have this album when Great-grandma died."

"She wasn't even around at the time."

"Did Hector give it to you?"

"Nope. Do you want to hear a secret? Nobody gave it to me, I took it."

"No lie?"

"I walked right out with it, after I visited my mama the last time. Callie knew about it; in fact, she was my accomplice. And nobody has ever said a thing, even though they saw I had it when they visited after the funeral. Who could say my mama hadn't given it to me?"

"I'd like to see them try."

"Don't be too hard on them, Mark. Hector might have seen to it that one of dad's kids got it, but I didn't want to take the chance. It meant too much."

"I can see why. Only I wouldn't like to look at pictures that reminded me of all that bad stuff."

"That's not all I see when I look at them, Mark." She shut the album and put it aside. "So. Did you come over to help me in my house of glass?"

"Yep."

For the next hour, Mark worked on the large, square table he was building to size for his grandmother's greenhouse extension, which had been completed two days previously. When Mark finished the table, he asked, "Do you want me to varnish it with marine varnish? That way it won't hurt if you spill water."

"No, don't bother. I don't want to wait any longer to move my plants. Besides, I'm not going to be using it long enough to worry about water rot."

Mark looked down at his feet for a minute, then said awkwardly, "Gram, Dad says you're real sick, but Mom says all we have to do is have the ward fast and pray for you. Which is it?"

"The answer to that is simple," replied Mae after a long silence. "Let's get my plants on that table so I can enjoy them for a while."

Mark had to clear his throat before he could answer, "Okay."

They worked together, setting the heat and sun-loving plants toward the front end of the table, the shade-loving plants toward the back.

"Bring the bonsai in next," said Mae after they had been working for a while. "And you be careful with them. They're my babies, you know."

"I know."

He began carrying the dwarfed trees into the extension and carefully setting them into place. As Mae watched him

41

bring in the trees, she marveled anew at the individuality and the inevitability of each bonsai. Of the several San Jose juniper she had, no one was the same, nor could one be the same as any other.

Next to the dignified juniper, the azalea was a blaze of color; the masses of pink blossoms on different planes were like clouds at sunset. The plant had been given to her thirty years earlier as a Mother's Day gift; after trimming the roots and repotting it the following spring, she had redesigned it as a bonsai. It was one of her earlier efforts, but her sensitivity to the plant's strengths had led to happy years of training.

Then came the cypresses. At Mae's request, Fritz had brought the two small Arizona cypresses home after attending a convention in California. "I want some bonsai I can enjoy all year round," she had explained. "The sort of plants I need are ones that grow in the temperate zones. That way I can have them in the house all the time without wrecking their metabolism." She had settled them near the edge of a round clay dish, the smaller of the two behind the larger—the effect was that of great space and distance.

"Put that one where it will get shade," directed Mae, as Mark moved the Kingville box. The Kingville, which Mae had purchased twelve years previously from a mail-order house, was the most majestic of Mae's bonsai. Barely seven inches in height, it stood exactly in the center of its container, a perfectly dwarfed tree. It had aged-looking bark and remarkable branching that bore new leaves of a beautiful light green—they looked almost like blossoms against the dark-green older foliage.

It happened as Mark bent to set the bonsai at the back of the extension. One minute the container was safe in his hands; the next, it slipped and smashed against the cement floor.

"Oh!" cried Mae, and Mark swore.

"I didn't mean to drop it, Grandma," he said, stricken. He righted the bonsai, and as he did, he saw that a branch had been broken. It hung by the barest strip of bark; it was not salvageable, not even by his grandmother. He swore again, his face bleak.

But Mae had a different perspective these days. "You go get a new pot, and let's see what's happened here," she said in a mild voice. While she was waiting for her grandson to return, Mae marveled at her detachment, for she knew that if the accident had happened earlier in the year, she would have felt the wounding of the tree echo in her own body. The Kingville was not only very beautiful, it was an extremely slow-growing tree, a characteristic that made it difficult to hide the results of accidents or mistakes in training.

Together, Mark and Mae repotted the bonsai. Then Mae clipped the strip of bark that held the broken branch to the tree.

"It looks awful," said Mark.

"It sure does, but that's because at the moment it's out of balance. See, when I work on a tree, I look at it very carefully. It comes with its own personality, you know. I have to use what's there. When I decide to let certain branches develop and to prune back or entirely eliminate others, I'm always thinking, What will it do to the tree? I want the tree to be a work of art when I'm done; I want it to have integrity. I can't superimpose a form on it—it tells me the form it is capable of reaching. I only help it along.

"Now, this poor tree has lost a branch, but it's not the end of the world. It only means that we have to change our plans a bit. We have to compensate by letting a different branch grow larger than was anticipated before. And maybe we have to trim back some of the other branches."

As she spoke, Mae clipped a bit here and there, pausing to look with critical eyes at the form that was left after the accident.

"Maybe if we had a little more air on this side . . . ," ventured Mark.

"Good idea. If we open it up a bit here, the tree won't look so naked on the opposite side. You see, we take what we have, and we make something of it. It's not every little needle and twig that counts; it's shape and form."

"Hey, Gram, I'm glad you're not mad at me. But don't tell Mom, she'd have a spaz."

"She'll never know. How could she? She never pays any

attention to my babies. There! Doesn't look too bad, does it?" They put the repotted Kingville in a protected spot to recuperate, then Mae and her grandson walked down the street to Sarah Louise's for supper.

After returning home later in the evening, Mae moved the albums and the boxes of photos off the table so she could write a letter before going to bed. As she took the old leather album in hand, she felt a surge of resentment, of thwarted wishes, of might-have-beens. Mark was right—in some ways it was difficult to look at the album. There were too many things that still hurt.

She shook off the hurt the way a dog shakes off water. "Come on, old girl, don't get so serious," she said aloud. "So you've been nipped in the bud a place or two; so you've had a broken branch. You should have listened to your own lecture—it was one of your best."

5

The afternoon deejay on Mae's favorite radio station had a little *shtick* that he had worked out with the station weatherman for use on sunny days. After the weatherman reported on temperature, wind direction and speed, and cloud cover, Dave Knoll would prompt him with "And the pressure is . . . "

"Iiimmense!"

That was what Mae often thought in the next days, and the unspoken words in her thoughts had the same cadence as the exchange between Dave Knoll and the weatherman. And the pressure is . . . iiimmense. She thought she knew the reason why: Sarah Louise had been on the phone. It was easy for Mae to imagine what her daughter had said in her breathy, unwomanly tone: "Mom's not fighting this thing, and she has to. I thought maybe if we all give her the support she needs, she'll snap out of this."

Of course, not all the visitors or calls Mae had were those set into motion by Sarah Louise. Some days so many people came or called, Mae was sure the whole town was descending on her; it seemed as if everyone knew of her condition. The neighborhood knew within hours after Sarah Louise had been told, since they had been asking what Mae's condition "really" was from the time the ambulance had spirited her away to the hospital. From there, it spread out with truly marvelous rapidity, for, like all small towns, Shelton had its own means of communicating necessary information.

A neighbor passed the information on to a gas-station

attendant early one morning; he in turn made it known to everyone else who stopped during the day, excepting out-of-towners. The customers then conveyed it to whomever they met in Ben Franklin's, Penney's, Safeway Foods, the Big Horn County Co-op, or the city park. Lack of fences between many backyards also speeded up the process.

The Church, of course, had an even more efficient network of its own. From Ron, the news went to Mae's home teachers, from them to the elders quorum presidency and the bishopric, then on to the Relief Society presidency, and then to Mae's visiting teachers.

In this manner the news spread. Only those living on the withered end of the grapevine are ignorant of what's happening, thought Mae wryly. Thus the visits and calls. And the inevitable pep talk, whether requested by Sarah Louise or not. Some visitors beat around the bush; others were more direct in their challenge. But they all gave Mae the "You've got to fight" speech, except for Keith Sullivan and her old friend Brent Weinberg.

That changed one lovely evening not long before Easter, when Brent Weinberg appeared at Mae's door unannounced. He was a compact man, well-dressed and groomed. His hair was a lively crisp grey, and his eyes were still strongly blue. Before retiring, he had been the superintendent of the Great Western sugar factory in Shelton, and the air of competence and dignity that had surrounded him still remained. He had known Mae for years and had been Fritz Thomlinson's best friend. He had made a point of keeping contact with Mae after Fritz died. In fact, since the death of his wife, there had been rumors that the two of them might marry.

"What a nice surprise," said Mae, taking the flowers he had brought. "They're beautiful."

"For a beautiful lady."

She put the flowers into one of the many vases she had and set it on the butler's table in front of the couch.

"Sit down, please. Would you like some lemonade? I've got some made."

"Yes, thank you."

She brought him a frosty glass, thankful that he had let her do what she had always done before. Not everyone allowed her to—she was often treated as if she were senile or incapacitated, although she wasn't. She thought that was quite strange, since the same people also expected her to fight against becoming either.

Brent sipped his lemonade as they talked pleasantly about their common past, what was being planned for Memorial Day by the committee he headed, and the latest scandal in Shelton, which was threatening to line up as a "Saints vs. Gentiles" conflict.

When their conversation slowed and hesitated and finally threatened to stop altogether, Mae said, "Brent, dear, will you please get to the point of this visit?"

He grinned, his teeth white against his new sunburn. "I don't know why I thought I could fool you. You're far too perceptive."

"And you're far too transparent. I can see right through you."

"Too bad you can't see why I'm here; then I wouldn't have to worry about finding a way to approach the subject."

Mae smiled at his discomfiture, but she made no move to help him. Finally he took a deep breath and said, "Sarah Louise asked me to come."

"I might have known," sighed Mae. "Well now, let me see if I can figure out what she wanted you to convince me to do. Or not to do, as the case may be."

"She's worried about you, Mae. She says the bishop offered to designate a special prayer and fast day for you, and you turned him down. Is that true?"

"Not exactly. Sarah Louise does have a habit of oversimplifying things, as you know."

"What did you say to him, then?"

"That it would be a lovely idea. *If* he would agree to make it clear that I don't want anyone praying for me to live."

"What? Why?"

"Listen, Brent. I know the faith that the Church members in Shelton have. I have no doubt they could move Sheep Mountain over to the other side of Powell if there was a good enough reason to."

"All the more reason to have a special fast."

"All the more reason to be careful about it, to my way of thinking. You see, there's something I know that not many people are willing to accept: I know this is it for me; I know it with complete certainty."

"Feelings can be misinterpreted, you know. You could be wrong."

"I know; I could be making a mistake, but I would rather make a mistake in trusting my own feelings than in trusting someone else's. And you have to admit, my dear friend, the doctor's chart gives me some powerful support."

Brent dropped his head and shielded his eyes with one hand. Mae sat down beside him on the couch and laid her hand on his shoulder as she continued, "I'm determined to live out my life the best way I know how, for as long as I have, but I don't want it to drag on and on because of the faith and prayers of the saints."

"I hear what you're saying, but I can't accept it. It seems to me if you have that kind of faith, you certainly have enough to be healed."

"Yes, I believe I do. But God grants the earnest, repeated supplication of the faithful even though it may not be in their best interest."

"Does he?"

"It must be a matter of law, I think. If certain criteria are met in the process of prayer, the petition has to be granted. Maybe God himself intervenes, or maybe the elements themselves respond to the criteria, I don't know. But I do think it's important to know that one's praying for the right thing."

"I'll grant you that, still—"

"Brent, what do I have to gain by adding more months? They may be terrible months, did you ever consider that?"

He shook his head.

"Remember the little Rawlins girl?"

"The one who had a brain tumor?"

"Yes. She was on the verge of death before we all prayed

her back to life. I'm not sure that's what we should have done. The next few years weren't very pleasant, if you remember."

"That's only your opinion, Mae. If you asked her mother whether those years were worth it, you might get another answer."

"True. But I've thought about this a lot, and I don't want my time artificially extended by any means."

"Is that what you want me to tell Sarah Louise?"

"I don't want you to tell her anything; I'll speak to her myself. She doesn't want to face this, you know. She went to you because she doesn't want to talk to me about it directly. But we have to."

Brent nodded.

"I would like to have all my family and friends fast and pray for me," Mae added wistfully. "It is such a privilege; it brings people together so. If they would be willing to pray just for the comfort of the Spirit . . . "

He took her hand. "We can do that, Mae. I'll see to it."

They walked to the door together, Brent slowing his stride a bit to accommodate her. At the door, he suddenly turned, and Mae was taken aback by the emotion in his eyes.

"Do you know I love you?" he asked.

"Yes. And I love you," she replied.

He cleared his throat and looked over her head. "You know, before all this happened, I was thinking that maybe we ought to satisfy the gossip mongers . . . "

"How?"

"By getting married."

"Brent, we've been through this before," she said gently.

"I know, but I was never convinced that the reasons you had for not getting married were good enough."

Maybe they weren't, thought Mae, resting against his solid chest. Maybe I was thinking about myself too much. But is it really possible to think about oneself too much? I'm not sure.

When she was young, she had been impressed by the necessity of putting the welfare of the family first, for it wouldn't have survived otherwise. It took the combined efforts of parents and children to care for the stock, to get beans and beets planted, watered, and harvested, and to cut hay. In addition, they also had to dry or can or otherwise preserve much of the food that was to sustain them through the winter, for there was never much money. Whenever Mae wished that she could have something just for beauty's sake or simply because she wanted it, she felt guilty. Did her mother have anything beautiful or frivolous? If she wanted to take a moment to reflect or read or just sit in the sun, her mother's harried, hurrying form was a rebuke.

Nor did she have a chance to think primarily of herself during her courtship, for she had taken over running the house the year her mother had begun teaching grade school in Shelton. So instead of sitting before her mirror experimenting with a new hairdo or with lipstick (which would have been so light as to defy detection, for good girls in Shelton didn't wear makeup), she was cleaning, mending, and making butter, cottage cheese, and bread. The family situation wasn't helped when Abe died.

After her marriage, which took place shortly after her father's death, Mae had her own household, husband, and children to take care of. This she did, all the while serving in various Church callings and actively participating in clubs and groups of one sort or another. And she was happy with her life; that is to say, she didn't think she had any reason to be unhappy, so when she felt depressed or empty or sad, she just kept going.

Mae didn't tell anyone how she felt after Fritz died, for who would have understood? What she felt, after the grieving process had been worked through, was great freedom. Freedom that was, at first, frightening. Suddenly, there was no structure to her day. Her household chores had dwindled to almost nothing, and there was no person with whom she had to clear the calendar. For the first time in her life, she could do what she wanted to do, when she wanted to do it. It was marvelous.

Sarah Louise thought she had gone crazy when she sold

the big house on the bench (she offered it to Sarah Louise and Ron first) and bought the little house across from the family homestead on Cook Street. "Why are you doing that?" she asked. "You don't have to; Dad left you enough money to get by very well."

"I know," Mae replied. "I didn't buy the house because I had to, I bought it because I wanted to."

Sarah Louise just shook her head.

Mae moved into the small house and went about feathering her nest. She set her favorite records on the shelf under the record player; she filled the bookcase with her own books and those of her husband that had special significance to her; she brought out the treasures she had always cherished and positioned them around the room. The result was an inviting semi-Victorian clutter that was completely opposite to the clean Danish modern spareness that Fritz had preferred. Mae felt the presence of the house around her like a warm blanket and was satisfied.

There was now time to indulge in all the activities Mae previously had had to squeeze in at odd moments. She read voraciously; she drove out into the desert to see the sunrise; she hunted fossils and grasses; she spent time with friends; she wrote letters; she immersed herself in the scriptures; she sat in her rocker with the cat on her lap, thinking. She felt herself growing, unfolding. It was delicious.

Brent was a part of her new life. In fact, he had always been a part of her life, beginning with kindergarten. They had been friends all their growing-up years, and when they both married, the two couples formed were surprisingly compatible. It was not surprising that they gravitated toward each other after both lost their mates. The tenderness and understanding born of maturity marked this new stage in their relationship. Mae often kidded him with the words, "You'd better watch out; next thing you know I'll be falling in love with you!"

Nevertheless, when Brent asked her to marry him, she was absolutely astounded. She cared for him a great deal; she even loved him, she supposed. But she was not willing to give up what she had. So, instead of answering his question, she asked one herself. "What time do you eat breakfast in the morning?"

"What does that have to do with it?" he asked, astonished.

"Indulge me, okay?"

"Seven-thirty."

"Always?"

"Probably. More often than not."

"And if we were married, would you still eat your breakfast at seven-thirty?"

"I don't know. I guess."

"Would you expect me to fix it for you and eat with you?"

He didn't answer, but the miserable expression on his face indicated he knew what she was driving at.

"Do you listen to the radio while you eat?"

He nodded.

"I do, too. I listen to a recital of Baroque music on the public radio station. What do you listen to?"

"The farm report."

"I thought so. Brent, I don't want to have to eat breakfast at a certain time every day with the price of feeder lambs in my ears. For as long as I can remember, I've scheduled my life around someone else. First my parents, then Fritz and the children. I don't want to do that again. I don't relish having to adjust to another person at this time of my life. Do you know what I'm saying?"

"Mae, do you love me?"

It took her a moment to quiet the quivering of her chin. "Yes," she finally replied.

"Isn't that all that matters?"

"When you're nineteen, maybe."

"Will you think about it?"

"I won't change my mind, Brent."

And she hadn't, though from that time on, they were even more tender and devoted to each other than before. They went to church together most Sundays except holidays, when she went with Sarah Louise and her family. They took long drives together. Once in a while, she fixed him his favorite foods; sometimes she fussed over him and sometimes she relied on him. But she was not his. Her life was her own, and he respected that. It was the only basis upon which their relationship could have continued.

Now, as he drew her tightly to him, she wondered for a moment if she had made a mistake in refusing his offer of marriage. "I did what I had to do," she murmured into his shoulder. "Everybody talks about finding yourself through serving others, but you have to serve yourself too sometime or another. How can you get to know who you are if you've never stopped to listen to yourself? Sometimes, when I'm very quiet, I can feel myself—my spirit, I mean. I can feel it reaching out beyond my fingertips . . . Do you think I'm crazy?"

"Crazy Mae," he murmured into her hair. "No, I don't think you're crazy."

He lifted her chin, and she accepted a kiss that was simple, yet unutterably sweet.

And then, because she was who she was, she started to laugh. "My, my! Aren't we a little old to be going in for dramatic scenes?"

"I may be, but you? That'll be the day."

6

Easter came late that spring; the day was already bright and warm when Mae awoke. Instead of getting up, she lay in her bed, listening to a special program on public radio. It was a little ritual of hers—she liked beginning her Sundays with Bach, Handel, and Brahms. She listened to the program with closed eyes, letting the sounds lift her up and out of herself. When the last tones ceased vibrating, she sighed with resignation: it was time to get up. She avoided it as long as her built-in aversion to lying in bed would let her, then rose reluctantly, knowing that the lovely, pain-free moments of early morning would give way to increasingly more intrusive pain and, as the day wore on, accompanying fatigue.

When she did finally get up, she put on her bathrobe and slippers and walked out into her garden. Encouraged by the warm spring sunshine, plants were coming up everywhere. Besides tulips, daffodils, and hyacinths, she could see the maroon tips of new peony shoots and light-green iris spears. Tiger lilies, poppies, delphinium, daisies, baby's breath, and lilies of the valley were all reaching up out of the loose, rich soil.

She made her rounds, then sat down on one of the stump seats, her eyes closed and face upturned to the sun. As she breathed in the bright morning air, she felt as if she were breathing in the sunlight itself. In an extraordinary moment, it was as if she were one with the earth and the flowers and the air and the sun. Thank you for the beautiful day, Lord, she thought. She was brimming with hope. The fact that hope could share the same inner space as knowledge of one's imminent death was a paradox, but a comfort as well.

In keeping with Easter tradition, Mae went to church with her daughter's family. Not long after they were seated, Brent Weinberg slipped into their pew and sat next to Mae. He leaned in front of her to shake hands with Ron and Sarah Louise, then put his arm around her shoulder.

"How are you?" he whispered.

"I'm fine."

It was an accurate report of her emotional state, for some of the morning's optimism still lingered. Besides, she always felt better when she went to church on Sunday. For Mae, going to church was not merely a matter of habit, or cultural response, or convention: it was a time of true worship. Taking the sacrament and renewing her covenants with the Lord was something she did with full awareness—a week minus that solemn confrontation with self and recommitment to principles was an empty week.

It was not accurate as far as her physical state was concerned. She had taken her medication according to schedule, and she had come to church confident that it would control the pain she knew would otherwise grow as the day went on. She was fine until after the sacrament was passed. Then pain ambushed her. She felt her muscles grow tense, and although she tried to stay relaxed, to keep her breathing even and to concentrate on the speakers, her fear of pain began feeding into a fierce cycle that only made it worse.

She was close to tears when she felt Brent's arm tighten around her. "Do you need to go home?" he whispered.

She nodded, grateful that he had sensed her discomfiture. She leaned toward Sarah Louise. "Brent's taking me home," she said softly. Sarah Louise picked up her purse as if to come along, but Ron shook his head. Mae and Brent slipped quietly out of the pew and left the chapel.

"What can I do?" Brent asked when he had her home.

"I don't know. Just sit by me." She took her painkiller, then lay down on her bed.

He pulled a chair close and took her hand. Instinctively,

he began smoothing it. "That feels good," murmured Mae, so he kept it up. Without realizing it, he began crooning to her as if she were an ill child or a wounded animal. She felt the medication begin to take hold, and Brent's soft stroking and repetitious assurance that "It'll be all right. The pain's going now. It's going right out the ends of your fingers" helped her to relax.

She awoke later to find him still sitting beside her.

"Better now?" he asked.

"Oh, yes. How long did I sleep?"

"About an hour. Are you going to try to go out to Howard's?"

"Yes," she said, sitting up. "It's probably my last family get-together."

He was silent for a moment, then his face contorted. Slamming his knee with his fist, he said, "I hate this! I hate to see what it's doing to you."

"I know."

"I don't know if I can stand it, Mae." His voice cracked on the last words, and he began to weep.

Brent's honest expression of emotion stunned Mae; it was the first time anyone had expressed to her their anger and sorrow over her condition. As he got control of himself, he tried to apologize, but Mae shook her head.

"Don't apologize, dear," she said, wiping the tears from his cheek. "You have no way of knowing how much those words mean to me. You're the only one who's been able to say them . . ."

He took her into his arms then, and they sat pressed together for a long time.

She rode out to Appleblossom Farm with Sarah Louise's family after church was over. By the time they stopped by to get her, she felt much better. The efficacy of the pills had been aided by her anticipation of the afternoon. She knew all of her brother Howard's family would be there, for none of them had moved out of the Basin, in spite of limited possibilities for employment. Some of her sister Susan's children would be there as well, although Susan herself had called to say she wouldn't be coming. The phantom sister, thought Mae now. But she knew it was going to be a great afternoon.

"Great to see you, Sis," said Howard, when Mae walked into the farmhouse. He had to bend down to hug her, for he was a large man.

"How you doing, you old sodbuster?" asked Mae.

"Pretty darn good, for an old sodbuster," he replied, grinning at their customary greeting. Neither one of them could have said how it got started, but it was already set long before either of them had even begun to entertain the idea that they would one day be old.

It was always like a step back in time to come out to the farm, especially at Easter, when the smell of the leg of lamb Howard's wife, Annabelle, was roasting brought back a flood of memories. The house was not the same as it had been then, however, for although Howard was like his father, Abe, in many ways, he had been blessed with an astute business sense and a wife who had inherited money. Using both of those assets, he had made Appleblossom Farm succeed in a way Abe had only dreamed of, and one of the first things he had done was add on to and renovate the farmhouse. In fact, everywhere Mae looked, Appleblossom Farm evidenced a prosperity never known when Abe was alive.

But the feeling on the place was the same as it had been then: it was as if one had been given permission to delight in life. Children scattered the minute they were released from the cars that had conveyed them thence, reveling in the freedom of the farm. The little ones crowded around the baby chicks Howard had bought from the Co-op, or tried vainly to catch the wild kittens that lived in the barn, while the older ones took turns in the tire swing hung from the big elm. Teenage girls arranged themselves decoratively on the bench beneath the giant flowering crab, while the boys congregated in the big barn, where the long sacks packed with wool from the spring shearing made a good place for lolling. The men's favorite spots were the stalls and corrals where Howard kept his thoroughbreds.

The main order of the day was conversation. Conversation had always been much prized by Abe, and he had passed this love on to his children. They enjoyed nothing more than a spirited discussion of current events, local happenings, farm business, and ideas. This exchange of ideas flourished before, during, and after the Easter feast, interspersed with jokes. "Did you hear the one . . . " was a common introduction. Terry would be the center of attention here, Mae thought. Nobody knows as many jokes as he does.

This propensity to tell jokes of any kind brought an uncomfortable moment into the proceedings. It happened while they were all sitting around the table. One of Susan's granddaughters, wishing to be a part of the adult repartee, asked, "Hey, did you read that column in Ann Landers about cowboy hats? It seems this professor had moved out to eastern Wyoming to teach in one of the junior colleges. He asked one of the other teachers what the custom was about wearing cowboy hats.

"'They never take them off in class,' says the teacher.

"'You're kidding. Do they take them off in church?'

"'They never go to church.'

"'But what about funerals?'

"'They never die!'"

Mae joined in with the laughter that greeted the punch line, but she noticed that the adults, who knew of her condition, looked highly uncomfortable. She smiled reassuringly at Howard, who was watching her with a worried expression, and said, "My, what a wonderful joke!" She meant it. The joke was funny, and it deserved the appreciation of the men and boys around the table whose permanently two-toned foreheads were the result of wearing Stetsons in the bright Wyoming sun.

After the dishes had been done up, all the family meandered into the living room, where they knew the requisite songfest would take place. First Howard and his wife sang some duets. Then everyone joined in when they began singing the old favorites. Mae especially loved this part, for her alto voice was still sweet and true, if softer than it had been. They sang the songs Abe and Lennie/Lenore had loved: "The Chieftain's Daughter," "Little Old Sod Shanty," "When It's Springtime in the Rockies," "On Top of Old Smokey." Then came "Whispering Hope," "The Old Rugged Cross," and "The Railway to Heaven." Later on, every grand- or great-grandchild who could sing or play an instrument or dance had his turn.

"Why don't you favor us with a little music, Sarah Louise?" asked Howard. "I haven't heard you play the piano for a long time."

"I don't play anymore," she said abruptly.

"Melody brought her violin," offered Ron.

"Then let's have some fiddling tunes!"

Late in the afternoon, when the pace slowed and the sound of conversations was a low murmur, Howard said to Mae, "Would you like to go for a ride?"

"When did I ever turn down a ride?" A Sunday afternoon turn about the place was something Mae always enjoyed. A farmer's daughter, she still had a keen interest in what was planted where and how the crops were shaping up. It gave her great pleasure to know that Abe Bateman had picked out a fine piece of land, even though he had not known how to coax it into yielding.

When Howard helped her into his new pickup, Mae said, "I don't know why they make them like this nowadays. You sure don't need something this fancy for driving out in the hills."

"Probably not, but they're all fancied up like this. Couldn't buy a plain old red pickup if I wanted to."

He drove her around the farm, indicating what was growing in each field as they passed: "That's alfalfa, that one there's beets, and in the forty down by the draw I'll be planting beans." Finally he took a road that went beyond the canal, which was the border between green and brown, and parked the truck in the shade of an old cottonwood. He stared out the window at Sheep Mountain for a minute, then asked, "How are you doing, Sis?"

"Fine."

"That's a terrific opener for a conversation."

"Sorry, but I am doing fine—"

"—for someone who's sick. More than just sick. I guess you don't want to talk about it."

"I don't mind talking about it, dear. I'm okay now, but I

did have some trouble earlier today. That's the way it goes—I can never tell when it's going to hit me."

"Have you seen your new doctor—Dr. Donnelly, is it?"

"Not yet. I'm not doing too badly, all things considered, so I thought I'd wait until I have to."

"Is that the only reason why?"

"Actually, no. I don't want to go to him, to tell the truth. I never have liked him, and I don't like him now. I'm not too thrilled about having him poke around on me."

"We could get you a doctor in Powell or Lovell. We could go to Billings or Salt Lake for that matter."

"That's sweet of you, but we don't need to. They wouldn't tell us anything more or less than Dr. Melton did."

"I just wish there was something I could do for you, Sis," he said, sniffing into his handkerchief.

"There is one thing," Mae said impulsively. "You could play the fiddle after my funeral."

Startled by the unexpected request, he laughed, though tears still seeped from his eyes. "Do you really want me to?"

"Bluegrass. Daddy and I would both be disappointed if you didn't."

"Okay, I will. Now come here."

She scooted over on the seat until she sat beside him, and he put his arm around her.

"It's been a long time since I've driven like this. Think I still can?"

"I doubt you've forgotten how—you did it often enough when you were courting Annabelle."

He drove back to the farm with his arm around her. When they got there, he helped her out, then held her in his arms for a long moment before they rejoined the others.

It was very late when the James van drove into Shelton. Mark turned the key in his grandmother's door and helped her in. In spite of the fact that she was leaning on his arm, she stumbled.

"Oops. Are you all right?"

"I'm fine. I'm only tired."

"We stayed out there too long," he said. "That was dumb."

"No. I'm glad we got a good visit in."

"Do you need any more help?"

"I can get myself into bed, but thanks anyway."

She kissed him as he left, then she checked to see that her cat was in, got into her nightgown, and fixed some hot chocolate from a mix needing only water. Before settling down in her chair, she put on the *German Requiem* by Brahms. Listening to it had been part of her private Easter tradition for many years, and she wasn't going to do without it no matter how tired she was.

She leaned back in the rocking chair, her cat on her lap, sipping the warm chocolate as the music began. She was not listening to the words as much as letting the lush sounds roll over her, until the second section, which began with the words "For mortal flesh is as the grass, and all the comeliness of man is as the grasses' flowers. The grass hath withered, and the flowers thereof hath fallen." The roll of timpani emphasized the words, and she felt a thrill run through her body.

The power of the section grew as both text and musical theme were repeated and emphasized: the words "For mortal flesh is as the grass" were sung again and again, in tones ever more penetrating, and the rumble of the timpani took on a threatening aspect. With every menacing roll, the fact that she was indeed going to die pierced deeper and deeper. She understood in a way she had never understood before that her little season was over; like the grass, she would wither and be gone.

She began to shake, and tears gushed from her eyes. She cried in the darkness long after the record player had clicked off.

She did not cry, "Why, Lord?" for that was the question of her youth, and she had moved far beyond that in the years following. She had long ago come to the conclusion that "Why not?" was an equally valid question. Besides that, the notion that everything has a reason and comes through the hand of God was foreign to her philosophy.

61

That fact in itself was a strong indication that Mae's philosophy was indeed her own, since Lenore Bateman Lamont had habitually praised or blamed God for everything that happened in her life. Mae had often heard her mother say, "Now, what does the Lord want me to learn from this?" Or, "The Lord's trying to tell me something." Lenore was also one of those who could say to distraught parents without compunction, "The Lord must have known you were a strong person, or he wouldn't have sent you a handicapped child."

It never set well with Mae.

While she was grateful to the Lord for the world, for life and love, for his Spirit and the gospel, she did not believe one should rightly give him credit for everything that happened, good or ill. She did not believe that God arbitrarily intervened in the affairs of men or nature. It was not a particularly popular belief, since it was the rare person in her community who could not relate instances of divine intervention.

When she was asked, "Where did you come up with that idea?" she would respond, "The Book of Job." If the person who posed the question were genuinely interested, she would elucidate:

"For a long time, that was the book of the Bible I liked the least. It was pretty difficult for me to feel kindly toward a god who would give Satan permission to make Job's life miserable. It didn't seem particularly fair, especially considering his faithfulness.

"Then when I was reading Job one day, I found the line, 'The thing which I greatly feared is come upon me.' There was Job, saying that he had lived in fear that he would lose his family and his wealth for a long time. As far as I was concerned, that cleared up the whole issue: Job's fear itself defined the area that Satan could influence or operate in."

Because she believed that, it was not surprising that Mae had now and then wondered if her illness was possibly the result of some thought pattern she had harbored, or some deep-seated, hidden negativeness that had been growing in secret, even as her tumor grew. But she had no time for recrimination or regret because she had decided to focus purposefully on dealing with the circumstances in which she now found herself.

So when Mae began crying that Easter evening, it was not "Why?" Nor was it for herself that she cried. She cried for the dearness and beauty of life, for the smell of freshly cut alfalfa, for the sweet, pithy taste of sugar beets, for the feel of crumbly, damp spring earth between her fingers. She cried for the faces of children, open and sweet, for all whom she loved and soon would leave behind. She cried even for ugliness and pain, for she had learned that they also, when integrated into oneself, took on a certain beauty and solidity.

She cried for all these things, but she did not change her mind.

7

Early on the first day of May, she went from door to door in her neighborhood with small baskets of violets nested in moss. The basket she took down the street to her daughter's house was larger and contained a small plush toy for each of the children, which her friend Edith had been kind enough to purchase for her. Still, Mae had the feeling she wanted to do something more in celebration of the day, but what? When the idea came to her, she laughed aloud.

They really will think I'm crazy Mae, she told herself, giggling, but I don't care. She knew that the children would love it, and it didn't matter to her what anybody else thought.

She found her old straw gardening hat, the one with the high crown and wide brim. Then she searched in her boxes of decorations until she found some crepe paper streamers. They were old and faded, but they would do. Working slowly, for her stamina was fading even though she felt fairly well, she measured off long lengths of different colors, cut them and then pulled one end of each length through a hole she had carefully punched in the top of her hat. She put a rubber band around the ends she had threaded through and taped them to the inside of the hat.

Humming, she went out into her front yard and set the hat down in the middle of the lawn. She fanned each streamer out from the hat three yards or so and rolled up the remaining length neatly. When she stood back to survey her handiwork, she nodded—she was almost ready. All that remained was to make the sign and then get some much-needed rest as she waited for the advent of the grade school children.

Laughter and calls preceded the children down the street, but when they came to Mae's house, they suddenly fell silent. For there on the lawn stood Mae, her hat on her head, streamers falling from the crown in all directions. On the picket fence was a sign penned in bright colors: "I'm a May pole. Wind me."

The children looked at the sign, then at Mae. She didn't move a muscle or blink or show by any motion that she knew they were there. A small crowd had gathered by the time Michael and Morgan turned the corner and began to walk up the street. When they saw their grandmother and the knot of children in front of her yard, they jogged up to see what was going on. They pushed their way forward, read the sign, and began to laugh.

"What are you waiting for?" Mike asked the kids. "Don't you guys know what a May pole is?"

"A-a-I do," Samantha struggled to answer. "W-we had one on the p-playground."

"So what did you do with it?"

"W-w-wound it up, like."

"Right on. That's what you do with a May pole, and this, THIS is a May pole."

They giggled and shuffled, feeling silly.

"You don't mean—" began a tow-headed boy.

"Would I lie?"

A slow grin widened the boy's cheeks. He looked at the youngster standing next to him and poked him with his elbow. The two of them joined Mike, Morgan, and Samantha in the yard and picked up one of the streamers. Other kids followed, and when the streamers were all spoken for, Mike said, "Go left, everybody." He winked at his grandmother, who was having difficulty maintaining her sober expression, as left they went, around and around, until they reached the ends of their streamers.

"Happy first day of May," the now-immobile Mae called to the children, who were clapping their hands with delight or rolling on the grass with laughter.

"N-now what are you g-going to do?" asked Samantha.

"Well, if some of the other kids will unwind me, I'll get you all some cookies."

A new crew scrambled for the loose ends of streamers and unwound Mae. They were laughing so hard they tripped over each other and tore the streamers as they fell. From across the street, a door opened as someone looked out to see what all the racket was about.

"Now, who will help me bring out the cookies and Kool-aid?" asked Mae when she was finally free. The little volunteers carried out trays, paper cups, and napkins; Mae carried out the pitcher. "Anybody who agrees to help clean up the crepe-paper mess and to throw their cup and napkin in the trash when they're finished, can join us for goodies," she announced. Everyone must have agreed, for all the cookies and Kool-aid were gone a short time later, and all traces of the celebration were consigned to the garbage bags.

"You're neat, Grandma," said Morgan, the thinner and quieter of the twins, as he stretched out expansively on the now-clean lawn. "You do things that no other grandma would do. Who else celebrates May Day besides you and the Russians?"

Mae laughed. "I like celebrating special days."

But she went to bed right after the twins left, taking with them the message that Mae would eat supper at home. Sarah Louise came right over to see what she could do to help, but Mae assured her she was only tired. However, she was so uncomfortable that she really couldn't rest until she had taken one of the pills Dr. Melton had prescribed.

The next day she asked Keith, who came by several times a week now, "Do you think I'm only doing this to make a black celebration out of dying?"

"I don't think so," he replied, setting his lemonade on the patio table.

"I wonder if I am, sometimes. It is possible that I'm choosing to live my last days this way just out of a perverse desire to make a grand exit, you know."

"What's so bad about that?"

"Nobody else would say that."

"Then it's a good thing you asked me, isn't it?"

Mae looked doubtful.

"Or do you want someone to tell you you're being a bad girl?"

"I don't know. It seems a bit presumptuous, somehow. It seems like I'm making a choice only God should make: the how and when of death. Maybe if I went ahead and had chemo, it would help. Maybe I would live many more months."

"Do you really think so?"

"No," Mae sighed. "But I wonder. People die of cancer, but people live with cancer as well. Am I being a coward for not choosing to fight for those months?"

"I don't think you're a coward, babe. Making choices, that's anything but cowardly. But I'm curious, why are you questioning it now?"

"Just something one of the M and Ms said. He said I do things that other people don't do."

"So keep it up; now's not the time to change."

Mae set her glass on the table and looked at him from sober grey eyes. "I'm taking more meds than I like, Keith. The pain's getting worse."

"We need to get started, then," he replied. "But I have to tell you, this isn't going to take the place of your pills. You're going to need painkillers, Mae. But it will help you keep the dosage down to a level that will allow you to function instead of knocking you out."

He had her sit in her favorite chair, her feet on the floor and her hands, palms up, on her lap. "Just start breathing slow and even," he instructed. "Breathe right down to your toes. Don't be in any hurry; just breathe in and out, in and out."

"Are you sure you aren't hypnotizing me?"

"No, Ma'am," protested Keith. "We're just going through a relaxation technique. I'm going to teach you how to hypnotize yourself, in a manner of speaking. Have you changed your mind about it?"

"No."

He began again, slowly, in a voice that was smooth and rich. "Relax the top of your head . . . relax your forehead . . . you feel the skin of your temples relaxing,

67

the tension draining away . . . now relax the area around your eyes . . . relax your jaw . . . "

He continued talking in his liquid voice. As she felt it pour over her, she was aware of the tension leaving one part of her body after another. When he stopped speaking, she was not immediately aware of it for some time. She was floating, more relaxed than she had ever been in her life. She felt no urgency; she just waited, breathing in and out. Finally, from far away, she heard him speak.

"Now, Mae, you are going to build a safe place inside of yourself. It will be a place you can come to whenever you need a break from tension or worry or pain. It will be your resting place. You will be able to come to it whenever you want to; you will be able to leave it and come back to the present whenever you're ready. Now, I want you to think about a place associated with pleasant memories. Think about it in as much detail as you can. See the color of the sky; hear the sounds; smell the smells."

When Keith had first told Mae about this method of dealing with and controlling pain, she had immediately decided that she would visualize the clearing around the mountain cabin her Grandfather Steward had built on his Wylie Creek sheep range up on the Big Horns. It was a place she had loved, and she had always gone there in the company of people she loved.

She took deep, slow breaths, and began visualizing the place as if she were lying on her back in the sharp-edged meadow grass. The sky was close and blue as a bird's egg, and her upturned face felt warm from the rays of the sun. Once in a while, when a wisp of cloud crossed over it, she felt the immediate and welcome cooling.

Mentally lowering her gaze, she saw the rounded top of Old Baldy, then the green spires of the pine forest that surrounded her magic circle of meadow. The ground was lumpy beneath her, and the grass spears pricked her bare arms. As she breathed in, she could smell the clear, cool air tinged with a piney scent. And in the distance, she could hear the muted bleating of sheep and the occasional bark of a dog.

She rested in her mountain meadow for what seemed a

long time, then Keith gently brought her back to the surface.

"How do you feel?" he asked.

"Wonderful. It's strange, but I feel better than I have in a long time."

"Here's that tape I promised you. It's pretty much like what we just did together. There's about five minutes of silence in the middle—that's when you do the visualizing."

"How often should I do it?"

"Maybe a couple of times a day. You want to get that image so fixed in your mind that it's easy to go there when things get tough. Use it whenever you feel a hint of pain; you'll be strengthening your mental response to it."

"Will it help when things get really bad?"

"I can only tell you what happened to me in 'Nam. I used the technique when I was wounded—"

"I didn't know you were wounded."

"I don't go around wearing my purple heart. Anyway, it's not something you advertise."

"Did it help?"

"Yes. It was odd, now that I look back on it. The pain made me think of the ocean. You know, you have to get up and over the breakers to get out where the waves support you instead of smashing you against the rocks. It was kind of like that. Meditating and visualizing took me out where I could float on the pain instead of drowning in it."

He paused uncomfortably, as if he had something to say, but didn't know how to put it.

"What is it?" asked Mae.

"I just don't want you feeling like a failure when you have to take something more."

"You're thinking about the morphine."

"It's not the same as doing drugs, you know."

"I guess not."

"I mean, you've got to take advantage of anything that helps you get through this the way you want to."

A sudden fear gripped Mae, and she reached instinctively for his hand. "Will I be able to?"

"You'd better believe it. And I'll be with you all the way."

"Why?" asked Mae tearfully. "Why are you willing to do so much for a virtual stranger?"

"That's simple. I'm not altruistic, babe. It's pretty lonely for me here. Oh, Melty is a good friend, but he's got his practice and his family and church . . . trying to be a Saint keeps him busy. As for the other people I know, basically, I think I scare the good folks of Shelton. I never thought it would be so hard for me to make a place for myself here."

"You know there's always a place for you in my home. You can count me as a friend."

"I do," he said.

"What are you going to do on Mother's Day?" she asked impulsively, drying her tears.

"Besides calling my own dear dam? Not much."

"Come to dinner—I'll finagle an invitation from Sarah Louise."

"Do you think you can do that?"

"Of course. You plan on coming."

The phone rang early on Mother's Day. It was Karen.

"Happy Mother's Day!" she said. "I've got a real neat surprise for you."

"What?"

"I got some time off—I'm coming out the second week of June."

"Karen, I don't want you to use up time off we might need later on—"

"Hey, I'm the star of Herschel and Mann—they'll give me time as often as I need it. Within limits, of course."

Mae chuckled.

"Mother, how are you, really?"

"I have my days, dear, but so far so good."

"I'm glad to hear that! Just so you know, I'll be flying into Billings, and I'll rent a car there. I'll call you before I start down, so you'll have an idea when I'll arrive."

"I'd appreciate that."

"Well, I haven't forgotten how you fret when you think someone is overdue. Now here's Jim."

"Hi'ya, Grandma . . ."

Mae talked to her two grandsons and her son-in-law,

then lay back in her bed, smiling. It was a lovely way to start the day.

Shortly before church, Morgan and his twin Michael came to her door. They were dressed in their Sunday finery, and Michael held a corsage box in his hand.

"Is that for me?" Mae asked, as her grandson handed her the box. "Oh, what a beautiful orchid! Will you help me pin it on?"

"I don't know if I can."

"I'm not surprised. There's not a man in my acquaintance who really knows how to pin on a corsage. That's because they don't get enough practice. Practice on me and on your mom so you won't stand there like a fool when you bring a young lady her first corsage. You watch too, Morgan."

Mae showed them how to secure the orchid corsage with the long, sharply pointed pin, then said with satisfaction, "That's the way. Don't you forget it, now."

Sarah Louise got out of the van as the two boys escorted Mae down the sidewalk. "Happy Mother's Day," she said, giving Mae a kiss before assisting her into the van.

"Happy Mother's Day to you, too. You look very lovely today, dear. And thank you all for the corsage."

Mae had an unusually keen sense of enjoyment that day. Riding to the church was a pleasure; walking into the chapel in the company of her handsome grandchildren was a pleasure; receiving the greetings of all who knew her was a pleasure.

The talks in sacrament meeting were unusually fine in her estimation. Too often in the forty plus years since the first child, she had felt inadequate as Mother's Day speakers extolled an ideal she knew she would never be able to live up to. The speakers this day, however, brought a smile to Mae's lips as they talked with unusual and refreshing candor about both the ups and downs of motherhood.

Mae didn't stay for the rest of the meetings, however. She no longer had enough stamina. It had been difficult for her to admit that; and it had also been difficult to admit that the bishop was right when he had gently suggested it was time to let someone else take over her Sunday School class.

"I know you're right," she had replied, "but it's like giving up part of myself."

As was becoming usual, Brent drove her home after sacrament meeting and sat beside her while she rested on the sofa. They talked quietly until shortly after noon, when the doorbell rang.

"Are you expecting company?" he asked.

"Keith Sullivan."

"Oh. The nurse."

"Now, Brent—"

"I know. If I would just take the time to get acquainted with him—"

"You'd like him," Mae finished in chorus with Brent. "He's been invited to Sarah Louise's for dinner."

"Too bad I'm expected at my daughter's. I'd enjoy seeing how Sarah Louise reacts to him."

Brent opened the door. "Keith?" he said in a tone of surprise.

"In the flesh—all of it. Or perhaps you didn't recognize me in my costume."

"You certainly don't look the same as you did when I met you in the hospital," said Brent as he stepped aside to let Keith come into the living room.

"This is an occasion," Keith said, grinning, "and I dressed for it." He extended his arms and turned from side to side. "Do you think I look all right?" he asked Mae as she came over to kiss him on the cheek.

"I certainly do!" she exclaimed.

There was nothing of Mae's "Jungle Boy" about Keith Sullivan that day. He wore a pair of grey slacks, a white shirt with an open collar, and a navy blue blazer. The clothes fit him well, neither binding nor puckering as they covered his great bulk. Not only was he well-dressed, he was freshly shaven, and he had somehow managed to groom his thick, curly hair so that it wasn't quite as wild-looking as usual.

"I'll have to tell my mom you approved. I asked her what I should wear when invited to the home of a very proper lady, and then I took her advice." He paused a moment before adding, "I confess to being a bit nervous about this."

Brent smiled. "I don't blame you. Sarah Louise can be formidable. But I don't think you have anything to worry about. She might have her moments, but Ron and the M and Ms will help you over them."

"The M and Ms?" Keith questioned.

"Mae's way of referring to her grandchildren," Brent answered. "Their names all begin with M—all seven of them."

About half an hour later the three of them left Mae's house, Brent to join his daughter and Keith and Mae to join the James family. When the latter two arrived, Sarah Louise was in the kitchen.

"Go tell your mother they're here," Ron instructed Melody. Then he shook Keith's hand. "Come in and have a seat."

Keith had hardly situated himself on the couch when the smaller James children crowded around him.

"Did you really give my grandma a foot rub?" asked kindergartener Matt.

"Matt! That's not an appropriate topic of conversation!" scolded Sarah Louise as she came into the room, wiping her hands on her apron. "I'm glad you could come, Keith," she said as she shook his hand. "Have you met the children?"

"We've made a start at it."

"Dinner will be ready in a minute. Matt, don't you pester Mr. Sullivan."

The minute she left the room, Matt asked, "Are foot rubs just for people in the hospital?"

"Nope."

"Then I want one."

The little boy climbed up on the couch beside Keith and began taking off his shoes and socks.

"That's probably not the best idea," suggested Ron, but Keith said, "I don't mind. I just need some lotion and a towel."

As one of the twins ran to get what he needed, Keith took off his blazer and rolled up his sleeves. Soon Matt's foot was propped on the towel covering Keith's leg, and the foot massage began. Morgan, Michael, and Margaret gathered around, and Mark watched over Keith's shoulder.

With an amused curve to her lips, Mae noticed the children's fascination. In spite of the fact that she considered the foot rub ill-advised, it had drawn all the M and Ms not busy in the kitchen around Keith like a magnet. They were fascinated by him, and that pleased Mae.

Sarah Louise was not pleased, however. She was furious when she saw what was going on in her living room on a Sunday afternoon that also happened to be Mother's Day. Her voice was icy as she informed them that the food was on the table, and Keith had a chagrined look on his face as he asked where he could wash his hands.

Things got better during the meal, though. Ron gave a little speech honoring Sarah Louise and Mae, and everyone toasted the two women with their glasses of sparkling grape juice.

"How about your mother?" Ron asked Keith.

"She's at my brother's in Charleston. I called her this morning—I was lucky to get through." He hesitated, then added, "I miss my mother a lot. I guess that's one of the reasons I enjoy Mae's company."

The words seemed to affect Sarah Louise. Her face lost some of its pinched look, and the rest of the meal was more pleasant than Mae had hoped for.

However, once the meal was over and the children had dispersed, Sarah Louise asked bluntly, "Do you always take as much personal interest in your patients as you have in Mother?"

"Not always."

"But you've taken a big interest in her, and you've influenced her to do things that aren't in her best interest."

"I didn't try to influence her one way or another, Sarah Louise. I just answered her questions honestly and let her know I supported her right to make an independent decision."

"That's really all he did, dear," affirmed Mae.

"It still doesn't seem right to me."

Mae started to defend Keith further, but she had no need

to. Quietly Keith replied, "I would never suggest anything to your mother that was not appropriate. Nor would I ever attempt to manipulate her into doing something that served my purposes only. I care about her too much."

The rest of the evening was spent enjoyably. Ron, perhaps because he was editor of the *Journal* and had become quite inquisitive, was especially interested in Keith's background. Sarah Louise occasionally joined in too, though a bit distantly.

It's up to Sarah Louise now, thought Mae later on as she got ready for bed. The afternoon had been a success. There was nothing in Keith's behavior that her daughter could fault, except perhaps the foot massage.

Nevertheless, Mae had the feeling that her daughter would probably continue to resent Keith. That resentment, she was beginning to understand, was misdirected: she herself was the person Sarah Louise was angry at.

Mae was still contemplating that thought when the phone rang. It was Terry.

"Hi'ya, Mom. Happy Mother's Day."

"Terry! I'm so glad you called. How are you?"

"Great. Couldn't be better."

"How are Ellen and the kids?"

"They're fine; everybody's fine. We're just doing a hundred out here. Vicky and Steve are doing great in school, and the twins are the cutest things you ever saw. Say, did you get the pictures we took on their birthday?"

"No, not yet."

"Darn. I meant to send them. I'll have to tell my secretary Pam to get right on it. She's the one who remembers little things like that. It's a feminine trait."

"What?"

"I read it in a book about women making it in the business world. They said women have a head for details, while men deal more with ideas and concepts."

"Oh."

"Really. That's what they said."

"I don't doubt that, but I can see how that little bit of information could be used in a pretty negative sense."

"Come on, don't take it personally. Hey, did you hear the one about the pig with the wooden leg?"

"You told me that one last time."

"Oh, sorry. How about the Texan who died?"

Mae closed her eyes as he told his joke. His animated voice sounded like a voice from the past: it was as if she were hearing Abe speak. Oh, she loved this son of hers who was so much like his grandfather, this man who was still a boy in so many ways. He was irrepressible and irresponsible and so engaging that he was irresistible. He was a very successful life-insurance salesman, thanks to the efforts of his secretary, who was an excellent businesswoman. Without her, he would have been a failure long ago.

"Well, the joke must not have been very funny," Terry's petulant voice broke into her thoughts.

With a start, Mae realized that she had missed the punch line.

"Oh, I'm sorry. You sounded so much like your grandfather, I got to thinking about him and—"

"That's okay. I'll just have to have a better joke ready next time. So, how are you doing? You know, I meant to send you a pretty something or other while you were in the hospital, but you got out too soon. I'll send it now, a sort of late Mother's Day present."

"That would be nice."

"Sarah Louise says you're still being stubborn about the chemo. I think you ought to listen to what she says. Let's get going on this, the sooner, the better."

"I've already started a program to help me out."

"That's great, just what I wanted to hear. I'd better hang up now. Ellen gets mad when I run up the long-distance bills."

"We don't want that."

"Nope. By the way, I'm working on getting some free days so I can get out there to see you."

"Oh, that would be wonderful!"

"Well, that's it, I guess. Take care of yourself, Mom."

"'Bye, dear."

Mae lay awake a long time after he had hung up. The call

was so typical of Terry: it reflected all his qualities, the endearing and the irritating. She was glad that he had remembered to call her, yet the sound of his voice conjured up the fears, worries, guilt, and sorrow she carried in the corner of her heart marked with his name.

You'll have to let go sometime, you old fool, she lectured herself, wiping away the tear that was tickling its way down the side of her nose.

But she couldn't, not yet.

8

Edith had begun showing up daily and staying a long time. It seemed strange to Mae, who disliked having a shadow, but the two women tolerated each other in large doses remarkably well.

In the routine that evolved around Edith's visits, they usually spent part of the morning on Mae's patio. This particular day was no different, for the patio was the perfect place to enjoy the cool hours of a June morning. Early summer flowers were now in bloom, marching in orderly fashion along her fence, only to rebel and break ranks in the garden itself. Tulips and daffodils had given way to irises, peonies, coral bells, and delphinium, which competed for attention with English daisies, columbine, coreopsis, and flax. It was very pleasant to have that lovely view before them as they enjoyed the Pero Edith had fixed.

"You do have a way of picking up strays, don't you?" said Edith, who then sipped from her cup.

"You're referring to Keith, I guess."

"Yes, indeed."

"You make it sound nasty, as if 'picking up strays' were in the same class as picking up a social disease."

"Mae!"

"What's the matter with liking people and wanting to know them better?"

"Nothing. It's just that you choose the most bizarre creatures to be the object of your charity."

"I assume you're using the word 'charity' in the sense of 'love.'"

"Assume it, if you must."

"Keith isn't bizarre, Edith."

"Isn't he? And how about Frank Nakamoto? Are you going to tell me he isn't bizarre?"

"You're a bigot," said Mae, but there was no condemnation in her voice.

"I suppose so. I've never said I wasn't. All I know is, I wouldn't have chosen either of them as friends. But then, I'm not you, am I?"

"No."

"Come on, you're not going to get mad at me for saying that, are you?"

"No, but I want you to give Keith a chance. He's not bizarre, and he's not a stray. He has a lot to give people if they'll just let him."

"Okay, I believe you."

"Besides, once you really get to know him, just think what you'll have to talk to the neighbors about!"

"Good material, huh?"

"A little will go a long way," said Mae with a smile.

"Okay, I'll give him a chance. And if he's as nice a guy as you say he is, I'll see if I can't improve his reputation."

Edith's mention of Frank Nakamoto put Mae in a pensive mood. As she gave her bonsai their afternoon watering, she stood for a long time in front of the juniper that had been a gift from Frank's grandfather. It was a venerable old tree; Mr. Nakamoto had reckoned it to be several hundred years old. His training of it had been an attempt to bring beauty and humanity into the grim surroundings of the Heart Mountain Relocation Center.

Mae had watched the camp go up; the hastily built barracks overlaid with black tarpaper were visible from the road she drove when going to visit her mother in Cody. Row upon row of ugly buildings sprang up among the sagebrush, behind which the beauty of the mountain was incongruous. Then, after evacuees from coastal areas had already begun to arrive, a barbed-wire fence and guard towers were built around the perimeter.

The first time Mae saw the fence and the eight towers, she was so shocked that she almost lost control of her car.

Pulling to the side of the road, she wiped away the sudden tears that had blurred her vision. The Relocation Center was not just an exceptionally ugly facility where people of Japanese descent were to wait out the war; the addition of the fence and guard towers had revealed it for what it was: a prison camp. She felt personally betrayed, and her heart went out to those confined there.

"I can't believe it!" she said later to Fritz, the tears coming to her eyes again. "It's the most awful thing I've ever seen. We have to do something."

"I agree with you one hundred percent. I can see the government's viewpoint, but this relocation thing has played right into the hands of greedy and bigoted people. I'm not at all sure it had to be handled this way." He looked at her quizzically. "What do you suggest?"

"You're a newspaperman, do what newspapermen do. Educate the public. Influence the way people around here think."

"I can do that only if George is willing to print what I write. But I think he will—he's more open-minded than some people I know, and he is a good editor. What about you?"

Mae drew her eyebrows together. "I haven't figured that out yet," she said.

"You will, I don't doubt that one bit."

Mae's opportunity to put her convictions into action came in an unexpected way some weeks later.

Not far into the sugar beet harvest, it became obvious that the crop was going to rot in the ground for lack of laborers. The logical source for the needed help was the internment camps, including the one at Heart Mountain. But even as the governor of Wyoming requested volunteers from the camps to work in the fields, he asked for assurance that the release of Japanese internees wouldn't in any way lead to future permanent settlement in the state.

"'Come help us, but don't settle down next to us,' that's what he's saying. Not very gracious of him, is it?" Fritz commented when he told Mae the news.

"Will some of them be coming here?" Mae asked.

"No doubt."

"I hope our mayor doesn't have the same attitude."

"I don't think he does," said Fritz.

"Well, we'd better find out for sure. I don't want my community to embarrass itself."

So Mae called up the mayor and suggested that he write a piece for the *Journal* welcoming the young Japanese men who were coming to Shelton. She was very satisfied when she read his statement, in which he encouraged his constituents to accord the volunteers all the courtesies due any other citizen of the United States. She was also in attendance the day he personally reaffirmed his stand in a welcoming ceremony.

But that wasn't enough for Mae. She liked doing things person-to-person, so she walked right up to some of the Japanese, introduced herself, and asked where they were going to be working. To her surprise, she found that one of them, Frank Nakamoto, was going to the Sidwell farm.

"That's my friend Edith's farm!" she exclaimed. "I drive out there often. Maybe you and I will get a chance to know each other better."

Frank Nakamoto only looked at her warily.

Suddenly, Mae wondered if she hadn't been too forward. All her life, she had proceeded on the assumption that people liked her and would welcome her company. Now she realized there was no reason why this young Japanese-American should trust her or even want to become acquainted with her. She was coming across like some busybody do-gooder.

"Well, uh, good luck," she stammered, then she made her retreat, feeling flushed and foolish.

She reacted by lashing out at Fritz.

"Why haven't you been to the camp? Why aren't you writing articles about it?" she demanded.

"I've suggested it, but George isn't too interested at the moment."

Not long after that conversation, however, Fritz called from his *Journal* office to tell Mae there had been a labor strike at the camp. The evacuees, who worked at all aspects of running their city, were very poorly paid in contrast to the wages received by the civilian administrative staff.

Angered by inequity following so closely on the heels of injustice, certain internees staged a strike, which had been broken when the instigators were arrested and sent to a camp in Arizona.

"George told me to get up there and find out what it's all about," Fritz said excitedly.

"I'm coming with you."

"Oh, no, you're not. George has arranged for Fritz Thomlinson to get a press pass, not Fritz Thomlinson and wife." She made a sound of disappointment, and he added, "I'll tell you all about it when I come home, right down to the last detail."

But Mae found she didn't want to hear every detail—it was too painful.

"You thought those barracks were awful when you saw them from the road, but they're even worse up close," Fritz told her after his visit. "You wouldn't believe it. Each family has a little room about twenty feet by twenty feet. Maybe that doesn't sound too bad, but Japanese families include grandparents, too, sometimes both sets. Some of those 'family apartments' have as many as thirteen people in them.

"And all they have in there are some cots. Mae, it's unthinkable! Cots and a potbellied stove. In some of those barracks, they don't even have insulation, and the cracks in the floor are so big that stoves won't do a bit of good in winter. It's cold enough now to need heat, and they don't have enough coal."

"How do they keep warm enough?"

"They don't. They huddle together under blankets, I imagine, but I doubt if that does much good. And they're hungry too. Most of the time, all they get for a meal is one ladleful of some concoction. They go to bed hungry too often."

"Then we'll need to get more blankets and food to them," said Mae.

"Mae, this is not like taking meals in to some needy family. There are *twelve thousand people* there! Unless you have the faith to divide loaves and fishes, anything you do will be a drop in the bucket."

"What if I went to visit just one family?"

"You don't know any families up there."

"I know Frank Nakamoto, that nice young man working on Edith's place. At least, I've talked to him once or twice since he arrived. I could drive out to Edith's and find out what his parents might need or want. How does that sound?"

"I don't know, Mae. You might be disappointed. They aren't going to welcome you with open arms. There will always be a certain distance, I'm afraid."

Remembering Frank's reserved, exquisitely polite behavior, Mae knew her husband was right. There were boundaries that she might never be able to cross. It was something she would have to deal with.

She called Edith the next day. "I'm coming out with a picnic lunch for the boys," she announced. "I want to talk to Frank and the others too. I figured lunchtime was the best possibility."

"Mae, what are you up to?"

"I'm forming my own relief committee of one. Unless you want to join."

"No thanks. I feel uncomfortable around them—I always feel like I should be apologizing for something. This is one venture you'll have to take on by yourself."

Mae met the young men under the tree along the canal bank where they were taking their midday break. She felt awkward, but no less awkward than they. They were halfway through the meal she had prepared for them before they really began talking to her. She was often close to tears as they told of boarding busses with only what they could carry in their hands; of the breakdown in family order caused by the ruling that only American-born and educated Japanese could take part in camp government, thus pitting the younger generation against the older; of the shame caused by lack of privacy; of hunger and cold.

Her compassion eventually won their confidence. After two weeks of bringing them lunches, the Japanese workers welcomed her suggestion that she visit their parents, taking with her the wages they had earned and personal messages.

"I'm scared," she told Fritz the day she was to drive to Heart Mountain.

"Don't be. They're just people."

"Will you come with me?"

"I can't, not today. If you want to wait . . . "

"No. I'll go by myself."

"Does David Bates know you're coming?"

"Yes." She had already talked to the director of community service, who had encouraged her visit. One of the few staff members who had come to Heart Mountain for reasons other than the good wages, he was doing everything he could to encourage contact and understanding between the evacuees and the local citizens.

Bates was waiting for her at the gate house when she arrived. "Welcome to the third largest city in Wyoming," he said as he shook her hand.

"I knew there were a lot of people here, but I never thought of it that way," murmured Mae, overcome by the sheer size of the camp. It was almost three times larger than Shelton.

"Come on. I'll show you part of our 'city' as we go. The mothers of the boys you've met are waiting for us at the Nakamotos'. Sorry about the dust," he added as they started down an unpaved street. "Just be thankful it didn't rain last night."

He talked as they walked, indicating what the various buildings were. When he pointed out the mess hall of one block, Mae noticed several women bent over a task at the side of the building.

"What are they doing?"

"They're sifting coal dust to find anything that might be big enough to burn."

"My husband told me there wasn't enough coal to go around, but I didn't really realize . . . "

"It's terrible, but can you imagine the logistics of setting up a camp this size? Not enough provisions were ordered to begin with, and we're overcrowded on top of that—this camp was meant to hold ten thousand maximum. Add the usual snarls and red tape, and we simply don't have what we need yet. But that will change, I assure you. It just takes a while. Eventually we'll have a couple of recreation centers. We already have our own school system, and we've even got some Boy Scout troops organized. Oh, here we are."

He led her to one of six stoops on the south side of a building and knocked on the door. A diminuitive woman opened it. "Mrs. Nakamoto, I've brought Mrs. Thomlinson to you."

Afterward, Mae could remember very little of what was said as they sat on the cots in the Nakamoto family's quarters. She had passed out the letters and given a personal message to each of the women there, assuring them that their boys were well. She spoke slowly, because she realized almost immediately that of all the women there, only Mrs. Nakamoto knew English well. Once the initial greetings were over, great silence settled in the room, broken only as Bates drew first one and then another woman into conversation.

Barely half an hour had passed before he rose to signal the end of the visit, yet to Mae it had seemed interminable. As she said good-bye to each woman, she wondered what had possessed her to think that a visit would be a good idea. But when she came to Mrs. Nakamoto, Frank's mother said in a gentle voice, "I thank you for all of my family. You are always welcome in our home."

It hasn't been a waste of time after all, thought Mae gratefully. "Thank you, Mrs. Nakamoto. Is there anything I can take to your son?"

Mrs. Nakamoto's eyes gleamed, and Mae knew she had said the right thing.

"That is most gracious. If you would please take this?" And she held out a small packet.

"Yes, of course. I would be happy to."

Mrs. Nakamoto bowed, and Mae impulsively bowed back.

That visit marked the beginning of Mae's crusade. For three years, she did whatever she could to make life at Heart Mountain more pleasant for the evacuees. Although she had found the person-to-person contact she wanted, she didn't limit her efforts to just the Nakamoto family.

When the mayor of Lovell invited the Heart Mountain high school students to play an exhibition basketball game, she badgered Mayor Edwards until he invited them to play at Shelton. Then she led the cheering for the five under-sized players who stuck it out through an unequal contest.

Then, when David Bates told her that the Associated Students of the University of Wyoming had written the Heart Mountain school superintendent indicating their willingness to accept qualified students, she went to work on behalf of Frank Nakamoto. She wrote letters to the camp director, the admissions office of the U. of W., and her congressman in a successful effort to get Frank and other students enrolled at Laramie.

And when she found out that the *Powell Tribune* carried "Heart Mountain Breezes," a column written by a camp internee, she convinced editor George Lenz to run a similar column in the *Shelton Journal*.

At the time she was doing this, Fritz was also covering stories at the camp. Both of them soon gained a reputation of being "soft on the Japs," as some put it. In fact, they were accosted on the street one day by a man who wanted to know why Fritz was "mollycoddling them Japs" instead of fighting like all the other able-bodied men.

Neither Fritz nor Mae could trust themselves to give a civil answer. The reason Fritz was not fighting should have been obvious: his right leg was visibly shorter than his left, the result of a poorly set break that had occurred when Fritz was thrown from a horse he and his father were training. It not only caused him to limp, but the stress it put on his spinal column had also led to chronic back pain. Consequently, his draft card read 4F.

"I know it's ridiculous," he fumed, "but comments like that do make me feel like I'm not doing enough."

"You are doing a lot," Mae assured him. "I know that some people have changed their attitudes because of what you've written."

"You've done as much as I have, when it comes to that."

"I think I have," said Mae proudly. But the most meaningful of her camp experiences was yet before her.

One day in the spring of 1944, as Mae approached the

Nakamotos' building, she noticed something was different. Curious, she quickened her step, only to stop, astounded, at what she saw. The space around the Nakamotos' stoop had been transformed into an oasis of beauty. Rocks defined a small pond around which various types of potted trees and bushes had been set. The plants were native to the area—Mae recognized juniper and sagebrush among them—but all had been pruned to the elegant perfection of the Japanese bonsai she had read about in *National Geographic*. The garden reflected a sense of balance, proportion, and restfulness that was a revelation.

"My father-in-law made that," said Mrs. Nakamoto proudly.

"Can he teach me how?" asked Mae excitedly.

"Bonsai is for old men."

"I still want to learn."

Mrs. Nakamoto smiled indulgently. "If you want to learn, perhaps he will show you."

When Mae told David Bates that the old Mr. Nakamoto was going to teach her the art of bonsai, he was surprised. "Did you know that bonsai is traditionally a man's hobby? I'm surprised he's willing to teach you. It must be because of what you did to help Frank get to Laramie."

Mae could hardly wait until the appointed day arrived. When it did, Fritz went with her to Heart Mountain, because he too wanted to see what the elder Mr. Nakamoto had done.

The small, frail, and balding man greeted his guests with great dignity—in Japanese. Frank's mother translated.

"I'm so glad you agreed to tell me about bonsai," said Mae. "What you have done here is lovely."

"It is not much," said Mr. Nakamoto, pausing so his daughter-in-law could translate. "These are not finished bonsai like the ones I left behind—they have just started training. Now that we are allowed to leave camp, I have been able to collect some trees in the hills."

Mae couldn't imagine how the delicate-looking man could have possibly done the hiking and climbing necessary to collect the trees. He seemed to read her mind for he added, "My children and grandchildren are my feet."

He pointed to a juniper that sat on the step in a homemade tray. "This is not the same kind of juniper we have in Japan, but it is beautiful too."

He explained to them how he had cut its roots back and planted it at the side of the barracks in the fall. This spring he had trimmed the roots again, potted it in a tray purchased in Cody, and done the initial pruning and wiring.

"Doesn't the wire hurt it?" asked Mae.

"No. Not if it's properly applied. You see? The branches have such a lovely plane. Now I will pinch the needles back next spring, and they will get very, very thick. Like this."

From his pocket, Mr. Nakamoto took photographs and showed them one at a time to Fritz and Mae. "Some of the bonsai I left behind were three hundred years old. They were passed on to me by my father, and I brought them with me to America in 1901. There was a master in our village in Japan. When he grew very old, he sent some of his bonsai to me."

"Who is taking care of them now?" asked Mae. Fritz poked a warning elbow against her ribs, but Mrs. Nakamoto relayed the question.

"I do not know. I think they must be dead now." The words were spoken evenly, as if devoid of meaning or emotion, but Mae thought she caught a glimpse of something in Mr. Nakamoto's eyes that made her ache.

"How long will this one be in . . . training, did you say?" Fritz changed the subject.

"Many, many years. The way of bonsai teaches the art of patience. One learns to appreciate slow, forward progress."

"I want to learn how to do that," said Mae.

"It is an old man's hobby. If one has many trees, it takes much time."

"But could I? Are there any books?"

"No one learns bonsai from books," said Mr. Nakamoto. When he saw the expression on her face as his daughter-in-law translated, he quickly added, "The theory is simple; for that you don't need a book. The tree is dwarfed because it is potted in shallow soil. We cut back the root system and prune the branches to keep the tree dwarfed and in balance. The art of bonsai is something else again—it can only be developed over years of practice."

Mr. Nakamoto picked up the juniper and handed it to Mae. "Look at it and learn. Keep it out of the hottest sun; water it twice a day. Put it in a protected spot in the winter so the roots don't freeze."

"But—" Mae tried to protest.

"Come back to me in the spring. Together we will trim the roots, change the wire, and pinch the new growth."

But the elder Mr. Nakamoto was not there to show her what to do with the juniper the spring of 1945—he had not survived his second winter in the internment camp.

After Mae got over her shock and anger at his death, she was gripped by a determination to train the tree herself as a memorial. Guided by an influence she could not define, Mae trimmed off as many of the juniper's roots as she thought prudent that spring. Then she took off the old wire and wrapped new, heated wire around the branches. When the wire had cooled, she moved the branches gently into the planes that Mr. Nakamoto had already set. Later on, she carefully pinched the ends of the spring growth, leaving only a few new needles. All the time she was working, she talked to the bonsai, reassuring it of her love and commitment to it, encouraging it to survive.

It did, and Mae was hooked. She talked Edith into juniper-hunting expeditions, and soon the lone bonsai in her garden was joined by companion trees. They collected numerous specimens, which spent their first year and sometimes their second in the rich soil of the garden before Mae transplanted them into shallow containers. She went by instinct, with uneven but interesting results, until the mid-1950s. That year, the Brooklyn Botanic Garden printed its handbook on bonsai, and the local librarian, aware of Mae's interest, included it in the library's book order.

The subsequent handbooks by the Garden also became part of the Shelton Public Library, but by then Mae had learned that what Mr. Nakamoto had said was right: you don't learn bonsai from books.

Now, on this lovely June morning, Mae reached out to touch the bonsai the old Mr. Nakamoto had given her, the bonsai that had been part of her life for forty-one years. She loved it with an intensity she would have found hard to explain, and she knew the fear that had suddenly struck her heart would be hard to explain as well. The old master in Japan had sent some of his bonsai to Mr. Nakamoto in hopes that they would be well taken care of, in hopes that they would survive many new generations. But the old master's tactic had not worked. Events never dreamed of had wiped out years, perhaps centuries of loving labor. Would her bonsai have any better chance of surviving after she was gone?

She had always wanted each of her children to have one of her bonsai; it would be her last, final gift of self to them and her last lesson. From her gift, she hoped Sarah Louise would learn not only to trim and prune, but also to allow the growth that the tree's unique nature required. For Terry, pruning would be an anathema, but there was always the hope that he might learn something from the process. And Karen, who already understood the principle of directed growth, could possibly learn quietude and patience. But that only accounted for three of her indoor bonsai. What of the others, and her outdoor trees?

"To whom shall I send you, my dears," she said, touching one of the exquisite old trees lovingly.

It was a question for which she had no answer.

9

She looked awful. She hadn't realized it before, given her *Tic* (as Keith called it in German) about avoiding mirrors, but she knew how awful she must look now, for it was reflected clearly in Karen's reaction.

"Why didn't you tell me?" Karen cried, vainly trying to keep control.

"What earthly good would it have done?"

"I would have known; I should have known!"

"Well, you know now. But this isn't the last hurrah, so let's not dwell on it. What do you think of my greenhouse?"

"Mother—"

"Do you want a tour?"

Karen gulped down a sob and said shakily, "Okay. Do it your way. We'll just pretend this is like any other visit."

"For now, anyway," amended Mae, leading her daughter into the house. The living room, which had always been so small, had opened up miraculously and was flooded with light. Instead of being an appendage to the other room, the greenhouse was part of it. The effect was marvelous.

"My word, Mother, this is beautiful!" said Karen, stepping into the plant-filled room. It seemed to be a jungle, for not only were there plants on the table, there were also lush, healthy plants hanging from the ceiling and standing on the tiled floor. Still, careful arranging left the extension spacious enough for a chintz-covered hassock, a small side table, and Mae's white wicker chair, which her cat occupied at the moment.

"It looks crowded, I know," said Mae, "but all my friends seemed to have sick plants that were sure to thrive if they took up residence here."

"It doesn't look crowded at all, it looks marvelous."

"It didn't look this good at first. For a long time I had only a cement floor and the table Mark made—I didn't even give him time to finish it properly, I was so anxious to get my plants moved."

"When did all the rest of this happen?"

"Well, when folks heard what I was doing, they all wanted to check it out for themselves. You know, they wanted to see what 'crazy Mae' was up to. One of my boys came by—you remember Dave MacArthur, don't you? He said 'What's the deal with this floor? You don't want ugly old cement. How 'bout if I lay some nice tile for you. At cost, of course.' It didn't seem like that much extra, considering how much nicer it looks, so I had him do it. 'Terra cotta,' he calls it. It's real pretty, isn't it?

"Then Mark's shop teacher came to help him finish the table off properly with stain and shellac and a metal lining. Margery Knoblauch down the street gave me the bamboo blinds—she said they'd been sitting in her attic for years. I did need something to block the sun on real hot days, but my! Those blinds were a lot of trouble. It took Mark and Ron a whole weekend to figure out how to rig them up."

"It's perfect, Mom. Scat, cat. I want to sit there. Shall we pull up your rocking chair?"

"Sounds like a good idea. You do that, and I'll get you something."

"You don't have to wait on me. I can get it myself."

"I know that," said Mae mildly. "I have milk, pop, and lemonade. Real lemonade."

"How could anybody pass that up? I'll take the lemonade."

Karen sat down in the wicker chair the cat had just vacated. "Oh, this is great. I can't tell you how much I needed to get out of Minneapolis."

"Is there anything wrong at home?"

"No, not particularly. Everything's pretty much the same. Too much to do and not enough time. We've got a new account at the ad agency, and that always means pressure and overtime, so I've been late getting home. Not that it makes any difference. The boys are always busy with afterschool activities, and right now is Cal's busiest time of year. I don't think they even know I'm not home at the usual time. So much for family life."

"It sounds like you're under a lot of pressure."

"That's what being in advertising is, Mom. Pressure. Be wonderful on cue. The job can get hung up a hundred different places along the way, from the ad manager to the art director to the printer, and you can't do a darn thing about it. Everybody knows that, but it doesn't stop them from dumping on you if the final proof isn't on the right desk at the right time. But there's nothing new about that. Otherwise, everything's okay."

"How's Greg getting along?"

"You'd have to ask that. Well, my dear son is doing fine, too, for a kid with studs on his belt and pants held together with wire, not to mention spiked hair that happens to be a particularly nauseating shade of yellow."

"You don't sound as worried about it as you used to be."

"I guess I'm used to it by now. Besides, his looks are the only thing that's really bizarre about him. He's basically a good kid. The only problem is, not many people take the time to find that out. He's done his normal good work in school this year, but his grades have dropped. Some of the teachers don't really see what he's doing; they just see what he looks like. It's sad."

"Does he realize what's going on?"

"Oh yes. But he's convinced that the teachers should change, not him. And he does have a point, there. His appearance shouldn't affect his grades."

"Unfortunately, that's not the way life goes, is it?"

"No. I mean, look at me. I like my image, don't get me wrong, but it's calculated to fit in the world of advertising. I wouldn't dress like this if I were trying to make it as a corporate exec. 'Course, this isn't exactly the outfit I would wear to work, but you get the idea."

Mae smiled and nodded. Only a tall, thin figure like Karen's could look good dressed as Karen was. She wore white pants that were yoked and pleated in the front and nipped in at the ankle, topped by a turquoise shirt that was tunic length and padded in the shoulders. A wide leather belt rested loosely on her hips, and her outfit was completed by a silver necklace of modernistic design and matching silver earrings.

"That's a new haircut, isn't it?"

"Chalk one up for diplomacy, mother dear. I was wondering when you'd mention it." Karen ran her fingers through her frosted, ash-blond hair, which was shorter than Mae had ever seen it. "It's a bit extreme, but it's easy to take care of. I think it brings out my eyes, don't you?"

"Since when did you ever need anything to bring out your eyes? Besides, the shirt does that well enough. It makes them look the same shade."

Karen chuckled. "Cal likes my hair like this, but Jim is not so thrilled. Greg says I ought to spike it with toothpaste just once, to see what Jim would do. He thinks it would be a good joke, but I'm afraid his brother wouldn't think it was funny at all."

"How is Jim?"

"What can I say? Jim's no problem—in fact, he's almost too good. He looks like a fashion plate whenever he steps out of the house, even when he's mowing the lawn. His room is always immaculate, and he's getting straight As in school. I'm worried about him, to tell the truth. Being perfect must be an awful strain. Both of the boys are doing okay, really, each after his own fashion. But living in a house with one punk and one prep is like living in a war zone. If it weren't for Cal, I don't think I'd be able to manage it. Somehow, he can relate to both of his boys, although I don't know how. Tell me, why couldn't I have just one average, run-of-the-mill kid?" After a moment of silence, Karen added, "Maybe Cory would have been."

"Is that what's bothering you, dear?"

"I guess so. I still get a bit down at this time of year, even after so long."

"I know what you mean. I have plenty of those anniversaries to deal with, myself."

Karen sniffed, then tried out a smile. "Do you mind if I change the subject? I don't want to get into that right now."

"What do you want to talk about?"

"Oh, you could tell me what Sarah Louise is up to. How is my dear sister doing?"

"Do I detect a hint of sarcasm?"

"Heaven forbid. Well, just a little, I admit it."

"I do wish you two could find a way to get over this childish snit."

"Is that what it is?"

"You're grown up now. Can't you be more tolerant with one another?"

"I'll try. So how is she?"

"Fine. Busy as usual. She's teaching Mother's Education in Relief Society; she's room mother for three of the kids; she works on the Bucket Brigade—"

"What in the world is that?"

"It's a volunteer tutoring service at the school."

"Well, knowing Sarah Louise, that's just a beginning. What else is she doing?"

"Nothing much. She has a 4-H group, and she's in Woman's Club, and—"

"Stop, stop! I may have a full-time job, but she's busier than I am. Maybe she'd have less to do if she went to work."

"Don't tell her that."

"What do you hear from Terry?"

"About as much as you do, I expect."

"Which is not much, except maybe at Christmas. He has called you since you got out of the hospital, hasn't he?"

"He called, but you know Terry. One time he was too busy telling me about his standing in the Million Dollar Club and about his stock market killings to really communicate; the other, he was trying to figure out what jokes he hadn't told me yet."

"Sounds just like him," Karen sighed. After a moment she asked, "Do you think he's happy?"

"Terry hasn't been really happy for years."

"Why is that? He's got so much going for him, why does he keep ruining it for himself?"

"I don't know. He's never been able to take responsibility for himself or his actions. Heaven knows how hard your dad and I tried to teach him. It just never got through to him. I wish he could realize one day that living the way he does takes far more energy than making choices and dealing with consequences."

"I worry about him."

"I do, too. I worry about all of you."

"Doesn't get any easier just because the kids get older, does it?" Karen grinned.

"No. And then the kids get married and have kids, and then you have in-laws and grandchildren to worry about. But you're all worth the prayers I say for you every day."

"Thanks. Speaking of grandchildren, where do you suppose the M and Ms are? I've been here a couple of hours already, and nobody's come over to say hello."

"I suppose Sarah Louise has forbidden them to barge in. But we're expected for supper in a few minutes, so you'll see them soon enough."

Indeed, Karen was surrounded by nieces and nephews the moment she walked in the door of the large, fully renovated farmhouse that was home to the James family. She was the immediate center of attention, for she was the aunt who lived in a big city; she was a copywriter for an innovative Minneapolis ad agency; she was the mother of their most notorious cousins.

"What did you bring for us?" asked Matt, with a calculated grin.

From her large bag, Karen drew out T-shirts, all of which had something to do with Minnesota. There was a scramble as the M and Ms started grabbing.

"Hang on," said Karen. "Here, these are for the little ones. Ron, why don't you pass them out? This one's for the baby, and these are for the twins. Mark, Melody, here are yours."

Mark read his, then laughed. "Hey, Dad, this is a Guindon T-shirt."

"What does it say, Son?"

"Minnesota, land of 10,000 lakes and a few weirdos."

"Do I get one of those?" Ron asked, laughing.

Karen took out a package. "Sorry. I didn't think that would be a gift befitting your station as the *Shelton Journal* owner and editor. This one is yours, and this is for you, Sarah Louise."

Ron opened his package, revealing a beautifully carved and stained wooden mallard. "For your office," Karen said.

"Wonderful workmanship," marvelled Ron, running his hand over the mallard's silky back. "Thanks, Sis. Open yours, Sarah."

Sarah Louise moved away from the others and turned slightly away as she opened the package. "Oh!" she gasped, and everybody crowded around her to see what was in the large package. She turned, holding up a two-by-three-foot woven hanging that integrated different textures and weights of natural yarns, as well as bits of polished shell and wood. It was a unique piece, one that Karen had loved herself and hoped her sister would love too.

"It's magnificent," said Ron.

"There's an artist in Minneapolis who does them for businesses. Once in a while she does smaller ones for homes. I was lucky to get this one—actually, I had to bribe her for it."

"Thank you, Karen. I'll hang it over the mantel, I think," said Sarah Louise.

"I'll put it up tomorrow," promised Ron. Then he herded the kids into the kitchen, leaving mother and daughters alone. Although she tried not to, Mae couldn't help comparing them as she watched them examine the hanging. Karen was tall, freckled, and fairly sparked with energy, while Sarah Louise was rather round, had flawless golden skin, and was more tenacious than energetic. But those differences were only the beginning. From the first, Karen had pursued life with an intensity regardless of risk, while Sarah Louise had always been the protector of the status quo. Karen had often said, "It's a good thing Sarah Louise lives in Shelton, not me."

"I'm glad you like the hanging," said Karen, stepping

forward to embrace her sister. But Sarah Louise's arms didn't really make contact with Karen's body, and her kiss was perfunctory.

"How was your trip out?"

"Not bad."

"How long do you plan on staying?"

"A week or so. I have two weeks off, actually, but there're some things that need my attention at home too."

"There's not much to do here—Shelton isn't a hotbed of activity, you know. We could go up the mountain. The passes aren't open yet, but we could drive as far as Five Springs for lunch."

"Don't worry about it, Sis. I really don't want to 'do' anything. I'm going to sleep in and fix fattening food—"

"Mother can't stand the smell of food cooking," said Sarah Louise sharply.

"Then I'll have rolls from the bakery and sandwiches. Still fattening, if dull," Karen replied coolly. Mae could see that she was making a conscious effort at remaining calm. "I'd like to take the kids out to breakfast one day and maybe take the older kids to a show."

"There probably won't be anything decent showing."

"Then we'll have to rent a video."

"I'd have to okay it first."

"Why don't you come with me when I get it?"

"Well, maybe. Do you have anything else planned?"

"Not really, but I'll probably help mother go through some things."

"What?" shrilled Sarah Louise. "Is that why you came out here? Just to make sure you got your pick of Mother's things before anyone else had a chance to say what they might want to have?"

"Sarah Louise!" reprimanded Mae sharply.

"No, dear sister, that is not why I came out," said Karen coldly.

"Sarah, listen. I'm the one who brought this up," said Mae. "I've decided I want to give each of my children the mementos I have of their growing-up years. I never intended it to be a private affair between Karen and myself—I hoped we could do it together. It could be a lovely experience, I thought. There're all those nice memories . . . "

"Oh, I don't know," said Sarah Louise in a distracted manner. "I'm taking meals into Julia Michelson—she has to stay in bed until her baby comes—and I'm camp director this year, so that means a lot of work . . . Oh, Ron! I smell something burning!"

And Sarah Louise dashed into the kitchen.

10

The next morning at about eight o'clock, Mae tentatively opened the door to the second bedroom.

"I'm awake," Karen said. "Who are you talking to?"

"Keith Sullivan. He dropped by on his way home from the hospital. I'd like you to come out and meet him, if you want to."

Karen sat up in bed. "Of course I want to. Just give me a minute, will you?"

Mae went back into the small kitchen. "She'll be out soon," she told Keith.

"Are you sure about this? I look pretty rough by this time of day." He ran his hand over his heavily shadowed cheek and tried to straighten his rumpled whites.

"You look fine. I don't think you need your blue blazer to impress Karen."

"I hope you're right."

Karen joined them a few minutes later, approaching Keith with a smile as Mae introduced them. "Thank you for taking care of Mother," Karen said as she shook his meaty hand.

"I'm not doing that much—"

"Don't discount it. Mom's told me all about you. You're doing a lot just by being her friend, and I'm grateful."

Keith smiled at Mae as he sat back down in his chair. "I see what you mean," he said.

"I told him he didn't need to dress up to impress you," Mae explained.

Karen chuckled. "I heard about your Mother's Day dinner."

"Well, you don't have to worry," said Keith ruefully, "I'm not doing impromptu massages anymore. I work strictly by appointment."

"That must have been something to see," Karen said. "So how do you like it out here in the boondocks?"

"A lot. I like lots of space—I think I'd get claustrophobia in a big city."

"I know what you mean. I always feel it when I return from visiting Mom. I get more and more antsy on the way back as the traffic increases. By the time I get to the Twin Cities, I'm usually ready to turn around. It always takes me a few days to stop noticing that it's never really quiet and that there's no dirt."

"No dirt?" questioned Keith.

"Everything's green in Minnesota. Out here, you can see the earth. Mom, do you remember the time we went out to Sheep Mountain and collected jars of all different colors of dirt?"

"Uh-huh."

"You wouldn't believe how many colors we found, Keith," continued Karen. "From purple to olive green to yellow."

"I'll watch for that when I go out there with Neal Larson," Keith said.

"Who's that?"

"You don't know him," answered Mae. "He came after you left. He teaches geography and history at the high school and is a real expert on the geology of our area. When Keith said he wanted to know more about Big Horn Basin, I introduced the two of them."

Keith nodded. "We're going fossil hunting next Saturday. Neal knows a place by Sheep Mountain where he says you can find fossils just lying on top of the ground. Should be interesting."

"I take it you're getting along here okay," said Karen. "In spite of the fact that you're one of the few non-Mormons around here?"

"Oh, I'm doing fine. What I don't understand is why you Mormons make so much of your separateness. You aren't · so different from other people. When it comes right down to it, I haven't bumped into any situations in Shelton that I wouldn't have found in a thousand other small towns. The truth is, there are things about me that put up initial barriers. I'd be looked at with suspicion no matter where I went, at least at first. Mae's helped out a lot there by introducing me to people like Neal. And the Boy Scouts have asked me to be their first-aid merit badge counselor."

"That's sounds fun."

"I've enjoyed it. In fact, I think I'll get more involved with them this fall. But the thing that's really made the difference is the fact that the head nurse on my shift finally trusts me. She doesn't watch every move I make anymore."

"That's good," said Karen. "I wouldn't like to think that someone with your capacity to care wasn't appreciated."

"Thanks," said Keith, a little embarrassed at the tears that came to his eyes. Then he pushed himself awkwardly out of his chair. "I guess it's time for me to go. Hope to see you again, Karen."

"You will."

Mae rose to accompany him to the door. As she passed Karen, she said in a low voice full of feeling, "Thank you."

Later on in the day, Mae and Karen went to help Sarah Louise get ready for the Young Women's fireside that was to be held there the next evening. That is, Karen did what Sarah Louise directed her to, while Mae observed the proceedings.

"Thank you for helping me," Sarah Louise said as they cleaned the kitchen, which was to Mae's eyes already spotless. "I know I should have started on this days ago, but I've been so busy with all the end-of-the-year projects at school, I didn't have time." She sighed enormously. "It just never quits!"

"Not if you don't want it to," murmured Karen. Then she said "Ouch!" as Mae jabbed her.

"What's the matter?" asked Sarah Louise.

"Nothing. I just got a splinter under my finger, but it's out now."

"We're always so busy," continued Sarah Louise, "I don't suppose you can even imagine, Karen. Oh, I know you work, but having two kids in a family is not the same as having seven. We're always going somewhere or doing something. By the way, I do want both of you to come over tomorrow night. All the girls in our ward love Mother, and I want them to meet you."

"You do?"

"Well, you're a good example of a successful business-woman—it wouldn't hurt them to meet one."

"I thought you disapproved of working women. Don't tell me you've changed your mind."

"Girls are much more career-oriented these days, Ron says. It's a lot different from the way it was when I went to college, that's for sure. BYU was just supposed to be a stopover on the way to matrimony—"

"Or a stepping-stone to matrimony," remarked Karen wryly.

"Whatever. The point is, I never really thought I would need my teaching degree. After all, we weren't told to go get some job skills; we were told to go get a husband. Isn't that the way you remember it?"

Karen nodded.

"But it's not that way anymore. Even the Church encourages young women to prepare for careers. Why, Melody and her friends talk about going to college and what they want to be as much as they talk about boys. They might as well meet a career woman who is also a good Church member."

"Okay. You can count on your token career woman being there. What about you, Mom? Will you be able to go to church, to the farm, and to the fireside, all in one day?"

"No," said Mae. "I'll probably forgo the visit with Howard. You go out yourself while I take a nap. That way we'll both be able to listen to Sarah Louise's talk."

Mae found that a nap and a pill were both necessary before she was ready and able to walk down the street with

Karen the next evening. Even so, while Sarah Louise was introducing her sister to the young women, Mae slipped to an upstairs bedroom where she could do her visualization without being interrupted. She felt much better when she joined Karen on the living room couch.

The room was filled with lovely young ladies. Karen sighed as she looked at the smooth faces and youthful figures surrounding them.

"What is it?" asked Mae.

"You'll think this is ridiculous, but they make me feel old."

Mae chuckled.

"Ah, well. I don't really wish to be fifteen again, even though it does seem tempting sometimes. I've invested too much in getting where I am. And I don't just mean in my job."

"I know," said Mae, patting her daughter's arm.

Finally, Heidi Inverhoff, the Young Women's president, arrived, and the girls started to settle down. The meeting got started the requisite ten minutes late.

"I'm so glad to see you all here tonight," Heidi said. "We don't usually have our firesides at the home of the person who is speaking, but Sister James preferred it that way. So we give her special thanks for welcoming us into her home as well as being willing to speak to us tonight. We're also glad to see Sister Thomlinson here. We all think she's a very special woman. And we welcome her other daughter, Karen Sikorski, who has come home for a visit."

After the introduction, Sarah Louise stood up before her audience. As she began speaking, Mae thought how nice she looked in her navy dress—so conservative compared to Karen's—which she had accented with a brightly colored scarf. She seemed confident and sure of her presentation, and she handled herself well in front of an audience. Although she had never had the rapport with Sarah Louise that had come so easily with Karen, Mae could appreciate the fact that her daughter had become in many ways a truly competent woman.

But Mae was not able to enjoy her daughter's presentation for long. Sarah Louise had barely begun when Mae felt Karen grow tense. She glanced surreptitiously at her younger daughter, and what she saw startled her, for Karen was furious. The signs were subtle, but they were there: the tightened cord in her neck, the slight flush that could have been caused by the warm evening, the widened eyes.

Mae was grateful that no one else sitting in the room would be likely to notice, not even Sarah Louise, who was woefully inept at reading expressions. She didn't know what had set Karen off, but she certainly didn't want it to ruin the evening in which Sarah Louise had set such store.

It was ruined for Mae, however. She was glad when the closing prayer had been said, and she could hardly stand it when Sarah Louise, all unknowing, called to Karen across the room, "Don't go yet; have some refreshments."

"Do you want something, Mom?" Karen asked Mae.

"No, thank you, but you go ahead."

Karen shrugged, then walked to the table where the refreshments were spread out. Her body, encased in a fashionable cotton frock, was tense with anger, and her hand shook as she took a cup of the frothy lime punch.

"Whatever is the matter with you," whispered Mae urgently when Karen sat back down.

Karen only shook her head.

Waiting for the girls and Heidi to leave was excruciating. Everyone had enjoyed themselves so much that no one was in a hurry to go. Finally Sarah Louise closed the door behind the last person.

"Well?" asked Sarah Louise, eyes bright with expectation. "How did you like it?"

"It was lovely, dear," said Mae, trying to forestall what she feared was coming.

"How about you, Karen?"

"It was nice."

"What did you especially like about it?" Sarah Louise persisted, and Mae felt painfully how much Sarah wanted her sister's approval.

"That's hard to say."

Still Sarah Louise waited.

Suddenly Karen swore. "What's the point of pretending!" she exploded. "I didn't like it at all—I hated it!"

Sarah Louise's mouth dropped. "But why?"

"You don't really want to know why."

"Mother, there was nothing wrong with my talk, was there?"

"I thought you expressed yourself very well," said Mae, glaring at Karen. She was astonished that Karen would be so hurtfully blunt. She herself did not agree with the viewpoint presented by Sarah Louise, but she had long ago ceased pursuing what would inevitably lead to confrontation, followed by bitter silence.

"I thought so, too, and everybody told me how much they enjoyed it. Karen, tell me what you didn't like about it, please."

"Do you really want me to?" asked Karen ominously.

"I don't think this is a good idea," said Mae, taking Karen by the arm, but she was too late. Karen had an awful grin on her thin face, and her turquoise eyes were gleaming.

"You know, I can visualize your whole talk, dear sister. It'd make a great ad campaign. Simplistic enough for the masses, with some great slogans. In fact, I can see it in headers. It's my professional mind-set, I suppose."

"What are headers?"

"Basically, headlines. You know,

GOOD GIRLS HAVE WONDERFUL LIVES

TEMPLE MARRIAGES GUARANTEE HAPPINESS

TITHE PAYERS HAVE NO MONEY WORRIES

"But what's wrong with any of that?"

Karen shook her head in disbelief. "You really don't know? Take your TITHE PAYERS HAVE NO MONEY WORRIES bit. When you said your lovely home was all due to paying tithing, did you ever stop to think that one of those girls might be living in a crackerbox, in spite of the fact that her parents pay tithing? Let me tell you, sister dear, not everyone who pays tithing off the top and then has nothing to live on the rest of the month gets a mysterious check in the mail that exactly covers the monthly expenses. There are plenty of good but nonetheless poor people who give their mite and still aren't financially successful. Granddad, for example. He always paid his tithing, didn't he, Mom?"

"Yes."

"And what did he end up with? Not much."

"If we had problems," Mae tried to explain, "it was mainly because Dad wasn't a very practical man—"

"You see? That's my point, exactly. There's more to it than putting your money in the slot and taking your pick. Circumstances exert power too. Sarah, you have a nice house because your husband is successful in what he does. He's a good newspaperman and a good businessman as well. Of course, it didn't hurt when he married the daughter of the man who owned the *Shelton Journal*, did it? All in all, I'd say he made some pretty fair choices. The fact that he tithes is not the only cause of Ron's good luck."

"Don't you talk about Ron that way—" began Sarah Louise, but Karen had built up a head of steam; she was nowhere near finished.

"Sometimes it's best to tell the truth," she stated.

"Mother—"

"For example," interrupted Karen in a voice vibrant with emotion, "instead of feeding those poor girls all those lies about life being logical and manageable, with cause and effect clearly related, you could have told them the truth. You could have told them that life is hard. That it's lonely, that all we have is ourselves. But no, Sarah Louise had to make it all seem like a weekend at the county fair: follow the recipe and win the blue ribbon.

"Those girls deserve to be told that a temple marriage guarantees nothing; that at any time, either partner can make a decision that makes a mockery of it. They deserve to know that all their good intentions or desires of the heart can remain just that when circumstances, or health, or family put up barriers. You know, sometimes you can try and try, but if the rest of your family doesn't want what you want . . ."

Karen was crying now, and the words sputtered wetly

through her tears. "Life is hard! It hurts! Why didn't you tell them that!"

There was a long silence, filled only with the sound of wretched, gulping sobs. When Sarah Louise finally spoke, she did so in a voice so cool, so controlled, so impervious to the painful words she had heard, it was shocking. "Honestly, Karen, you get so dramatic sometimes, just like Mom. I confess, I don't know what you're talking about. Do you, Mom?"

"Oh, yes. I do," said Mae softly.

"Well, I don't. I suppose it's just another one of those 'Karen and Mae in the red corner vs. Sarah Louise in the blue.' But I've lived through them before, I can live through this one too."

"Oh, you're a smug one, aren't you," said Karen through gritted teeth, pulling her arm out of her mother's warning grasp. "You think your life's so perfect! Well, I can tell you a thing or two—"

"Karen, let it go."

"No, Mom."

"And what could you possibly have to tell me about my life?" asked Sarah Louise with pursed lips.

"Quite a bit, my dear. Like the fact that you live in a dream world. You can't see what's in front of your face. You rush all over the stake with meals, you spend hours sewing costumes, you find something to keep yourself busy every minute of the day. Do you know what that is?"

"I like serving—"

"That's not service—that's nothing but a defense mechanism to keep from seeing what you don't want to see. If you looked hard enough, you would see a husband and seven kids who need attention, but you'd rather give it to someone else than to them; it's safer."

"How can you say that! I take care of my family!"

"Oh, yes. You keep them fed and wash their clothes, but when do you ever give them a hug or hold them on your lap? When do you ever listen to them? Why do you think they love to come over to Mother's? I've always known you resent the fact that she can give them something you can't."

Sarah Louise's gaze faltered.

"And when it comes to avoidance and denial, here's the biggy. Our mother is dying, and you don't want to face it."

The sound Sarah Louise made was like the popping of a bubble.

"No, Mom, I'm not done yet," said Karen harshly. "I am so sick of getting those phone calls from my dear sister telling me that everything's 'just fine.'" Karen mimicked her sister's breathy, immature voice. "Well, it isn't just fine. We don't have much time left, and I don't want to lose that time playing games with you, Sarah Louise. Let's put the cards on the table. I am here because I want some time with my mother before she dies. I didn't have the chance to say good-bye to Cory, you know."

Her voice cracked, but she kept on. "I was washing the dishes when they called . . . I still can't believe it happened that way. You send your child off to catch frogs in the pond, and the next thing you know, you're getting a call from the police saying your son has drowned. I don't even remember if I hugged him before he left. . . "

She was crying softly now; Sarah Louise and Mae waited silently until, finally, she took a shuddering breath and wiped her eyes, smearing mascara down her cheeks. "I'm not going to miss the chance I have with Mom. I'm going to say good-bye to her the way I need to. I'm not going to have nightmares after all this is over. And you'd better think about it yourself, sister dear. I think you have some things that need to be said and done."

The words were strong and solid, but the electric emotion had lost its charge. Karen stood up slowly and moved to the door. Without turning around, she asked, "Are you coming, Mom?"

"I don't think I want to, Karen. If this is what you call making good use of our time together, I don't want any of it. Go back to the house and cool off, Miss. I'll talk to you in the morning."

Karen left without a word.

After she had gone, Mae put her arms around Sarah Louise. "I'm so sorry this happened," she said. "Are you going to be okay?"

Sarah Louise rested in her mother's embrace a surprisingly long moment, then she moved away. Her eyes were full of emotion she was not willing to acknowledge verbally. "It was such a lovely day—I don't know what happened to it."

"It's no excuse, I know, but things are a little tough for Karen right now."

"Maybe if she stayed home and took care of her family—"

"It's not that simple." Mae sat back down again, weary to the bone. She knew that a good deal of what Karen had said was valid, and she hoped that some part of Sarah Louise's mind had stored it up for future reference, though it wasn't likely she would do anything with it now. Now she was just feeling angry and resentful that her sister had ruined what was to have been a lovely evening. Still, Mae tried to explain one of her daughters to the other.

"Karen doesn't allow herself many escapes from reality, Sarah Louise. She forces herself to look at everything straight on. Sometimes that's very hard and frightening, but sometimes it's necessary, and it's always courageous."

"But it's so morbid and intense!"

"Perhaps." After a pause Mae added, "Tomorrow is the day Cory died, Sarah."

"Oh! So that's what it was all about."

"Not entirely."

"Poor Karen," said Sarah Louise. Her face cleared—she simply ignored her mother's qualifying statement. "I forgot all about it. We'll have to think of something to do tomorrow to keep her mind off of it."

"I can't imagine anything could do that, Sarah Louise."

"Well, we can try, can't we?"

11

The next morning Mae stayed in bed. She heard Karen open the door to her room, but she didn't open her eyes or in any way indicate she was awake. She was lying on her side, which was her habitual sleeping position, but in that position her stomach protruded a bit out onto the mattress. With all her weight loss, she had enjoyed a time during which she had a figure that went in and out where it was supposed to. Now, while the rest of her remained thin, her abdomen had begun to swell disconcertingly.

One hand was under her head, the other rested on the bed, where she could easily see it. Against the white sheet, the skin of her hand looked odd. It was very dry and beginning to flake, but that wasn't what bothered her: it took her some minutes to realize that the color was wrong. She held up both hands and examined them; she looked at her arms and then her legs as well.

She lay back with a sigh. It wasn't just her hands that looked funny. Her whole body was taking on a strange yellowish hue. She didn't need a doctor to tell her what that meant. Everybody knew that jaundice made a person's skin yellow.

So, the old liver's going, Mae thought. Then there's not much time.

She started to rise, but an enormous lethargy bound her to the bed. She lay back down, frustrated that she didn't have the energy to use the time she did have. Finally she called out to Karen, who fearfully assisted her into the bathroom and then back to bed.

111

"Should I call the doctor?" Karen asked uncertainly, as she sat down by her mother.

"That old Donnelly? No. If I don't feel any better after a while, maybe I'll have you call Keith."

"This is all my fault. How can I ever apologize for what I did yesterday?"

"By apologizing."

Karen hid her face in her hands, and the words came out muffled. "I'm sorry, I really am. I don't know what got into me. I guess I'm more stressed out than I thought I was. Will you please accept my apology?"

"Yes. But you have one more apology to go."

"I know. That one will be harder. I doubt if Sarah Louise will ever speak to me again. The silent treatment would be well-deserved."

"It won't be as hard as you imagine. She thinks it's all because of Cory."

Karen dropped her hands and looked squarely at her mother. "You know it isn't."

"Yes. Some of what you said was valid, Karen, but you picked a lousy time and place to confront your sister. Given the circumstances, I'm sure she was so defensive, she didn't even hear you."

"You're probably right."

"And whatever became of love? Never in your life have you seen me deal with another person that way. I would never dream of it; life is too short and people are too fragile."

"Not Sarah Louise. She's strong, like stone."

"Come now, girl. We all have our own ways of coping. Hers is a firm belief that 'God's in his heaven, and all's right with the world.'"

"Don't I wish. But Mom, she has to wake up and smell the coffee sometime—in a manner of speaking."

"She may not. She's doing what she has to do in order to survive—she's honestly doing the best she can. And that's not bad, really."

"I suppose not, but I couldn't live like that."

"Nor could she live your life."

"Ah, Mom. How do you make it through the vicissitudes of life?"

Mae laughed, and was immensely relieved to find that she still could. "Karen, nobody *says* that word! I've read it, but I've never in all my life heard anybody say it until now."

"Just answer the question, Mom."

"One day at a time."

"That's not funny."

"I know. It wasn't meant to be."

"We all live one day at a time whether we want to or not."

"No, some people spend their days hanging on to what used to be or trying to manipulate what will be."

"I guess that's directed at me. You're thinking about Cory."

"You do have a problem there."

"It's just that I lost so much when I lost him," Karen said, her tears welling up again. "He was so special, so sweet and loving. It seemed like he set the balance for all of us, which we've never regained. We've all spun off in different directions: Cal's inactive in the Church; I'm working; Greg and Jim have so little in common and spend so little time with each other, they might as well be living on opposite sides of the country."

"Your family is different now, that's true. But is this new family structure really all that bad? It isn't just that Cory is gone, my dear. Your family is also growing up—your boys are beginning to think about going to college or on missions. Even if Cory were still alive, there wouldn't be the kind of cohesiveness that you see in younger families. Teenagers have to begin pulling away sometime."

"I suppose."

"And as for Cal, he is a good man. You couldn't ask for better. He's honest and committed and caring. I know it's hard to sit alone in church when all around you there are complete families, but don't let those feelings poison the relationship you have."

"Oh, it's more than hard. It's excruciating. It would be

bad enough just not having Cal there, but on top of it, there's Greg."

"Yellow hair doesn't go over too well, I take it."

"That's the understatement of the year. He stands out like a sore thumb. You can't imagine how hard it is to have people look at him the way they do. I get the feeling that everyone's thinking, 'If that were my kid, I wouldn't put up with that sort of behavior. I'd chloroform him and dye his hair brown again.' But it's not that easy, believe me. There comes a time when a parent can't force a kid into conforming. I mean, am I supposed to ground him for the rest of his life? Or kick him out because of his hair?"

"No."

"That's what I think. Nobody would believe it, but Greg isn't as mouthy or belligerent as Jim. Everybody thinks Jim is wonderful."

"I suppose the comparisons don't help."

"I really think Greg would dress normally if people would stop asking him, 'Why aren't you like your brother?'"

"He's a good boy. He'll turn out all right."

"Yeah, I think so. Mom, when you asked me if everything was all right at home, I guess I wasn't exactly truthful. Nothing's really wrong—I've just run out of gas. I bought a mag to read on the plane; it had an article about parent burn-out. I took their test. In fact, I did wonderfully on it!"

"I hear the sarcasm."

"They said that anyone scoring over 86 was in need of help. I scored 92."

"Oh oh."

"Oh oh is right. I'm way over the boiling point. I'm so tired. I don't have any energy; I don't have any emotional reserves." Her voice wavered as she began sobbing. "And I'm fresh out of hope."

Mae held her daughter, patted her back, ran her hand over the short frosted hair, and murmured sounds of comfort. When Karen's shoulders finally stopped shaking, Mae sent her into the bathroom for a cool, wet washcloth. Karen handed it to Mae, but Mae shook her head. "It's for you," she said. "It'll make your eyes feel better."

"Thank you. Sorry about that. I'll feel better tomorrow, and I'll just keep plugging along, but right now, it all seems like too much."

"I don't doubt it. You were right when you said you were stressed out."

"Did that ever happen to you? I mean, who ever talked about stress and parent burn-out when you were raising kids?"

"Nobody. We had to have our breakdowns in private. It was too embarrassing to admit we felt like we were going crazy. We just tried to bury our feelings and keep on going."

"When you say 'we,' do you mean 'I'?"

"Of course."

"I never saw you looking like I do right now."

"Probably not. I tried to make sure that nobody did, except my horse. When I thought I was going to split in two, I knew it was time to go riding. Chico and I would fairly fly down the back roads! It was marvelous with the wind in my face and the sound and smell of the horse. And when we both finally felt like slowing down, we'd just mosey along. She'd eat grass from the ditchbank, and I would listen to the cicadas humming. I always felt better when we finally got back home."

"I remember that now. All of a sudden, you would disappear, just go off by yourself. I asked Daddy about it once."

"What did he say?"

"Something about you needing to ride like a drunk needing his bottle."

"That's not exactly complimentary, but it's accurate, I guess."

"When was it the worst for you? When we were all little, or later on?"

Mae pursed her lips and thought for a minute. "It was pretty hard when you were all babies—I had you so close together. But it was a happy time too. In a way, I was still playing at being a mother and wife. The first really bad time I can think of was when I was making all those trips to Cody, but I don't remember wishing I could run away from home then. That feeling came the year your dad ran for the legislature. That was the worst, oh yes."

Mae thought back to the day Fritz stood excitedly in the large living room of their second home (it was in a new development on the bench) and told her he had filed for the race.

"Come on, Mrs. Thomlinson, let's dance," he said, whirling her around the room.

When they finally flopped down on the new, sleek Danish modern couch, he said, "Mae, just one thing. Don't do anything silly, please."

"What do you mean, silly?"

"You know what I mean. No questionable jokes, no risqué language. No dressing up like the Statue of Liberty, and no demonstrations of your prowess with the Hoola Hoop."

"You didn't like that? But you laughed just as much as the others."

"I know I did. I don't mind a few shenanigans among friends, but this is different."

Her smile faded.

"Listen, doll. I don't want to hurt your feelings, but running for public office is serious business. Almost everyone in Shelton has known you for years. They know what to expect from you. I just don't want you to take the rest of the county by surprise."

"You're afraid 'Oh, that crazy Mae,' might turn into 'She's as loony as they come!' Is that it?"

"Put that way, it doesn't sound very nice, does it?"

"It certainly doesn't." She pulled away from him and got up.

"Mae, this is important to me."

"My own self is important to me, Fritz. I can't be what I'm not."

"Can you tone it down a bit, maybe?"

"I'll try."

The first major function was a fund-raising dinner, at

which Fritz was to speak. He was incredibly nervous, a fact she first noticed as they were getting dressed. "Hey, handsome, you're going to do just fine," she encouraged him, but her words did little to lessen his tension. They finished getting ready, said "good night" to the kids, and started off.

"Hey, smile once," said Mae, as he stared down the road grimly.

He looked at her as he was about to reply, but the words never got out of his mouth. Instead, he burst out laughing, almost losing control of the car. When his guffaw finally quieted down to chuckles, there was no trace of the tension left. Fritz grinned at her and said, "Thanks, I needed that."

She smiled at him, and he started to laugh again.

She had blackened out one of her front teeth.

That was Mae's last spontaneous act for many weeks. During the club meetings, dinner speeches, and rallies that followed, she was charming and careful. "Good girl!" Fritz said with an appreciative smile. But the campaign went on and on; after a while every meeting seemed endlessly boring.

Still, Mae kept her promise: she was as prim and decorative as possible while still remaining a living, breathing creature. She was so careful, in fact, that after one informal get-together among folks who knew them well, someone came up to Fritz and asked him "What's the matter with Mae? Is she sick?"

She found that out later when Fritz said to her, "Hey, doll, I have something to tell you." He recounted the remark, then admitted, "I think I've been asking too much from you. You are who you are; part of the reason I married you was your humor, the way you can make something fun of every occasion."

"Almost every," she amended.

"Let me apologize, will you?"

"Of course; go on."

"I only ask that you consider the time and place before you display that talent. Fair enough?"

She grinned and reached for him. "Fair enough," she said before she kissed him.

But it wasn't over so easily. Her wholeness was shattered; she was constantly on guard; her spontaneity dried up. It wasn't just because of what Fritz had asked of her; many more things added their own unique pressures. For one thing, Mae took pride in keeping the house spotless, a difficult task with three teenagers who were in and out, leaving trails behind them. She tried to enlist their help, and Fritz gave them a weekly pep talk, but it didn't seem to take. They would improve for a day or two, but it was always up to Mae to push and prod and nag.

At the same time that she was trying to be a help to her husband in his campaign and to keep her family and household in order, she was president of the local chapter of the Wyoming Woman's Club and a 4-H leader. Then there was the Church. Despite the pressures of her personal situation, Mae's consciousness of an obligation to the Church never lessened. She could have had someone else teach her Sunday School lessons for the duration, but it didn't occur to her that she had that option. Such a request would fall in the same class as asking to be released from or refusing to take a Church calling.

Mae felt herself slowing down, but she didn't know what to do about it. Never one to cry, she often felt her eyes glaze with unwanted tears. It was too hard, all of it, and she simply didn't care any more. Still, she didn't quit; she kept on, dogged and humorless. She rode as often as she could in those days, leaning low over Chico's flattened neck while she pounded out mile after mile. Only her concern for the faithful animal prompted Mae to draw Chico up— she didn't want to ruin a good horse.

Then she would ride home to her family, to face Terry's tantrum when she said she was too tired to bail him out with the paper that was due; to face Sarah Louise's slow-burning disapproval and Karen's exhausting energy alone. For Fritz was out almost every night, if not campaigning, then working at the *Journal* office or doing his Church work. When he did come home at a decent hour, she only shrugged. It didn't make any difference because she had nothing to say to him. Nor did she desire him. She slept as near to her edge of the bed as she could get, her back a barrier.

Recalling that part of her life was painful for Mae. Her fingers picked nervously at the bedspread, then she sighed and looked up at Karen, who was sitting quietly, waiting for her to continue.

"Your dad lost the race, as you know. It was a great blow to him—he was so certain that he would walk off with it. He was a Republican, and he had the endorsement of the man he was hoping to succeed. He was still darn good-looking, had impeccable credentials, and was a faithful churchgoer and tithe payer. How could he miss?"

"What happened?"

"Underneath his Republican colors, your father was really very liberal in his thinking. His prospective constituents understood that about him, and they voted for the more conservative of the two, rather than for the party ticket. He didn't understand—or didn't want to, so he blamed it on me—crazy Mae."

"That's terrible, Mom!"

"Yes, it was. It almost destroyed our marriage. Fritz mourned that seat in the legislature as if it were a stillborn child, and I couldn't comfort him, knowing how he felt about me. And then I got sick."

"Is that when you went to the hospital with pneumonia? I didn't realize that much was going on at the time."

"How could you? All you could think about was Ralph Richardson."

Karen shuddered. "He had buck teeth."

"You didn't notice it at the time. Anyway, going to the hospital was the best thing that could have happened. It gave us some time away from each other, and it gave me a chance to get some rest. I was so tired! I was in there for a long time, remember? I just slept and ate and read and listened to good music and talked to God. He and I got on pretty good terms after a while. By the time I came home, I had learned one very important thing."

"What was that?"

"That taking care of myself came first. Oh, I know it

doesn't sound very revolutionary now, but in those days, it was tantamount to being the most selfish person imaginable. But God and I, we worked it out between the two of us. I knew it was the right thing to do."

"Did you ever have that kind of crisis again?"

"Do I have to count? Over and over again, but never to that degree. It seems like every stage of life has some pressure that just squeezes and squeezes until a body can figure out what to do about it."

"And did you?" asked Karen.

"What?"

"Take care of yourself?"

"I've tried, but it hasn't always been easy. I wasn't used to asserting myself when it came to my own needs. I never knew it was all right to think of myself, you know."

She paused, then sat up a little straighter. "Now pay attention. What I'm about to say falls under the category of taking care of myself. I will not put up with any more unpleasantness between you and Sarah Louise. I have my own agenda, and it does not include spending my time and energy playing referee. Do you understand?"

"Yes, Mom," said Karen meekly.

12

Mae Thomlinson's two daughters made their peace. They had to, considering the ultimatum she had given them. The sorting of family flotsam and jetsam took place in a rare atmosphere of togetherness. It began with the bookcase drawers, which held yellowed, folded, or faded pieces of paper.

"My word, I can't believe what you've kept all these years," said Karen, holding a valentine she had made for her parents when she was in grade school.

Mae smiled and shrugged. "All those things were precious to me."

Indeed, it was difficult for Mae to turn from one thing to the next. Once she had a memento of the past in her hand, it became the most important of all the papers that jammed the bookcase drawers. Looking at a note or a drawing or a homemade card, she could conjure up the giver's face at the very age the child had been at the time. She could feel the chubby, childish hands clasping hers, or the lovely, sweet skin pressed against hers in an abandoned hug.

"Each of you should take at least one of the cards you made, don't you think?" she said. "It would be nice to have them in your scrapbooks."

From the piles, Karen and Sarah Louise chose some mementos of their own making, setting aside Terry's so he could choose some as well. The rest were ostensibly to join the rejects, but neither daughter mentioned the fact that few found their way into the trash can by the table.

There were, besides handmade valentines and cards

commemorating Father's and Mother's Day, letters the three Thomlinson children had written to their parents. "Take your own letters too," said Mae. "It'll be like having an instant journal—you can use them when you write your life story."

"Won't help me out much," murmured Sarah Louise, whose pile was very small. Except for three years at BYU, she had never lived more than a few miles away from her mother.

"How about your life story, Mom? Have you written it?" asked Karen.

"Not really. I've kept a journal off and on, and I've started my life story a hundred times, I guess, but I've never finished it."

"Why not?"

"I didn't quite know what to put down. You get to a certain point, and the lives of your children take over. Mainly you record their achievements or problems. Besides, looking at my life in detail wouldn't be terrifically exciting. She pantomimed reading a volume held in her hand: "Got up. Fed Fritz, cleaned the house, read the paper. Went out to work in the garden, ate lunch, visited with Edith. Her arthritis is bad today. Made lasagna for Fritz. Spent the evening watching TV and writing letters, went to bed early."

"But that's not all there is," protested Karen. "Maybe instead of a journal approach, you could write about the main events or the things you've done."

"Which would be?"

"Modesty doesn't suit you, Mom. There're your grass exhibits, for one thing. You didn't get a whole banner full of ribbons by doing nothing."

"Yes, but would anyone be interested? All you have to do to compete in the Sheaf Forage for Hay category is keep an eye out for likely-looking clumps."

"Oh yeah, tell me all about it."

"I guess there was a bit more to it than that, wasn't there? Remember when you helped me set up my booth at the county fair? We drove down to Basin . . . "

"We" meant Mae and Karen. Fritz thought "gleaning the

grasses" was just another one of Mae's strange kicks, an opinion shared by Sarah Louise, and Terry rarely went anywhere with "the women." (He had developed a dreadfully chauvinistic attitude at a young age.)

It had taken the two of them a whole day to arrange the almost thirty-five sheaves of beautifully bunched grasses in the booth. Blue grass, Canada wild rye, fescue, red top, reed canary, slender wheat, timothy: the thick sheaves of headed-out grasses covered it from side to side. After the judging, almost every sheaf sported a ribbon, most of them blue.

"I did have some lovely sheaves," mused Mae. "One year I even had a sheaf that the county agent himself couldn't identify. Remember that? I really had him stumped. I've got several pictures of us in front of the booth, Karen. Be sure to take one home with you."

"Maybe what we should do is put the nicest pictures in one album, and then we can get copies of it made," suggested Sarah Louise. "Once in a while Ron gets someone at the *Journal* to make a stat of things we want copied for each of the kids. Then we make photocopies of the stat. It works out real well."

"That's a great idea," said Karen. Excitedly, they began to pick and choose from the pictures. They decided to leave the leather album belonging to Abe and Lenore Bateman as it was and concentrate mainly on the photos of Mae and Fritz and their family. That meant going through numerous albums and several shoeboxes of loose snapshots.

"Ugh. I think I'll throw away every picture taken of me before I was twenty," said Karen. "My nose looks humongous in all of them."

"Some people take good pictures, and some don't," said a satisfied Sarah Louise.

"Now, your daddy was real photogenic," remarked Mae. "I can't think of a single picture where he doesn't look just fine. Take this one," said Mae, looking at a youthful picture of Fritz Thomlinson astride his horse, Sourdough Sam.

"He was a handsome man," said Karen.

"That's just what I thought, the first time I saw him. He

was sitting on a horse then, too, and I thought, My, what a handsome man. 'Course, your granddad wasn't impressed with him much. He was more impressed by the horse Fritz was on. That was because he and his sorrel had just beaten your grandpa's horse in the most important race of the Shelton Roundup."

Mae smiled, remembering the look on Abe's face as he said, "Let's go see the horse that beat Danny Boy." But while he was looking at the sorrel with the swift feet, Mae had been looking at the handsome young man in the saddle. He had coal-black hair, hazel eyes tending toward green, darkly tanned skin, and a broad grin that showed off white teeth.

Only when he dismounted did Mae notice that one leg was shorter than the other, so that the man limped when he walked. His name was Fritz Thomlinson. He was the son of R. B. Thomlinson, who owned the Bar B spread near Meeteetse.

"Who trained that horse?" Abe asked.

"My dad."

"Do you have more like him?"

"We've got some good-looking colts."

"What say I drive over to the Bar B next weekend. I'd like to take a look at them." Mae nudged him and he added testily, "I'm just looking, Mae. And to prove it, I'll bring you along. That should satisfy your mother, too. My wife's not much for horses," he added in an explanatory tone.

They drove over in the disreputable pickup Abe had managed to purchase for himself. Under the palest of blue skies, the Bar B sprawled up to the foothills of the Absaroka mountain range, which formed part of the western rim of the Basin. The very size of the ranch house and the outbuildings intimidated Mae. She felt they had no business being there. But while her discomfort rendered her silent, her father was his most expansive, loquacious self.

Abe began by telling the story of the man who left his pickup on the road and walked out onto a fenced range to check a herd of cattle.

"This was typical Montana range, you understand," said Abe. "Nothing but grass—not a tree in sight. Well, the man had to walk quite a ways before he saw the herd because they were down in a draw. That herd was mighty fine, all good stock. Especially the bull."

"A-hah," said R. B.

"You can guess what happened. The man saw the bull about the time the bull saw the man. That bull just lowered his head and started pawing and snorting something fierce. Well, the man started walking back up the hill as fast as he could. 'Course, when the bull took out after him, he found out he could go a whole lot faster!

"Now, this poor fellow had spent too much time on his horse or in his pickup. He wasn't very fast on his feet, and since he kept slowing himself down by looking over his shoulder to see where the bull was, every time he looked, that old bull gained ground.

"Well, he knew he had only one chance, and that was to get to the fence before the bull got to him. But the bull was closing in on him fast, and those horns were aimed right at his behind. He knew he wasn't going to make it. Suddenly, he saw a tree—"

"Hey, hold up there," said R. B. "You said there wasn't a tree in sight."

"Why, R. B., when you're being chased by a bull, and he's about to take you for a ride on his horns, there's just got to be a tree!"

Abe's charm worked. He really had nothing to offer R. B. Thomlinson, yet before leaving, arrangements had been made for him to bring two of his best mares to the Bar B when the time was right. R. B. would have the pick of the two resulting foals.

Hoping to see Fritz, Mae went with her father when he took the mares to the Bar B and again when he went to pick them up, but by then Fritz was back at the University of Utah, where he was pursuing a degree in journalism. Her disappointment made her ill, and both times she had ended up weeping herself into a migraine.

She couldn't believe her eyes, then, when she saw him leaning against the top rail of the corral in her own back-yard many months later. She only paused long enough to comb her hair with her fingers before joining him, shyly inquiring what brought him out to Appleblossom Farm. She found out that he was home from the University of Utah, waiting for his mission call, and had come with his dad because R. B. wanted his opinion as to which of the two fillies they should take back to the Bar B.

The fact that he hadn't come to see her didn't bother Mae—he was close enough to her that her shoulder touched his arm, and that was all she was aware of. The sweet pain she felt at his nearness flustered her, yet she couldn't bear to move away from him, and when the filly was loaded up and the deal concluded, Mae felt close to tears. She was sure she would never see him again. She was fifteen at the time.

Four years later, she looked up to see who was sliding into the pew next to her, and to her surprise, she found herself looking into those greenish eyes she had dreamed about so many years ago. After church was over, he said, "You'll be seeing quite a lot of me from now on. I've got my degree in journalism, and I've been hired by the *Shelton Journal*."

"How nice," she had responded inanely. Her heart was thumping so loud she couldn't even hear the words she was sure her mouth had formed.

"I intend to own it one day," he'd added.

Their courtship was quick. There was no critical future mother-in-law to complicate things, since Mrs. Thomlinson had passed away some years previously, and Fritz was encouraged in his choice by R. B., who liked Mae.

Although she was quiet and deferential in his presence, R. B. sensed in her the steel he admired in many Western women. He knew she would have the kind of loyalty necessary to build strong families. She would also keep her own council.

He had no notion at the time that she also had a mind of her own and a sense of humor slightly on the raw side. That wouldn't have changed his mind about the impending marriage to his son, however. He detested wimpish, overly delicate women.

Then, when Abe Bateman died unexpectedly of a heart attack right in the middle of making another of his deals,

R. B. offered to pay all the wedding expenses for Fritz and Mae. He bought the newlyweds a small home on Canal Street and had Fritz pick what he wanted from the furniture and household objects that had belonged to his mother. "Might as well take what you want now, Son. It's all yours anyway."

Three months after Mae's wedding, Lenore—always a practical woman—married Hector Lamont and took Susan with her to Cody. Howard, then nineteen, convinced his mother to rent him the farm. "I don't need to go to college to find out how to farm, Mom," he said. "I watched Dad make all the mistakes in the book. I'm not likely to make them over again." He didn't. He was like his father only in his love for good fiddle music and horses.

As she saw her family split apart, Mae's love for Fritz grew even stronger. In fact, the next years were so good, Mae often felt like pinching herself, just to make sure she was not dreaming. She knocked on wood many times and sedulously avoided tempting fate. Fritz adored her, and for the first time in her memory, she didn't have to worry about money. He often teased her about her frugality; he could never convince her that he was doing well enough to afford something just because they wanted it. For her, an item was judged on need. If it wasn't necessary, it wasn't purchased. She did, however, consider flowers, records, and good books to be absolute necessities, "hyacinths to feed the soul."

The children came as soon as possible according to the laws of nature: first, Sarah Louise; then, Karen; and last, Terry. In the years following, Fritz and Mae were completely absorbed in the challenges of their respective worlds: Mae was intent on raising a good family, and Fritz was determined to reach the goals he had as a newspaperman.

Both of them were successful. Only a few years had passed before Fritz was made assistant editor of the *Shelton Journal*, and he became a member of the city council and a member of the local quorum of seventy in the Church. Mae was pleased with the progress of the children, with her home, and with her activity in Woman's Club and the

Church. They still found some time for each other, however, because their love of horses, camping, and fishing offered them many hours of mutual enjoyment.

But as Fritz became more prominent, a rift developed between them, for the differences in their education began to bother him. Whenever she slipped and said, "I ain't," or "I never," he would grimace with embarrassment. Mae adored him, so she determined to rid herself of that habit as well as her habit of mixing up the usage of "I" and "me."

It was at this point that Mae undertook an elaborate self-education program that she pursued the rest of her life. She checked out piles of books on every subject imaginable, but more often than not history books outnumbered the rest. She read much on the history of Wyoming and of the Basin; she even studied the unique geological features of the area. She also read the *New York Times* and *Time Magazine,* to which Fritz subscribed. She was quite well informed, although Fritz, out of habit perhaps, never acknowledged it.

When R. B. died, Fritz sold the ranch in Meeteetse and with the proceeds bought out the owner of the *Shelton Journal.* He was in a position at that point to begin building a political base, which he did. The Thomlinsons entertained often and were often invited to the homes of those prominent in the Basin. To his chagrin, Fritz found that the invitations were due as much to his articulate, funny, and occasionally outrageous wife as to his distinguished person. He never criticized her about it, however, until his disastrous race for a seat in the Wyoming state legislature.

Their relationship, which had been so devastated by that experience, was rebuilt on horseback. Their love for riding brought them together in the neutral and hopeful arena of nature. It was difficult for either of them to remain angry or depressed with the sun warm on their shoulders and the comforting creak of leather in their ears. But Mae did not let the unfair accusation he had leveled simply slide into oblivion. Before peace was finally reestablished, Fritz had had to humble himself and apologize. He did, for, as he told her, her illness and hospitalization had shaken him deeply.

As the years went by, Fritz became an extremely distinguished man. Mae, however, grew softer in the course of time, though not exactly fat. Her face assumed a look of dignity, although it could unexpectedly turn impish, and her eyes were steady and full of compassion. The picture taken on their thirty-fifth anniversary showed a handsome, loving couple.

Mae had been holding the anniversary picture before her during her musings; now she set it in the middle of the table where her daughters could see it. "I guess we ought to get copies of this one," she said. "We look quite the couple, don't we. You'd think we were really something."

"But you were," said Karen.

"Oh, I don't know. When you come down to it, we were just plain folk."

"Hardly. Mom, how can you say that? If you think about everything you've done, it's very impressive."

"I don't know about that."

"Just take what you've done in the Church, and your years as president of the Wyoming Woman's Club," added Karen. She grabbed a scrap of paper and began writing.

"What are you doing?" demanded Mae.

"Just putting some of this on paper. Maybe I can help you organize your life story while I'm here. Tell me the dates of your stint in Relief Society and as the president of Woman's Club." Karen wrote while Mae talked, and before long, the dates of her years in 4-H and Girl Scouts and as a Den Mother in Cub Scouts were added to the list as well.

"That sounds pretty impressive," Karen said.

"Yes . . . " Mae replied, but her voice held a note of doubt. "But it sounds too much like those 'superwomen' described in so many articles lately. I definitely was not one."

"Of course you were," protested Sarah Louise.

"No, absolutely not. That looks good on paper, but my real accomplishments aren't even listed."

"What are those?"

"Surviving a house full of teenagers for nine years. Staying married to your father for thirty-seven years." Mae's eyes twinkled as she added, "And loving him for most of them. Keeping my sanity for sixty-one years—with only minor lapses along the way. Keeping the faith.

"Those are the positive things—there were plenty of negatives too. Like the arguments I had with Fritz and the days we spent not talking to one another. Plus the fights I had with Terry and with you, Sarah Louise. I wasn't exactly your favorite person."

"That's been done and over with for years. Why bring it up now?" demanded Sarah Louise.

"Because that's part of it. Karen, you put down that I doubted myself all those years. Was I a good enough wife? Was I a good enough mother? Was I a good enough daughter? I didn't think I was such hot stuff. I still wonder—"

"All those daily ups and downs don't mean that much, for heaven's sake!" said Karen. "Everybody's life is littered with the kind of things you're talking about. Why get hung up on them?"

"Because I wonder. I'm nearing the end and I wonder, 'What was it all about?' Sometimes I don't think I know."

"Of course you know," stated Sarah Louise.

"Wait a minute," said Karen. "You said something yesterday about every stage having a pressure that pushed you to some sort of resolution . . . Isn't that what this is, one of those pressures, I mean?"

Mae's eyes widened—her words came back to her with sudden and absolute rightness. "You're right. Now that I think of it, I don't know why I didn't realize that before now. I'm certainly not the only person my age—or in my situation—trying to make some sense out of life. It's part of the process, I guess."

"I'm not with you," complained Sarah Louise.

"Mom is so smart, she doesn't even recognize her own genius," said Karen. "Yesterday she said something absolutely brilliant, but she didn't relate it to her own experience."

"All right. What did she say?"

"It's about ages and stages: every stage in life has something that comes with the territory, no matter where or who you are. Maybe doubt comes with the territory when you're Mom's age."

"It's not just doubt," said Mae thoughtfully. "It's a need to find some pattern, some meaning to everything you've

130

gone through. It's frightening to wake up one morning and realize that my one and only chance is almost over. I wonder if I've made the right choices, if I've made something lovely of my life."

"Mom, you remember what you always used to tell us about trimming your bonsai?"

"Probably not the exact words . . . "

"Well, I remember them. You said not to look at the individual needles, because then you would lose sight of the overall shape you were working toward. 'It's not the part, it's the whole,' you'd say. Isn't that right?"

"Yes," said Mae slowly, thinking, Why is it so hard to understand what you already know?

13

Karen's June visit had lasted only one week, yet to Mae it was both too short and too long. She had enjoyed most of the time with her daughter, but she was exhausted by the time she kissed Karen good-bye. Her routine had been disrupted by the visit, and she had not been getting sufficient rest, nor had she been doing her visualizatons. With her back turned so that Karen couldn't see, she had swallowed down pill after pill, yet often it hadn't been enough to mask the pain that sometimes started with a small hot pinpoint and grew increasingly severe, or other times assaulted her in full fury, taking her breath away.

In the days following Karen's departure, Mae tried to rebuild her emotional and physical reserves by resting a great deal. Edith, who had not visited while Karen was there, resumed her daily drop-ins; Mae was surprised at how important her friend's presence had become. She was even more surprised when she realized the reason: Edith was not only willing but determined to take care of her. If she felt lousy on a given day, Edith didn't try to talk her out of it. If she felt like staying in bed with the covers over her head, Edith didn't chide her, but simply went about with her birdlike movements weeding and watering.

After a week of rest and recuperation, Mae felt considerably better. She was back on her every-four-hours medication schedule, her stamina had increased, and she felt once more in control. Thus she was up and dressed when someone rang her doorbell one morning. She opened the door to find Dr. Lee Melton standing there.

"Nobody makes house calls anymore," she said, smiling a little.

"This isn't a house call."

"No, I suppose it isn't, since you're not my doctor."

"That's what I wanted to talk to you about."

She invited him in, but instead of sitting down, he stood awkwardly in the middle of her cheerful, flower-filled living room, shifting his weight from one foot to the other. Twice he started to speak, only to have the words trail off.

"For heaven's sake, do sit down."

Dr. Melton obeyed. "I'm sorry I made it so tough on you when you decided to stop treatment," he finally said.

"I think I understood why."

"I don't know how you could; I didn't even understand it myself. I reacted way out of proportion." His lips made a puffing sound as he exhaled. "Keith's been after me ever since. He talked to me again last night; in fact, he really laid it on. I, uh, I finally had to admit he was right."

"About what?"

"About the reason I flew off the handle." Dr. Melton had crossed one leg over the other, and the foot not on the floor bobbed up and down nervously. "You know I was in Vietnam?"

Mae nodded.

"I was a medic too. It was . . . I can't forget it, no matter how hard I try." He paused and Mae waited silently.

"The odd part is, I could handle most of it, like being away from home, the heat, the jungle, the *strangeness* . . . Even being under fire. But not being able to help the wounded, that was what got to me. Some of those poor guys were nothing but chopped liver. We'd do what we could, but too often it wasn't enough.

"The unpredictability was worst." Although Dr. Melton's voice was firm, his foot was jiggling even faster. "I mean, you never knew when someone would get it. A guy could make it through the worst patrol and then get shot by a sniper while he was walking down a village road where kids were playing in the dust . . . And Keith and I were in on all of it. It was a long time before I got the smell of blood out of my nose."

Dr. Melton straightened his collar nervously before continuing, "I'd always wanted to be a doctor, but after 'Nam, I wasn't sure I could go through with it. Med school was different, though. Everything was neat and clean and orderly. I mean, all the diseases are listed in the index—all you have to do is look them up. Symptoms and cures, all in black and white. The disease in question might be ugly, but what it does to the human body is predictable. It's not messy, like what a mine does when a kid steps on it."

"There are freak accidents out here too, Dr. Melton. Farm accidents, hunting accidents."

"Not every day, day after day. Freakish things were the norm over there. I felt safe when I came back here. I wrote prescriptions and presided over birth . . . and death. But death didn't bother me so much. Even when it was inevitable, I was still controlling to a certain degree what went on. That was the main thing, you see. I was in charge. I didn't get ambushed every time I turned around. You ruined that."

"Oh. I'm sorry."

"Why should you be sorry? You were within your rights to make the decision you did. Uh . . . Donnelly says you haven't been in touch with him."

"No, not yet. Up until a few days ago, I was doing pretty well with the medication you gave me. And Keith—"

"I know. Keith's been teaching you to hypnotize yourself."

"You think that's all right?"

"If it works." He looked at her appraisingly. "Mae, uh, *Mrs.* Thomlinson, do you need a change of medication?"

Mae sighed. "Yes. You said disease is pretty predictable. Well, mine is doing its thing." She held out her hand. "I've got jaundice now too. That means the liver is involved, doesn't it?"

He nodded.

"I guess I'll have to give up and go to Dr. Donnelly—"

"Not if you don't want to. If it's all right with you, I'd like to continue as your doctor."

Her eyes filled. "I would like that," she said.

"This'll be new for me. I don't know much about home

care, but Keith has had hospice training. Keith has had training in just about everything that could be classed under 'alternative,'" he said, smiling. Then he turned sober. "There's a lot we'll need to be talking about, like getting a private nurse lined up, but we can do that another day."

"That sounds fine to me."

He shook her hand gravely before he left.

The next morning Keith stopped by after work. When he found out that Mae hadn't eaten yet, he made her a scrambled egg and toasted a slice of bread while she sat outside where the smell wouldn't upset her stomach. Then they sat at the picnic table eating breakfast together.

"You'll never guess who came to see me yesterday," Mae said.

"Sorry to spoil your game," he said between mouthfuls of food, "but I already know. He told me."

"He's agreed to go along with us, did he tell you that?"

"Uh-huh."

"He talked to me about being in Vietnam. In his own way, he's had as hard a time getting over that war as you had."

"Who hasn't." He leaned back in his chair and wiped his mouth. "There's a whole generation of Vietnam vets who feel isolated, I mean *totally* separated from the normal life everyone else is leading. It's pretty hard to deal with something like that, especially when you can't talk to anyone about it. Just like the main character in *Im Westen Nichts Neues*."

"What's that?"

"Sorry, I always think of it in German. I was going to get a degree in German once, did I ever tell you?"

She shook her head.

"Anyway, it's *All's Quiet on the Western Front*. I'd read it before 'Nam in one of my literature classes, and after I got out, it kept going through my mind. So I read it again. The way the main character felt when he was home on leave was exactly how I was feeling. Somehow it helped to know my reaction wasn't so unique."

"How did he handle things after the war?"

"He didn't have to worry about after the war."

"Oh. Has Dr. Melton read it?"

"I suggested it to him, but I don't know if he has."

Mae fiddled with her napkin. "He said we needed to talk about getting a nurse."

"Doesn't necessarily need to be a nurse, at least not for a while yet. But I have been getting a bit nervous about you being here alone."

"I'm not really alone—Sarah Louise is just two minutes down the street."

"Two minutes isn't close enough, as far as I'm concerned. Is there someone you know who might agree to move in with you?"

"I don't know. I've been trying to avoid thinking about it. You know, sometimes I think living with cancer is a whole lot harder than dying of it will be."

Keith's head jerked up, and he looked at her intently. "Really? What makes you say that?"

"Something that happened yesterday. A sweet little neighbor girl named Samantha was on her way to town. I've always liked Samantha; I make it a point to talk to her, because I know most everybody else is too impatient. She stutters, you know. Anyway, I just happened to be in the yard, so I spoke to her like I always do. And she made the longest speech of her whole life."

"What did she say?"

"In a nutshell? That her mother didn't want her to talk to me anymore."

"Why not?"

Her eyes glistened as she said, "Because I'm a crazy lady who doesn't have the sense to go to the hospital to die, like I ought to."

He swore, then was instantly contrite. "Sorry, but that's exactly how I feel about it." He reached across the table to take her hand. It was not the same elegant hand he had held shortly after they had first met. It was very bony, and the skin felt dry and too warm. The effects of her illness were also visible in her face: it was thinning inexorably into gauntness, and her eyes were not so lively as before, as if a dimmer switch had been turned down. Her hair stood out around her face in a dry, wispy halo.

"Don't take it personally, babe," he consoled her. "It's stupid, but it's not unusual. Most people have an irrational fear about cancer, especially now with all of this talk about viruses being the cause. People are afraid that they can somehow 'catch' it, and some go to great lengths to avoid an ill person."

"Don't I know," said Mae.

"Besides that, you're violating another unwritten tenet."

"What's that?"

"Dying should take place behind closed doors."

"Oh."

"I don't think it's quite as bad here as it is in big cities. I think it has something to do with the fact that this is still pioneer country."

Mae raised her eyebrows.

"Well, isn't it? Let's say for argument's sake that the real development of the area began in 1900. That's just eighty-five years ago—not long for a place to be civilized. A lot of the old values are still strong here: family, home, self-reliance."

"That's true."

"And the influence of the Mormons strengthens that. You know, in many ways, your church operates as if there were no welfare or social programs in the country. The support from the church structure is amazing. People can come into the hospital in the morning, and by evening their visiting teachers, their home teachers, and the bishop will have all been there." He grinned. "See how much I've learned about Mormons since I got here?"

She smiled. "Not bad."

"I tell you, I'm amazed at the way people rally around. Just offhand, I'd say that members of your church do better because of the instant support system."

"Instant mashed potatoes."

Perplexed, Keith said, "Either I missed something, or that's a non sequitur."

"That support system is like instant mashed potatoes:

good only when they're fresh. It cools down mighty quick over the long run."

"Really? I wouldn't have guessed that."

Mae avoided his gaze by fiddling with her napkin again. "Don't listen to me," she said finally. "Everything I'm liable to say is going to be negative right now. They have given me a lot of support."

Such as the fast, which had been conducted as she had requested and had imbued her with a sense of peace and strength beyond her own. Such as the regular visits of her home teachers and visiting teachers. Such as the sweet, serious young men who brought her the sacrament on Sundays when she didn't feel well enough to go to church.

"What's getting you down, babe?"

"I've just realized that doing this at home is not going to be as easy as I thought," she said in a thick voice. "There's more to it than ordering a bed." Mae began to cry. "I can't get down on my knees to work in my garden anymore; and if I do, I can't get back up. I don't have enough strength."

Keith's eyes teared up, and he stroked the back of her hand lovingly as she cried.

"It's not pain that gets me," she said after regaining control. "Between the new pills and my quiet place, I'm not doing too bad. It's the little adjustments I have to make every day, such as getting up a little later each morning because it's becoming a chore."

Each day it did take her a little longer to get up. Then, when she finally was dressed and ready for the day, she was too tired to want to eat, much less fix herself something. More often than not, she prepared only a cup of herbal tea and a piece of toast. Sometimes she opened a can of peaches and added a few slices to her breakfast. By the time she had dumped the uneaten portions of toast and fruit in the trash and rinsed the dishes, she was ready to sit down.

Often, as she sat in her rocking chair, she dozed off. She was sleeping more during the day than before, but less soundly at night. It was not unusual for passers-by to see the light on at a late hour.

Her little rituals had become even more important. In the

morning, after resting or dozing in her chair for a bit, she usually went out to one of her gardens. The day she couldn't get up from her knees, she wept among the fragrant blossoms until Edith found her. The incident, despite its implications, changed her routine in only one aspect: she used a hoe instead of her fingers when she went out in the mornings.

She usually came in from her gardening at lunchtime, although the thought of food was anything but enticing. It was much easier just to lie down and go to sleep than to fix a meal, even though Karen had insisted upon buying a microwave before she left. However, Mae usually forced herself to have something. Often she put a small potato in the microwave, marvelling that it could be ready to eat so quickly. Other times, she warmed up a package of the leftovers Sarah Louise fixed for her to heat up when she was hungry. After cleaning up, she took her afternoon nap.

It was almost as hard to get up after that nap as it was to get up in the morning. She woke to the hottest part of the day groggy and enervated, even though her room air conditioner kept the inside temperature moderate. When she was finally moving, she usually read her scriptures or tended the flowers and plants in her greenhouse, where it was still pleasant, thanks to the effect of the ceiling fan that was Ron's latest addition. The bamboo shades Ron and Mark had installed had also proved their worth: they cut the scorching sun, which would have long since cooked her plants to death.

She spent much of her time with her bonsai. She studied each one, slowly turning the pots, so that she could see them from all angles. Sometimes, she picked up her small clippers and snipped a bit here and there. More often, she simply observed them. Depending on how she looked at them, they seemed alternately deformed and almost grotesque or elegantly honest in their simplicity. It all depended on her point of view at the time.

When the weather was good, she spent the late afternoon or early evening sitting on her front porch, waving to the people and cars who went by. She was often visited by children in the neighborhood during those cool hours.

They came by with cookies or meadow flowers or just to chat. She found that the children were her measuring stick: their words measured the changes that were visible.

"You don't look too good."

"Did you always have that many wrinkles?"

"H-how come you don't l-laugh so m-much anymore?"

She finally decided that the only way to deal with their questions was to answer them honestly, without playing a game, without telling a story. It was a mistake, she thought later, because her honesty prompted the unhappy comment by the neighbor woman.

"I don't laugh so much because I'm not feeling very well," she said to Samantha the stutterer, who was the woman's daughter. "The fact is, I'm getting ready to die."

"D-do people have t-to get ready to d-d-die, like getting r-ready for school or church?"

"Well, it's nice if you can, but not everybody gets the chance to."

"H-h-how do you do that?"

"I'm not really sure myself, you know. Nobody ever told me how to, either. But I think a person gets ready to die by learning how to live."

"I don't g-get it."

"It's finding out what's really important."

"D-do you know, n-now?"

"I think so."

"Can you t-t-tell me?"

"That's the thing about it, you can't really tell other people. They have to find out for themselves."

She thought it was a mighty fine speech until Samantha reported her mother's assessment.

The final hours of a normal day were usually as unexciting as the first. One of the M and Ms always came for her when supper was about ready at Sarah Louise's, and slowly they would promenade down the street. The promenades were taking longer now than before, though she walked with determination.

After the meal, she often rested there a while, talking to Sarah Louise or to the M and Ms while life whirled around her. Just watching them exhausted her. Sometimes Mae found herself thinking that she was glad life slowed down, that it had its flow and ebb. She felt herself slowly pulling back from life, like the tide ebbing from the shore.

But on this day, she suddenly didn't feel like ebbing at all. She was sitting across the table from Keith, a person she cared about, having the most enjoyable breakfast in weeks. The sun was warm but not yet too hot, and life seemed worth the effort.

"You're smiling. That's good," said Keith, smiling too.

"I feel like today's going to be one of my good days, so I might as well enjoy it. But I'm curious—do dying people sort of withdraw from life?"

He nodded. "It seems to be part of the process. Some people need to do it before they can finally let go. Why?"

"Just wanted to know. By the way, what you said about getting someone to live in? I'll see if I can't get someone by the end of the week."

"Sounds good. And listen, you're right on my way home from work. Is it okay if I stop in more often?"

"Certainly. I enjoy your visits. But you don't have to—"

"It's not a question of 'have to.'"

14

Several days later, Mae was awakened by the shrill insistence of the phone. As she picked up the receiver, her hand shook with the fear that strikes whenever the phone rings at an unusual hour.

"Hi, Mom."

"Terry?"

"Himself. So how're you doing?"

"For someone just frightened out of a solid sleep, not too bad. Is something wrong?"

"No, what makes you think that?"

Tears of relief filled her eyes as she said, "It's midnight here. That's not exactly the time I'm used to getting phone calls."

"Sorry about that. I just had a great idea, and I couldn't wait to tell you. I need to be in Seattle for a training seminar July 9th, and I've got a day or two to play with. I've scheduled a stopover in Billings, so I can be right there in Shelton on the seventh. How does that sound?"

"Wonderful! I've been hoping you'd come."

"Well, that's all I had to say, so *adios*. Hope you can get back to sleep."

"Fat chance," she murmured as she hung up. Then she noticed Edith standing in the doorway. "Sorry you woke up," Mae said. "I got the phone as fast as I could."

"That's what I'm here for, remember?" said Edith. "Who on earth was it, anyway?"

"Terry. He's coming for a visit."

"It's about time. I was beginning to think he'd never come."

"He's so busy—"

"You don't need to explain him to me—I've known that kid since he was in grade school. He's been avoiding you, hasn't he?"

Mae shrugged sadly. "It's not a very happy thought, but you may be right."

"Of course I'm right. He doesn't want to deal with what's happening, so he pretends that it isn't. Why not? He's gotten away with that ploy often enough in the past. Actually, it wouldn't surprise me if he didn't come up with another excuse."

"Oh, Edith! He can't. He has to come. I've been waiting . . ."

"I know, dear." Edith sat on the bed and put her arm around Mae.

"If he doesn't come soon . . ." Mae's voice trailed off.

Edith tightened her arm around Mae's shoulders and smoothed back the lifeless hair. After a while, she asked, "Would a cup of warm milk help you get back to sleep?"

"I read somewhere that it isn't the warm milk that does the trick; it's the toast most people eat with it."

"So I'll throw toast into the bargain."

"That does sound good," said Mae, surprised that the very thought of food had not brought on nausea, as it did so often lately.

After Edith went into the kitchen, panic set Mae's heart racing again. What if I were alone, she thought, chewing her knuckles.

But she wasn't. From the kitchen came the sounds of Edith's preparations. Mae heard with relief the homely clatter of pan against stove and the rush of pouring milk. Bless you, Edith, she thought. She was incapable of expressing what it had meant to her a few days ago when Edith had asked, "Don't you think it's about time I moved in?"

"What?" Mae had asked incredulously.

"Well, how else do you think this is going to work out?

You certainly don't think you're going to finish this marathon on two feet, do you?"

"No, but—"

"You're not going to move in with Sarah Louise, are you?"

"Heavens, no!"

"And hiring a private nurse is a waste of money, even if you do have it to waste. Now, I've been reading—"

Mae burst out laughing.

"It's not funny, you idiot! I had to find out what taking care of you was going to involve."

"Edith, we haven't even talked about this."

"That's not my fault. I gave you plenty of time. Why do you think I've been hanging around here every day?"

"Oh, Edith!" cried Mae as she threw her arms around Edith's narrow, determined shoulders. "What would I do without you?"

"And what will I do without you?"

For Edith Sidwell and Mae Thomlinson had been friends ever since the day they literally bumped into each other in the library. As they sorted through the pile of books that had landed on the floor, they found that their tastes in reading material were similar, that is to say, eclectic. That common interest was the beginning of a long, supportive relationship between the two, despite the difference in approach that soon became obvious.

They both read voraciously and with great interest, but Mae always read with a lively skepticism. The only time that skepticism was laid to rest was in cases where she felt a responsive ring of truth deep in her soul. She recognized that to some, such a subjective weighing of truth was invalid and, moreover, fraught with danger. But she had a firm belief that she was more than her cognitive capacity, that part of her was eternal and had been eternally sentient. That part recognized truth no matter what guise it came in.

Edith, on the other hand, was willing to believe anything in print, and she loved to startle solemn and conservative Sheltonians with the most outrageous of the things she read. She found plenty of material, since she read indiscriminately. She drew no distinction between the validity of such different publications as *Newsweek* and the *National Enquirer*.

Reading was life to Edith. If something was bothering her, she checked out every book she could find on the subject. She read them all and then proceeded to proclaim the solution. If she was not able to implement it, she would read to find the reason why.

When Edith found out that her dear friend had terminal cancer and had made up her mind to live out her life at home, she checked out and read everything the library had—books by Elizabeth Kübler-Ross on death, and other books on hospice and home care. She had only been waiting for Mae to ask for her help before moving in.

Now they sat in comfortable silence, eating their toast and drinking the warm milk, which Edith had sweetened with honey and sprinkled with nutmeg. When they were finished, Edith asked, "Do you need another pill?"

Mae nodded, knowing how important it was to take the medication necessary to insure a pain-free night. She took the Dilaudid, then fell asleep feeling warm and good for the first time in weeks. In the last second, she wondered, Will Terry really come?

He did.

He arrived earlier in the day than Mae had expected him, flushed and jubilant, red hair standing up as it always did and blue eyes intense.

"How did you get here so quickly?" asked Mae as she hugged him.

"Boy, that's some story! I was just about to rent a car when Carl Witsoe came in to return one. He'd flown up to Billings in the little two-seater he uses for crop dusting. And guess what? He invited me to fly home with him. He even let me take over the controls! What a kick! I know what I'm getting next, Mom."

"Not a plane!"

"Why not? Man, that was great stuff. And you know my motto: if you can, do it!"

"But can you?"

"Sure. I've got it all worked out. First, I'll get my license, then I'll rent planes for a while until I know which kind I want to buy."

"It sounds exciting, but is it practical? Can you afford it?"

"No prob. I'll just sell a few more policies or play around on the stock market, that's all."

"You certainly are optimistic."

"I am. I have to be. The world is full of negative people, and they all want to drag everyone else down with them." He flopped on the couch and put his feet up on the butler's table. "Even you. I tell you something exciting, and the first thing you say is, 'Can you afford it?'" He wagged his finger at her. "Negative, negative."

"Sorry. But anyone who has to be so careful about making long-distance phone calls probably can't afford something as expensive as a plane."

"Don't make a big deal out of something that's not. You take things too seriously, you know."

"Terry! You can hardly accuse me of being serious."

"Maybe not. But here you are thinking in terms of limitations. I say the sky's the limit."

"Sometimes limitations force people into being more creative than they would otherwise be."

"Maybe. Hey, aren't you going to feed me? I'm starving!"

Mae hadn't been in her kitchen for weeks; nothing got cooked or otherwise prepared in that kitchen unless Edith or Sarah Louise did it. But Mae was so used to waiting on Terry, she actually pushed herself up out of her rocking chair and took a few steps toward the kitchen before realizing what she was doing. With great effort, she forced herself to sit back down.

"No. As a matter of fact, I'm not going to feed you. I don't cook anymore. I hardly eat at all, to tell the truth, and when I do, it's something Edith or Sarah Louise have fixed, or that nasty supplement my doctor wants me to drink. By the way, we're expected at Sarah's for supper tonight. In between, you can reconnoiter the cupboards and raid the fridge to see if there's anything you'd like."

"Oh. Well, I'll just wait until we go to Sarah Louise's, I guess. If I can."

"The cupboards aren't completely bare, Terry. There's probably a can of tuna fish and some bread, at the very least. Do you still like tuna fish sandwiches?"

He brightened. "Sure."

"Look in the cupboard left of the sink. If I have any, it'll be in there. The bread's in the bread drawer."

She made no move to rise, and his face fell.

"I guess I won't," he said petulantly.

"It'll only take you a minute to make one. Really, Terry! You *can* make yourself a sandwich, can't you?"

"I can, but I don't have to, at least not at home. Ellen takes good care of me."

"You mean she waits on you. She must be awfully busy with the twins. How does she find time to baby you too?"

"She's a great little gal, Mom. A perfect wife. She supports me the way a wife should support a husband. I can't believe what a lucky day it was when she said 'Yes.' Let me tell you, I never have to ask her to iron a shirt, and she fixes my supper, no matter what time I get home."

"I suppose if you wore slippers and smoked a pipe, she'd bring those to you too."

"That's about right," said Terry, who had missed the tartness in his mother's voice. "And even when the twins keep her up at night, she still gets me off in the morning."

"Do you mean to tell me that you don't get up to help when the twins are fussy?"

"I don't even hear them. Unless she says something, I usually don't even know when she's had a bad night."

At this point, Mae wondered why she had been so anxious to have Terry visit. In her weakened condition, which he hadn't even noticed, the strong anger that flooded her veins set her shaking. Still, she tried to lighten the mood by asking, "How do you manage that? Do you sleep on your good ear, like your dad did?"

Terry laughed. "Probably," he conceded. "Are you ready for my latest joke?"

Mae wasn't listening as Terry launched into his recital. She was thinking of Ellen, the sweet, loving girl Terry had swept off her feet. She was wondering how long Ellen would put up with her son before she demanded some changes. Just thinking about the childish outbursts and verbal abuse he resorted to when trying to avoid responsibility embarrassed her. No doubt Ellen had long since gotten used to that and to the aggravating push and pull necessary to get him to do anything around the house. His affected helplessness reminded Mae of the folk song "There's a Hole in the Bucket." He never got any job really done.

How did he get to be like that? Mae had often asked herself. She had no doubt that she and Fritz were partly to blame because they had been taken in by the bright blue eyes that could grow so huge with innocence or indignation. From the first, it had been difficult to discipline him. It was always easier to forgive, after which Terry rewarded them with the wide grin of the victorious. The oft-repeated scenario complicated every aspect of family life, causing contention between Mae and Fritz and infuriating the girls.

By the time it was clear to Mae and her husband that they needed to set stricter standards for Terry and follow through with them, the problem had become more serious than either one had imagined. Terry had the idea that he could do anything he wanted to—with impunity. Worse, he was committed to his own innocence in every situation, whether it was something as simple as a request to put away the bologna he had left out—"What makes you think I left it out!"—or as serious as a demand that he return the money taken from Mae's purse. If he did finally admit his culpability, he would go to unimaginable lengths to shift the responsibility—"It's really your fault for not giving me enough allowance!"

He did very well in school but at the cost of much turmoil, for he was a dedicated procrastinator. He almost always put off reports, reading assignments, and studying until the very last minute; then, being in a bind, he would refuse to do his chores, arguing that he had too much to do.

"You've had all sorts of time to do your work," Mae would counter. "I've watched you wasting time all week long. Do your chores and then study."

"You don't understand," Terry would protest. "If I waste a lot of time, then I have even less time for studying.

148

All the more reason why Sarah Louise should do the dishes and not me."

Striving to be firm, yet reasonable, Fritz and Mae asked Terry to be home after dates and dances at a certain hour. If he wasn't able to keep his curfew for some reason, he was to check in. He never did, even though he was often late. Over and over again they told him the rules. He would agree to them and promise to abide by them. Yet over and over again as he came home late, he would begin his explanation with, "But . . . " If they refused to let him drive, he would say, "If I can't drive, I can't go to work. It's your fault if I lose my job." No matter how justified their disciplinary measures were, they always ended up feeling like rotten parents.

He never learned how to stop talking and to just do what he was told, thought Mae now. He never learned to accept boundaries. Could we have helped him by being tougher? Or was he born with a congenital inability to relate actions to consequences? "You have to learn that there are limits!" she remembered having shouted at him one day.

"Who's going to make me?"

"Life will, if we can't," Fritz had said. "And life is a good deal less compassionate than we are."

But the fall they thought would come when Terry was on his own had never materialized. Lucky Terry had so far avoided the head-to-head with reality, thanks to those who were always ready to take on the job of protector—his mission companions, his secretaries, his wife.

Mae's thoughts trailed off, and in the silence she realized that Terry was looking at her oddly. "Look, Mom, if you're tired of hearing my jokes, just tell me, okay?"

"I've done it again, haven't I? Oh, I'm sorry! Lately I seem to spend as much time in the past as I do in the present. Maybe it has something to do with being so sick . . . "

She had given him an opening as broad as the proverbial barn door, but Terry did not use it. He acknowledged her illness only once, when it was time to go to Sarah Louise's for supper.

"Can you walk that far?" he asked.

"Just barely."

149

That was as far as they got. The rest of that day and most of the next, Terry talked nonstop about every unimportant thing that came to mind. Mae indulged him and restrained the outspoken Edith from attacking him straight on. She knew it would do no good to force the issue. Only when he was about to leave did she finally speak.

"Will you be able to visit again soon?"

"Probably not. I've got a heavy schedule the next few months. Maybe Christmas."

"Christmas will be too late." She felt a surge of hope as understanding flashed in his eyes; it was just as quickly extinguished.

"Now, Mom, you don't know that."

"Yes, I do. Terry, look at me! What do you see?"

"My own dear Mama, who is worrying too much, as usual."

"Terry, if this is the last time I'll ever see you—"

"It won't be, I guarantee it. Only next time I come, you have Edith stock that kitchen first. I'm hungry for your specialties, like that spectacular devil's food cake you used to make."

He smiled at her and then straightened his tie in the mirror of the hall tree that stood by the front door.

"I have something for you," Mae said, choking back tears. She picked up the azalea and held it out. "Here. I want you to have this. Karen and Sarah Louise will get one too."

He took the proffered bonsai gingerly, holding it at arm's length. "Are you sure? You've had these things for years."

"As a matter of fact, this particular one is over thirty years old. It's my favorite, although I can't say exactly why."

"Then you keep it, Mom," he said, thrusting it at her. "I can buy a bonsai when I get home."

"But I want you to have something of me. This lovely old plant and I have shared the same space for many years. Sometimes, in a weird way, I think it is me . . . "

"It's magnificent, and I appreciate it, but I'd rather leave it with you, okay?" He pushed the ceramic pot into Mae's hands. "I don't like plants anymore than Sarah Louise does. I'd probably kill it before the year's out. Maybe you should give them all to Karen."

Mae hesitated a moment, then she set the bonsai back in its place. She did so in a manner oddly ceremonial: when she took her hands from the container, she felt that she was letting go of far more than that. She felt years of guilt drop away as she realized her son was who he was by choice. Terry was Terry; his life was his own. She had said that often enough, but until that moment, she had not really accepted it.

She accepted it now.

It was just as well that Terry refused the bonsai, she thought. He would never appreciate it, he whose life had grown without direction, like an unpruned tree. Whose life, thought Mae sadly, had a malignancy of its own.

"Wait, if it means that much to you—" began Terry.

"No, it's all right."

She said her farewell in full consciousness of the fact that she would never see her son again. Later, as she lay in bed, she realized that although the self-recrimination was gone, the sorrow was not. That, she thought, was the only constant besides love.

15

Not long after Terry's visit, Mae called up Sarah Louise. "Do you have any use for my sofa?" she asked.

There was silence on the other end of the line. Finally Sarah Louise said, "You're getting the bed, aren't you?"

"Yes. I seem to need an awful lot of rest lately. I don't want to be stuck off in my bedroom, and the couch isn't that comfortable."

"When is it coming?"

"Tomorrow."

"I'll send Ron and Mark over tonight. We can put the couch in the TV room downstairs."

Mae could see her lovely camelback sofa with mahogany trim languishing in Sarah Louise's TV room, cushions flattened and springs protruding from the bottom, but she closed her eyes against the image and said, "Good. I'll be expecting them then."

The bed came on schedule, and Mae directed the men to position it so that anyone lying on it would have the front door before them, the greenhouse to the right, and the north windows to the left.

"I'll really have my back to the wall, won't I?" said Mae to Sarah Louise and Edith. She appraised it, arms akimbo, then added, "It's ugly."

"When we get it made, it won't look so bad," offered Sarah Louise. "We can put your Gram's quilt across the foot of it for color, or your favorite afghan."

Mae nodded. "But no white sheets. I don't want to look any worse than I have to."

Melody had color-analyzed her in February: "You're a 'summer,' Grandma. You should be wearing mauve and blue and lavender and stuff like that. Forget white and black."

"There goes half my wardrobe."

"Right."

Melody had begun pulling articles of dubious color from her grandmother's closet, and before long a pile lay upon the bed.

"Well, I was going to get rid of a bunch of this stuff anyway," said Mae.

"Not this jumper—I get it." Melody pulled it over her head. She was shorter than her grandmother, so on her it looked like a drop-waist, calf-length jumper, just funky enough to be in.

"Super! And look at this coat. It's got humongous shoulder pads! I want it, too."

"Melody, that coat must be forty years old. Your grandfather picked it out for me; that's why I kept it." Mae ran her fingers over the fabric.

"He had good taste."

"Do you really think your mother will let you wear those things? They were nice once, but—"

"Sure, why not? What else have you got stashed away?"

Together the two of them went through the rest of the closet, putting things in two piles: "old enough to be in" and outright reject.

"There's not much left," said Melody, when they were done. "Maybe we ought to put some of these back."

"Let's see. Oh, it's not so bad. There're three dresses, a suit, and some blouses. At least I've had some things I looked good in. That's a relief."

"You always look good, Grandma," said Melody, hugging her. "You'll just look better now. All you need are some scarves and accessories in the right colors."

"Well, I'll tell you what. Why don't you go shopping for me? That way I know I'll be getting the right colors."

Thus, when she began spending a large portion of her day in bed, Mae sent Melody shopping again, this time to get her a new bathrobe and two more nightgowns. "In the right colors, mind you." Melody brought home a gown of pale lavender, one sprigged with pink flowers, and a lilac-colored bathrobe.

"Thank you," Mae said. "Now I'll be able to hold court in high fashion."

Only the queen's throne, now that it was installed, was ugly.

"There's not a heck of a lot you can do with a hospital bed, Mae," said Edith, contemplating the bare ugliness of metal and mattress.

But Sarah Louise was already there with flowered sheets in hand. "What else do you want on it, Mom?"

"That lightweight flannel blanket, probably."

When the bed was made and the sheets folded down invitingly, Sarah Louise said, "I guess you'd better try it out."

Mae got onto the bed, and Edith raised it to a comfortable height. "How's that?" asked Edith.

"Great. I've always wanted to be elevated. But I really need to have a nap on it before I'll be able to say for sure."

"You're tired, aren't you?" asked Edith. "Why don't you put on a nightgown and really rest?"

She changed into the lavender gown, and Edith helped her into the bed, guiding her emaciated limbs ever so carefully. "Can I get you one of your malts before you sleep?"

Mae wrinkled up her nose at the thought of the food supplement Dr. Melton had suggested, but capitulating to the concern evident in Edith's eyes, she drank down a glass of the stuff. Then she closed her eyes, hoping that the combined effects of painkiller and visualization would move her to that spot beyond the breakers Keith had spoken of.

Her strategy against pain was no longer always successful. She was learning that regardless of the medication she took and the mental ploys she tried, pain could at any time break through her defenses. When it did, something as simple as the touch of sheets could be excruciating.

Thankfully, this was not one of those times.

"We can have bedtime stories all the time now, can't we?" said Matt to his grandmother, who was propped up in the bed.

"Anytime you want one," said Mae.

But the M and Ms' visits had to be regulated; Mae was not really strong enough anymore to enjoy the usual flood of little people she had entertained so many years. They were allowed to visit any time between two and four, unless the stoplight Edith had made of construction paper and hung on the front door was red. That meant "Don't you dare ring this bell!"

"I don't like that," protested Mae. "After all these years of encouraging them to come, it doesn't seem right to stick a sign on the door like that."

"We're not saying they have to stay away. We're just saying 'Not now.' There's nothing wrong with that," Edith replied firmly.

Sarah Louise agreed. "I'm glad you're here, Edith. You take such good care of mother."

"I'm just like a little baby. I need someone to fix my food and get me to the potty on time," said Mae dryly. "And even then, I don't always make it."

"Mother!" protested Sarah Louise with a pained expression.

"Well, it's true, isn't it, Edith?"

Edith nodded.

"In fact, we have just about decided it's time to buy some diapers. Seems I'm coming full circle. At the rate I'm regressing, I'll get a chance to see what it's like to be a baby again."

But no one laughed—Edith's lips were drawn together in a firm line, and Sarah Louise had fled.

A comfortable routine had developed since Edith's advent. Sarah Louise usually called the first thing in the morning, then dropped by both late mornings and afternoons when she could. Sometimes she stopped just to chat, sometimes to pick up the wash or to bring over something she hoped would tempt her mother to eat. Sometimes she sat with Edith for a while in the quiet, semi-darkened room after her mother was ready for the night.

The room was not always quiet. A comfortable little group had begun meeting around her bed early in the evenings. Howard had gotten into the habit of stopping by often, and Keith usually dropped in on his way to work. Brent came once when both Howard and Keith were there and found it so pleasant that he joined them more often than not. And so there were three. The men talked to each other as much as they talked to Mae, an aspect that made it easier for all of them, for when the focus was shifted from Mae, conversation took a less intense, halting course. It meandered comfortably down whatever path presented itself, and Mae found it lovely to lie in her bed listening to the flow more than to the words themselves.

Things were more lively when the grandchildren and their friends visited. Mae tried to make those times enjoyable, although she was not energetic enough to do much besides listen to them as they tried to amuse her. She did manage a few things, though: she often had Edith get her something from her box of costumes. One day the kids entered to see their grandmother in a witch's hat, another day in a crown. But the most successful headgear Mae wore was a white bedcap.

She was wearing the bedcap and some old wire glasses the day the twins came (Sarah Louise would only let two of the M and Ms come at any one time). It took them a moment before they could collect themselves enough to know what was required of them, then Morgan said, "Oh, what big eyes you have, Grandmother!"

"All the better to see you with," Mae replied with a sly chuckle.

"And such big teeth you have!"

"All the better to *eat* you with!"

As the room filled with laughter, Mae knew she was doing what Sarah Louise had accused her of so many weeks ago: making an entertainment of her dying. But she didn't care. Such antics brought some lightness and laughter into days that were becoming too long. There were times, however, when Mae suspected that her sense of humor was failing along with the rest of her. When she complained once about "this old bed," little Matt said reproachfully, "But Grandma, it can be anything you want it to be."

She wasn't so sure about that anymore, but she didn't want to disillusion him, so she asked, "What do you think it should be?"

"It could be an island. Or a ship."

"I know," said Michael. "I'm reading *The Voyage of the Dawn Treader*. Why not make this bed into the *Dawn Treader!* You could be Lucy, going on a voyage with King Caspian to the end of the East world. I'll be Caspian, of course."

"It doesn't look much like a boat," said Mae doubtfully. "I think you'll have to spruce it up a bit."

They took her suggestion seriously. When the older children came the next day, they had with them a prow made of cardboard. "Do you like it?" Michael asked. "We made it out of a giant box!"

"It's wonderful," said Mae, admiring the dragon-head prow, which had fierce eyes and bejeweled sides. The twins attached it to the end of the bed (right where it was in everybody's way) with masking tape.

"What are you doing—" began Edith, when she saw them at work.

"It's all right," said Mae.

"Hey! Oh neat! I can't believe it!" said Morgan, fairly jumping up and down.

"What are you having a spaz for?" asked Michael disgustedly.

"It's the bed! What direction is this bed pointed?"

Michael looked at him as if he had gone crazy. Then his eyes widened in recognition. "East! Hey, Gram, your bed's even going in the right direction! You are going on a voyage to the end of the East world!"

Her eyes misted as they took turns reading to her from *The Voyage of the Dawn Treader*. She couldn't help thinking of the many times she had read aloud to them. Everything was backwards, the tables were turned, and there was nothing she could do about it.

Though she had never been much of a TV fan, Karen, Terry, and Sarah Louise had gone in together to buy her a VCR. "That way, you can pick out what you want to watch," said Karen. It's just like the microwave, thought

Mae. It's a wonderful idea, if you want to eat. The VCR would have been wonderful, too, had she had any interest in movies.

But the M and Ms did. They loved movies, and the older kids spent a lot of time in the homes of friends who had VCRs. So, on evenings when she felt up to it, Mae would have Edith invite the M and Ms to pick out a movie and bring it over to watch on her VCR. The only stipulation was that they had to bring their own popcorn and drinks.

Sarah Louise had final approval on what was chosen, which meant they saw a lot of Disney and PG movies. Sometimes Sarah Louise picked out one of the good old movies she enjoyed, starring Bogart or Gable, or Cary Grant, though these were not so old as far as Mae was concerned. Actually, Mae didn't watch so much as lie back with eyes closed, enjoying the sounds of her family around her. She did notice, however, that more often than not, Mark and Melody weren't there.

"Those are dumb movies," said Mark when she asked him about it. "Only a dipstick would go for those."

"A dipstick?"

"A nerd."

"Oh. Well, what kind of movie would you like to see?"

"Something you wouldn't want to watch, Grandma."

"Like what?" she demanded.

"Like *The Breakfast Club*."

"And why wouldn't I like that?"

"The language isn't too good."

"But there must be something good about it, if you like it."

"Yeah. There is."

"Then maybe I would like it too."

"I don't think so. It's too real."

"And I couldn't take it?"

"Face it, Gram. Most parents would just as soon not know what it's like for teenagers now."

"I would. Give me a try."

"It wouldn't work. Mom was mad enough when she found out Melody and I had seen it at a friend's—she'd get furious if she found out we saw it again over here."

158

"We can't go behind her back, you know."

"Yeah, well, that just means we won't do it at all."

Mae had been struggling to resolve the conflict between her desire to remain part of life and the bone-weary need to withdraw into peaceful oblivion. She opted for life.

"You get the tape, I'll talk to your mother."

"All right!"

Sarah Louise was furious. "Mother, you're undermining everything I've been telling the kids! It's bad enough that they saw the movie at all, but to see it again with your approval, in your house? No way."

"Calm down, Sarah," said Ron, who had been warned about the problem by Melody. "It's not as big a deal as you're making it."

"How can you say that? That's not the kind of thing we want our kids to be watching. The language is terrible!"

"Sarah, our kids hear that sort of language every day. They don't respond to it the way we do. I don't even think they hear it anymore, to tell the truth."

"That doesn't change the principle."

"No, but I think Melody is right."

"And just what has our daughter been saying?"

"She's angry that we assume she's going to go off the deep end just because she sees a movie or two. And I have to agree with her. If I had to put it on a scale, I'd say that kind of language isn't as pernicious as a movie full of sex. Anyway, Melody's a sensible young lady, and her values are strong."

"But why does she want to see that junk?"

"In some ways, that junk is the voice of her generation. It taps in on her feelings and concerns. I'm not saying we should give the kids free rein, I'm just saying we ought to give the older kids a chance to exercise their judgment in this thing. I think it's come to a case of judging each show on its own merit."

"Well, you're responsible if they go ahead with this!"

"Still want to, Mom?" Ron asked Mae.

"I said they could," replied Mae.

"Then it's on."

So Mae Thomlinson, lying in her hospital bed, got a

glimpse at the world her teenage grandchildren inhabited. This movie she didn't doze through. Although she had decided to be open-minded, the offensive words were like squeaky chalk on a blackboard, and she shut her eyes against a few scenes she felt were more than she could tolerate.

"Hey, Gram, we can turn it off if you want to," suggested Melody, who had noticed Mae's closed eyes.

"No. I'm doing all right." In spite of the things she felt were inappropriate and unnecessary, Mae recognized in the five teenagers and the teacher portrayed on screen people she really knew, pains and sorrows she understood.

"Well, did you like it?" asked Mark as the video tape rewound. He didn't have to include Edith in his question— she had left after the first fifteen minutes.

"Yes. As a matter of fact, I did," said Mae, wiping the corners of her eyes. The last poignant moments of the movie had been a forceful argument of the need to look beneath the differences that separate people and to make the connections that are so enriching. And in those last moments, Mae thought of Keith.

Still, there was much about the movie that had repulsed her, and the fact that Mark thought it an accurate representation of what things were like for his generation made those aspects even more troublesome. Her heart ached with compassion and the need to protect her grandchildren, all of them. But she knew she couldn't. The most she could do now was to love them and to say a prayer for them.

The VCR played an even more important part in the days to come. Keith brought Mae a copy of the book *Anatomy of an Illness* by Norman Cousins. He had underlined the sections that explained Cousins' notion that laughter is the best painkiller of all.

"I know the pain's getting tougher to deal with all the time," he said. "I thought maybe we could hold back on increasing your medication if laughter does help."

She read the underlined sections, and later she told him, "It sounds like a good idea."

"Do you want me to get you some tapes of comedies?" he asked.

"I guess. It might help, Keith, but I'm so tired. I don't know if there's anything that can really make me laugh anymore."

Keith brought everything he could lay hands on that had a reputation of being funny. Abbot and Costello, the Marx brothers, Charlie Chaplin (Mae thought the Chaplin video was sad, rather than funny), Cartoon Classics from Disney, the Apple Dumpling Gang, and others. He also brought audio tapes of *Who's on First* and *Baby Snooks at the Opera*. Mae listened to or watched a tape after the morning routine was taken care of, and often at night, just before going to sleep. They did help, but they didn't help enough. She had long since progressed up the medication scale from codeine to Dilaudid. The laughter therapy was another attempt to forestall the next step of painkiller—morphine.

She was able to put it off by two weeks.

16

It's strange how unreal it all seems, Mae thought. Edith had already helped her shampoo her hair and wash her body, but Mae insisted that she could do the rinsing with the newly installed, hand-held spray nozzle. "I'll stay sitting down," she promised, patting the plastic shower stool beneath her.

Now, as she rinsed herself, Mae saw her distorted body clearly. Her stomach seemed to have a life of its own, swelling roundly. She had been proud of such smooth swelling during her three pregnancies, but this was the result of a dreadful, malignant growth. In contrast, the rest of her was nothing more than bones thinly covered with skin. She had the look of starvation about her.

Her body didn't seem to have anything to do with Mae Thomlinson. She felt the same odd disjunction between self and body that she had felt at other times: she was the person who lived inside; she was not the body.

"I never really got integrated with you, did I?" Mae said to her body, patting it dry lovingly. "Here we've been together 'lo these many years,' and we're about to be separated soon, and I'm not even sure we ever understood each other."

"Mae, are you okay?" called Edith nervously from the other side of the bathroom door.

"I'm fine, I'm just talking to myself, that's all."

Here I am talking to myself as if I were partners in a long marriage about to be dissolved, she thought wryly. But we'll have another go at it, and maybe we'll do better the second time around.

When she made the same comment to Keith that evening, he looked at her oddly. "Do you believe in reincarnation?"

"No, why?"

"What you said sounded like it."

"I was talking about resurrection. Do you believe in reincarnation?"

"I don't know for sure. I'm leaning toward it, mostly because I like the idea of karma."

"I've read a little about karma," said Mae, "but I'm not sure I know exactly what it is."

"Basically, karma is your destiny. It's what you bring with you into this life from your previous go-round. It's as if whatever fixations or passions you have indulged in get marked in the debit column: you bring that karmic debt with you, and until you have worked it off, you have to keep coming back."

"Do it till you get it right, is that it?"

"Something like that."

"What do you like about the notion of karma and reincarnation particularly?"

Keith frowned, his heavy, curly eyebrows drawing up into his forehead. After a long hesitation, he finally spoke. "It's the only idea that satisfies my need to know there will be justice somewhere, somehow."

"'Oh, yet we trust that somehow good will be the final end of ill . . . '" Mae quoted.

"There was a time when I didn't believe that. I guess I did when I was a kid, but too many things happened in between." He leaned back reflectively. "I grew up in a little farm community in Kansas, did I ever tell you that?"

"No."

"It was like Shelton in a lot of ways. Hardly anybody lived there who wasn't connected in some way to the original settlers. Life was pretty predictable—I figured I understood it all by the time I was nine. You got born, you got married, you got kids, you got old, and then you died. No

163

big deal. You hoped you didn't get in trouble, and you prayed from planting to harvest that the tornados and hail and heavy rain would hit some other corner of Kansas.

"Then I got drafted—safe in Kansas one minute and plopped down in the middle of hellfire the next. I never knew what hit me." He shook his thick, heavy hair and grinned slightly before adding, "I spent three nights in the supply shed searching for ruby slippers, but no luck."

Mae smiled.

"I saw more there than I ever wanted to see, and I don't just mean the fighting." He was silent for a minute, then asked, "Do you know German?"

"Almost nothing. *Macht nichts* is about it."

Keith laughed. "Then I don't suppose you ever heard the word *Weltschmerz*?"

"No. What does it mean?"

"In ten words or less? We don't have a direct translation for it, it's such a preworld war German concept, such a part of the German soul . . . *Schmerz* means pain. *Welt* means world. *Weltschmerz* is a kind of exaggerated existential pain. When you're suffering from it, you've taken on yourself the pains of all people on earth."

"I thought someone else already did that," said Mae.

Keith shook his head. "Nope. Christians—and you Mormons are Christians despite rumors to the contrary—believe that Christ bore the sins of the world. The pain is something else again. We have to help one another with that. Unfortunately, we can only do so much—that's another part of the definition. You are so weighed down by the pain of humanity, you can't do anything. You're helpless."

"But you can help the people around you."

"You could if you weren't completely overburdened by awareness."

"And you were?"

He nodded. "I couldn't stand it, so I took the easy way out. I got my head so messed up, I didn't care what was happening to the rest of the world. Melty tried to get me off the drugs, but it didn't work. I was still hooked when I got out."

"You told me once it wasn't love that made the difference."

"I said it wasn't a woman. That's not the same. But a woman did help me get turned around.

"That was a strange relationship. She wanted enlightenment, so she said, but she was going about it in a strange way: she was using drugs for a shortcut. I didn't agree with that, but what she told me about karma and enlightenment and reincarnation made sense to me. I started meditating. The day I realized I was doing more meditation and less drugs, I knew it was time to surface. I hadn't really done anything since my discharge, so I needed to find someone who would take a chance on me. That's when I called Melty."

"You don't have this . . . what did you call it?"

"*Weltschmerz?*"

"You don't have it anymore?"

"No. If the circumstances a person is in are a reflection of his karmic debt, then he is right where he needs to be to work that debt out. No matter how awful a situation looks to be, it is just and offers the possibility of release. I guess that sounds pretty weird to you."

"Maybe a little, but I understand its appeal. You and I have worked on the same problem, Keith, and maybe the solution we've come up with isn't so different."

Slowly Mae began explaining. She told him how she had struggled with the question of ultimate justice for many years. It all started with the awareness that the condition of man was so different depending upon time and place as to defy comparison. It didn't seem at all fair, and she wondered how a just God could judge men whose conditions were so disparate. Even though she had a keen appreciation of the mystery surrounding God and the inability of finite man to comprehend his ways and means, she felt the need to create some personal philosophy that would satisfy her in this regard.

It has to do with individual response to circumstance, she decided. That's the only way it could be fair. And if that's the case, the circumstances don't really matter. Only the response matters.

She concluded that there were basically only two possible responses to any given situation: toward good or away from good. That was to say, toward God or away from God. It was a notion she found tremendously liberating.

For as long as she could remember, Mae had been throwing herself against a brick wall of Why? When something dreadful or sad happened, she demanded an answer, which of course presupposed that there was a reason behind every occurrence, from not getting the house she wanted, to having a miscarriage. It was an understandable supposition for someone who had grown up with a mother whose constant question was "Now what does God want me to learn from this?"

She was a mature woman with many of life's experiences behind her when she finally came to the conclusion that not everything could be blamed on God. The idea that God was arbitrary or capricious, visiting good and ill upon his children as his pleasure dictated, offended her. Also, if God could only be God by operating in complete accord with law, which she believed, there was no place for such tyrannical behavior.

Mae found a clue to what she was searching for when she found the unheralded line in Job: "For the thing which I greatly feared is come upon me, and that which I was afraid of is come unto me."

Ah-ha! she thought, now that's interesting.

Her mind began working. Unknown to her husband or her children, she followed different lines of thought while vacuuming, washing the dishes, or driving. The joy she felt when she found a concept that fit was like nothing she had experienced before.

Her solution was simple. God did not, she concluded, arbitrarily intervene or refrain from intervening in the life of his offspring, man: man created in himself the conditions that allowed God to operate in his behalf. She also concluded that good and evil were not only a matter of individual will, but were also called into existence because a person created in himself the conditions that allowed their presence.

This conclusion she was not entirely happy with, for it implied that *nothing* was random. She wasn't sure anyone could have such ultimate, and in most cases unrecognized, power over the course of his own life. Anyway, was it always possible to say that a person's freak accident or sudden, fatal illness was brought upon himself by himself as a result of his habitual thought patterns?

That was distasteful to her, so Mae allowed that both evil and good could also come into one's life as random events. After all, didn't the rain (or hail) fall on the just and the unjust alike?

She was tremendously excited and satisfied by the conclusions she had reached. She wrote them in her journal so that she could refer to them, but she never spoke of these thoughts to anyone. Only now, as death began its patient watch, did she decide to unfold them to Keith. She knew that he would listen to her in a way her husband had never listened, and that he wouldn't make fun of her attempts to create a satisfying personal philosophy. Like Fritz had.

One of the great and abiding sorrows of her life was that Fritz had never granted her any intellectual credibility. As a journalist, he of necessity had honed his thinking processes sharply. He was educated in logic and rhetoric, so any thought that was intuitive or unsubstantiated was not worth his time. Besides, he had the words of the great philosophers and essayists as well as of scripture to rely upon: his job was to measure others' words and thoughts against each other. He had never felt the need to develop an extensive philosophy of his own. He thought it amusing that Mae did.

She had found that out when she made her first venture into the realm of philosophy. She was in her thirties when she stopped to wonder at the implications of a comment she had made to herself: "That was a dumb thought."

She had said those very words often and unthinkingly, as everyone does. However, this time she heard what she said to herself, and in astonishment she asked, "If there is a part of me that can assess my thoughts, then that part of me is obviously beyond my thoughts, something different all together."

Up to that time, she had vested most thoughts that crossed her mind with 100% validity. Now she watched her thoughts with interest, wondering where they came from and how they affected her life. She was thrilled when she saw a quote by Joseph Krutch that was a filler in a magazine: "The brain does not create thought (Sir Julian Huxley has recently pointed out this fact); it is an instrument which thought finds useful."

"Oh my!" she said aloud.

Later she thought, Yes, it works.

Through the scriptures, which she had studied all her life, she knew that her most essential element was intelligence, which could neither be created nor destroyed. That intelligence now resided in a physical body, which had a certain masking effect on it. Of course, the brain was necessary: through the instrumentation of the brain, one learned to cope with the world in which one found oneself.

When one felt that there was no other means of apprehending knowledge, one relied on the brain and the assumptions and connections—all highly subjective—that the brain made as it fielded the experiences life offered. But Mae realized that there was something more.

Her inner life changed at that point. She began to observe the workings of her mind with more objectivity and, sometimes, with grim humor. "My brain is doing a number on me," she said when feeling the tyranny of habitual, baseless thoughts. She began to realize that everyone remade the world in his own image and that essentially the world one inhabited was a dream world, in which one had nightmares as well as lovely fantasies. She took as her own the statement she had heard somewhere, "Life may be dangerous, but it's not serious."

She tried to share her discoveries with Fritz. She told him excitedly that she had just come to the conclusion that the world of ideas was the real world, not the tangible arena in which she was to play out her probation.

Fritz responded to her philosophical musings with the comment, "That's just Plato."

"You crumb!" she howled. "I've never read Plato! It has nothing to do with Plato—I came up with it all on my own!"

168

"It is still Plato."

"Thanks a lot."

The joy and excitement of discovery shriveled. She never spoke to him about such things again.

But it was hard not to share what was most important to her, so one day in Sunday School, she responded to the teacher's question concerning wealth and righteousness with a purely Platonic answer.

"How can we keep the proper perspective about wealth?" he had asked.

"First, you have to have a sense of humor about it," Mae responded. "It doesn't do to take wealth all that seriously. We have to remember a person isn't essentially his wealth, nor is a person his lack of wealth."

She paused, waiting for an affirmation of her response, but she got none. It was as if she hadn't spoken at all. The teacher moved on to someone else who had a more conventional answer about using wealth for doing good.

"I'm not surprised," Howard said laughingly when she told him. "You really walked into it."

"Why? How?"

"Sis, the attitude of some Church members toward wealth is basically obey and grow rich. Most Saints of Shelton 3rd Ward make a direct connection between riches and righteousness, and here you are, telling them they aren't their wealth! To them, their prosperity is a clear reflection of their self."

It was strike two. Still she tried some of her ideas out on Edith who said, "Mae, you think too much."

How can a person think too much, wondered Mae.

So she kept her thoughts to herself, and she tried to bring her actions into correlation with them. Sometimes she could, but more often, she still railed and fretted over life's difficulties.

It became easier for her to hold a steady course when she expanded her philosophy with the notion that there were really only two responses possible in any situation, toward good and God or away from them. She felt that it made a lot more sense to make the choice for God and good right from the first.

"You know," she said to Keith once she had aired her tale of philosophic adventure, "I've often wondered if it was a waste of time to struggle with those questions. Fritz used to laugh at me for worrying my 'uneducated head with philosopher's conundrums.' But when I learned I had cancer, I knew it hadn't been a waste of time. Those years of trying to come up with a meaningful understanding of the human condition gave me an advantage, you know. I'd already accomplished, under easier circumstances, what I would have been struggling to accomplish under the worst."

With a twinkle in her eye she added, "Of course, I may be all wrong."

17

Mae was glad to have her bed. As the month of July progressed, she spent more and more time in it. In fact, she would have ceased leaving the house at all if it had not been for Brent. Often he would appear, nattily dressed as usual, and offer to take her for a ride. Edith objected to the continuation of their drives at first, as did Sarah Louise, but Brent had potent ammunition: "Keith says it's all right. As long as Mae feels up to it, of course."

So, slowly and carefully, they would help her out to the car, where they would lower her onto the lambskin Brent had bought just for her, thinking it would help protect her fragile skin from the pressure of sitting so long in one position. The rides were never too long. Sensitive as he was to Mae's every expression, Brent always knew when it was time to turn back.

Sometimes he would head south up on the bench and drive out past the fields and farms. When that was the case, he would pick drives where Mae would see some horses. She especially liked that, and she would comment knowledgeably about them.

Other times, he would take a lane leading down to the Shoshone River and park under trees, where the cooling shade and flowing water took the edge off the July heat. Then, they would talk. Watching her fail was difficult for Brent, she knew: he had been through the same process with his wife not many years earlier. But their conversation didn't mire in her present circumstances, for she still had access to the curiosity and the ability to enjoy the moment that had served her so well up to now.

Only once did Brent and Mae misjudge what was possible. For some reason, Mae had an insatiable need to drive up the Big Horns once more.

"Impossible!" said Edith, and this time Keith concurred.

"Can't I at least go up as far as Five Springs? Brent's got air conditioning, and if I get tired, I can lay down in the back of the car. I can take my medication with me. Why would it be so different from staying at home?"

"Mae, it really doesn't make sense to take such a risk—" began Keith, but she interrupted.

"Have you been up the mountains since you came here?" she asked.

"No," he admitted.

"That's why you don't understand. I want to smell juniper in the mountain air; I want to put a piece of salty sagebrush between my teeth; I want to drink cold mountain water from my cupped hands . . ."

"Okay. But only if I come," said Keith, realizing how important it was to her.

They started early on a day when Mae felt strong and able to go, and the trip itself went remarkably well. But the next day, the effects of the exertion made themselves manifest—Mae was in agony, and Dr. Melton had to come. When he heard what they had done, he was livid.

"You should have known better," he said angrily to Keith.

"I did know better, but she wanted to go so badly . . ."

"It was my fault. Keith said we shouldn't go, but I didn't listen to him," said a visibly distressed Brent.

A weak voice from behind them brought their argument to a halt. "Don't get mad at them. I wanted to go, and even if I have to pay for it, that's all right with me."

It took Dr. Melton several days to stabilize Mae; the price she paid for her last trip up the mountain was high.

That incident served to point up how weak she had become. She needed help with many things now, and what Edith didn't do for her, Keith did. Sarah Louise, who came briefly three different times a day—mornings, late after-

172

noons, and again in the evenings—expressed her thanks to both of them often.

"I don't know how we'll ever be able to repay your kindness and generosity. Really, I have no idea how I would ever be able to take care of my family and Mom too if I didn't have your help. Of course, Melody and Mark are old enough to take over at home, but there are some things that only a mother can do."

Such comments led Mae to believe Sarah Louise understood and agreed with the schedule that had evolved.

"I'm glad she doesn't object," said Mae gratefully after Sarah Louise left.

"So am I," said Keith, "but I've got to tell you, Mae, I don't get it. I thought she'd hit the ceiling."

"I don't think she has the slightest idea what's going on," said Edith, shaking her head. "And if she ever does find out, there'll be the devil to pay."

"But there's really no other way to do it," protested Mae.

"Sure there is," said Edith. "I could do it myself. I'd only need Keith to move you."

"We could do it that way," agreed Keith. "Well, Mae, do you want to try it?"

"No." Mae was embarrassed at her childish voice and quivering chin. "I'm so afraid . . ." For her skin was becoming increasingly sensitive: the pain that a thoughtless hand could cause was at times so severe that she had become fearful of being touched by anyone but Keith, whose foot massage had won her confidence from the first.

"It's all right, we won't change," Edith hastily assured her. "I know you feel safe with Keith—you know he won't hurt you. I just hope Sarah Louise doesn't find out."

But one day Sarah Louise came over to the little house earlier than usual. Because she did, she learned exactly what Mae had meant when she had said, "Keith gets me ready for the day." She stood in the doorway, utterly speechless at what she saw. Mae's sheet had been arranged so that one of her legs was exposed; Keith was washing it with smooth, gentle strokes.

"Good morning, Sarah," he said, looking up briefly before continuing to bathe Mae's leg.

"Come on in," said Mae. "We're almost done here, aren't we?"

"Almost. Are you going to join us for breakfast?" asked Keith.

"Breakfast?" echoed Sarah Louise.

"Yeah. We usually have breakfast after I get done taking care of Mae." He sniffed the air. "Smells like we're having something special today. Hey, Edith, are those blueberry muffins you're cookin'?"

Edith stepped out of the kitchen. Her face reflected momentary panic when she saw Sarah Louise, but she said smoothly to her, "Someone told me they were his favorite. Join us, Sarah Louise. There's plenty."

"Thank you, but I'm on my way to the *Journal*. Ron forgot some papers he needs," she said in a strangled voice.

Keith finished patting Mae's leg dry, then he asked her, "Do you want a back rub?"

"I not only want it, I need it."

Keith helped her roll onto her side. He was careful and sure, treating her with immense dignity, respect, and love. He pulled the spread over her buttocks before pushing up her nightgown to expose her emaciated back. Sarah Louise gasped.

"What's the matter?" Mae asked, trying to turn so that she could see her daughter.

"Nothing . . . I just didn't realize you were so *thin*."

Mae could sense the tension in the air, and the normally therapeutic back rub was not enjoyable this morning. She was glad when Keith finished and settled her in the fresh bed before taking the basin from the room.

When he was gone, Sarah Louise hissed at Mae, "Mother! How could you let him do that?"

"Do what?"

"*Touch* you like that!"

"Is that what you're upset over?" said Mae. "Good heavens. For a minute I thought something awful had happened."

"Believe me, it was awful to walk in and see that . . . man!—bathing you. Edith should be doing it, and if she can't, I will. He certainly doesn't have to."

174

Mae leaned back on her plump pillows and closed her eyes. "You're right. He doesn't have to. But he comes over after work every day, you know, so when he offered to do it while Edith fixed breakfast for us all, I said okay. I really don't see what's so awful about it. He doesn't see anything he hasn't seen before. Besides, he has such gentle hands—"

"It just doesn't seem right."

"It's no different than having a nurse bathe a man, is it?"

"I suppose not, but—"

"Chow's on!" said Keith with forced cheer. He was loaded down with plates and utensils, which he set on the round wicker table in the greenhouse extension. Edith followed him with a basket of muffins and a plate of eggs. She pushed the hospital table in front of Mae and put a plate with a bit of egg and half a muffin onto it.

"Do you want juice, dear?" she asked.

"Yes. But I don't really think I can eat this," she added.

"Please try," said Edith, touching Mae's cheek gently.

"Just for you. And Jungle Boy, there."

Keith grinned.

"It looks like I fixed way too much food," said Edith. "Are you going to help us eat this, Sarah Louise?"

"No. I've got to go, but I'll be back later."

"Oh oh," said Keith when Sarah Louise had gone. "We're in trouble now."

"I'm afraid so," said Edith.

Strangely, Sarah Louise didn't bring up the subject of Keith when she returned to visit in the afternoon, but Mae knew her daughter was deeply disturbed by the relationship she had formed with the outsider. Later on in the evening, when Edith suggested to Mae that she could just as well give her her bath, Mae was suspicious. "Whose idea was that, yours or Sarah Louise's?" she demanded.

Edith admitted that Sarah had suggested it.

Still, Mae was surprised a few days later when little Matt asked, "Do you know Mom watches Keith out the kitchen window?"

"What?"

"She watches him come, and she stays right by the

kitchen window no matter what until she sees him leave."

"It's that bad, is it?" murmured Mae to herself.

"Now you're doing it too," Matt said disgustedly.

"I'm sorry, dear, what did you say?"

"I said you're doing it too. Mumbling to yourself, I mean, just like Mom. It gives me the creeps."

Oh dear, thought Mae. This is getting out of hand.

Two days after that conversation, Sarah Louise burst into the living room of Mae's home and flew to the bedside. Her face was ugly with rage as she ripped the washcloth from Keith Sullivan's hand.

"Move out of the way! I'll do this," she said through bared teeth. "I'm her daughter—I'm the one who should be doing it, not you."

Keith started to protest, but Mae shook her head warningly. He stepped back, giving Sarah Louise room at the bedside.

Sarah Louise began washing her mother where Keith had left off, muttering to herself, "See, there's nothing to it. It's no big deal. I don't know why you all have to make such a big deal out of it." She washed the thin, sensitive skin quickly and efficiently, but without gentleness. She was so consumed by her own rage that she didn't realize she was hurting Mae until her mother flinched. She looked up from her work to see tears in Mae's eyes.

"I know it's ridiculous, but every little thing seems to hurt now," said Mae apologetically.

Sarah looked from Mae to Keith, then back to Mae. Then she burst into tears, collapsing in a chair. "I can't do anything right," she sobbed. "Everything I try to do to help you is wrong. You don't like what I fix to eat; you don't appreciate the fact that I want to be with you. You just want to do this your own way—with nothing left for Sarah Louise."

"Sarah!"

"It's true. You could have moved in with us, so that I could take care of you, but what do you do? You take up with a certifiable weirdo and the town gossip."

"I'm just trying to avoid being a burden—"

Sarah Louise laughed. It was an ugly sound.

"As Melody would say, 'Give it up, Mom.' You're not

doing this for my benefit. You've never cared that I felt left out. It was always you and Karen and Terry. Now it's you and Keith and Edith, and I'm left out again. I shouldn't be surprised, actually. That's how it's always been."

"I didn't mean to leave you out—"

"Maybe not, but you did! I couldn't write, I couldn't sing or play the piano very well, I didn't get into books the way the rest of you did, so you just pushed me off to one side. But there are other things besides that, you know. I can knit and sew and quilt; I can do crewel and macramé, which is more than you can say for Karen. And I know how to manage money, something Terry never has been able to do, or your precious daddy, for that matter."

"Hey, I don't think this is a very good time—" began Keith, but Sarah Louise cut him off.

"It probably isn't, but since we've never got the truth out before, maybe it's a good idea to get it out now."

"What is the truth?" whispered Mae with quavery voice.

"The truth is, you've never loved me. I've needed a mother all my life, and I've never had one. I needed you to approve of me and to spend time with me, but you never did. In spite of that I thought, What the heck. Mom needs me now, and I'm going to be there. But you won't let me."

"I want you here, I do!" protested Mae. She was sitting up now, and her eyes were no longer flat and colorless. Her voice, when she continued, was strong. "I love you very much, Sarah Louise, but I'm still living and breathing, and I don't intend to be managed. I don't want to be treated the way you treat your children—"

"You stay out of this!" Sarah Louise said to Edith, who was standing with open mouth in the doorway. "This is between my mother and me! Now, just how do I treat my children?"

"Like pawns on a chess board. You wash them and dress them and schedule them and move them where *you* think they ought to be. What matters most to you is that they're clean and in place. It's easier for you to do the wash than it is for you to give a hug!"

"So all the times I did your wash don't count, is that what you're saying? Thanks a lot. It wasn't easy doing it,

177

you know. I mean, if you've got five washes a day, adding another two a week seems like an awful lot," Sarah Louise said, the words tumbling out of her mouth almost faster than she could articulate them.

"Sometimes I didn't want to do your wash, but I did it anyway. I came over and picked it up and washed it and folded it and brought it back, because it was a way to tell you that I cared about you. Maybe that is the only way I can, did you ever think of that? I even put it away where it belongs: the towels in the kitchen, the sheets in the linen closet, the bath mat in the bathroom. And in all that time, I never complained, even though I felt like it.

"I mean, here I am, wishing my mother would take care of me for once, but before that happens, I end up having to take care of her. The one that lives nearby is the one that has the most responsibility, you know. Karen can come and have a good time, Terry can flit in and out without a trace, but I'm here. No matter what I've got planned, no matter how busy the family is, I'm the one. I stop in the middle of what I'm doing—"

"I've never asked you to do that—"

"I stop in the middle of what I'm doing and come, no matter what. Only once have I ever really thought, What's the use? I can still remember that day. I was folding your wash, and I noticed that the rubber rings on that stupid nonslip bath mat were loose. I could have fixed it right then, I suppose, but I thought, Just for once, it can wait. Any old bath mat will do—"

Sarah Louise stopped in the middle of what she was saying as the words penetrated her consciousness. "Oh! It was that old blue bath mat! I just threw it on your bathroom floor because I was in a snit . . ."

"Oh no," whispered Mae.

"It was, wasn't it? It was that old blue bath mat! I put it in your bathroom because I was tired of always taking care of everybody else—it was my fault you slipped and fell!"

"Sarah Louise—"

"If I hadn't done it, you wouldn't be in that bed right now," cried Sarah Louise, her voice rising hysterically.

"That's not true. They would have found it sooner or later."

"You'd be out in your garden, pulling up invisible weeds. You'd be riding up to Five Springs for a picnic with Edith. You'd be planning to visit Terry or Karen."

"I'd be right where I am, anyway."

"It's true, Sarah Louise," interrupted Keith. "Your mom's fall is entirely separate from her illness. They have absolutely nothing to do with each other."

"I don't care what you say, you, you . . ." Sarah Louise searched her vocabulary and came up with the worst thing she could imagine: "You fat, crazy queer! It's my fault. Do you understand? It's my fault!"

She turned and raced from the room.

"Keith, help her. You heard her. She thinks she's to blame for this," pleaded Mae.

"I heard her quite clearly," he said coldly. "And she is to blame for your falling."

"You know she didn't mean what she said about you. And so what if she made a mistake—that's all it was, and it's not important now. But Sarah Louise is important—she can't handle this."

Keith finally nodded. "Okay. I'll go see if I can find her. Edith, take care of Mae."

"I will, you can count on it," said Edith, moving toward the bed.

Keith was already out the door when Mae called, "Tell her that I love her."

179

18

Is there no jumping-off place, no point of departure from which one can quietly leave without being tugged ever backward by some mortal tie? Mae wondered wearily.

She had thought she had done with all that. She had accepted or understood or at the very least made sense of the things that still weighed heavily. She had said what needed to be said, done what needed to be done. It obviously had not been enough.

Maybe Sarah Louise was right, she thought. Maybe I have been too busy doing it my own way to think of her. And it is true that I've always been more concerned about Karen or Terry. It always seemed like she didn't need me that much. But things aren't always as they seem—axiom number one of child-rearing theory.

She hadn't known that as she held her first child, cuddling the plump, pink infant to her, reveling in her baby-powder warmth. She had wanted a child so! As the time of delivery neared, she had anticipated the moment when she would finally be able to lavish her maternal love on a new human being. But it was not to be as she had dreamed. To her immense disappointment, she found that her baby girl didn't like cuddling. More often than not, the child pushed against Mae, seeking a certain distance.

It hurt the young mother, and the hurt didn't diminish as Sarah Louise grew. Though she knew she would be rebuffed, Mae touched the child whenever she could, reaching out to tousle the blondish hair, to hold a hand, to comfort a hurt. She was glad (and felt guilty that she was glad) whenever Sarah Louise fell ill, since that gave Mae her only chance to rock the child. She would rock and sing, then rock and sing some more, heedless of the tingling in her feet or the cramp in her arms: she was holding her child, whose limp, warm weight pressed against instead of away from her. The fact that Sarah Louise would tolerate and even welcome her father's embrace didn't help any.

In many ways, it was a relief when Karen arrived, scrawny and squalling, demanding the immediate touch of her mother's flesh against her own. Karen's need for Mae made it easy for Mae to let the cool, self-sufficient Sarah Louise have the privacy it seemed she wanted. Perhaps because of that, Sarah took the presence of Karen in stride. There was no sibling rivalry. Fritz was inordinately proud about the fact that his girl was not in the least jealous of baby Karen. It seemed inevitable that he spend so much time with Sarah Louise when he was home, glad enough to leave the never-quiet, never-still Karen to her mother's care.

That arrangement continued even after the birth of Terry: Fritz and Sarah Louise, Mae and Karen. The only thing that changed was the amount of time either parent had to give to the girls—it was considerably less than it had been because Terry drew a good portion of it to himself.

The distance between Sarah Louise and Mae grew even greater as the girl's natural preferences became known. She did not share her mother's love of nature and music. Worse still, she couldn't enter into the fantasy play that Mae loved to engage in with the other children. She thought it was stupid, and she didn't hesitate to tell her mother that she was an embarrassment.

"Why do you always have to make a game out of everything? Can't you ever be serious?"

"That's when I'm the most serious," Mae had replied.

"Daddy, can't you do something? Mother's making herself the laughing stock of Big Horn County."

"I doubt if it's all that bad."

"You're as ridiculous as she is!" fumed Sarah Louise, for she had caught her father winking at Mae.

"I just learned a long time ago that if I want your mother,

and I do, I have to take all of her—the outrageous part as well. Otherwise, I would have tossed her out the day she sewed one sleeve of every suit jacket shut."

"Only with the basting stitch!" Mae said, joining him in laughter.

"I don't think that's funny at all!"

"She wanted to get my attention, and she did," said Fritz.

"Doesn't she embarrass you?" Sarah demanded of her father.

"No. Not any more."

"She does me. How would you like to be known as the girl with the 'crazy mother'?"

"Nobody means that seriously."

"Maybe not, but it's still embarrassing."

"Okay. Point made," said Mae, no longer able to ignore her daughter's cold seriousness. "What do you want me to do?"

"Just stay out of my way, will you? I don't need any of your 'fun and games.'"

Sarah Louise was thirteen at the time. After the campaign debacle, she was even more removed, convinced that she had been right about her mother all along.

So it was that Mae watched her firstborn grow up, an observer of, more than a participant in, Sarah Louise's life. She was lovely but unreachable. She was intelligent but without warmth. She was successful in almost everything she undertook, but underneath it all she was sad.

Mae sensed that something was amiss, but being unable to identify what it was or what she should do, she chided herself for imagining things. After all, in other respects Sarah Louise was the kind of child other parents wished they had. She decided that their estrangement was only a case of differing personalities—it was just the way things were between parent and child sometimes.

There was more to it than that, Mae knew now. The scene that had just played itself out at her bedside was proof enough. Her daughter had needed something from her that she had not received. Or was it a case of not accepting what was given? It didn't really matter at this point.

The only thing that matters is getting Sarah Louise to give up the crazy idea that all this happened because she put the wrong bath mat on my floor, Mae thought. I just hope Keith can find her and talk to her.

It was a great relief when Keith called to say Sarah Louise was home and he was with her.

"I'll stop by when I leave," he assured Mae.

"You won't get much sleep today, I'm afraid," said Mae. "I'm sorry about that."

"No problem."

When Keith did come back to Mae's some time later, she asked anxiously, "How is she?"

"Not so good. Finding out she caused your accident has pretty well wiped her out."

"Couldn't you convince her that the accident and my sickness weren't connected?"

"In her head, she knows that already, Mae. In her heart, she feels guilty."

"But I'm not angry at her. I don't blame her for any of it."

"She knows that, too, but there's more than just the accident."

"What do you mean?"

"Are you sure you want me to go into it now? This hasn't been the best morning for you."

"I feel all right. In fact, I feel better than I have for days. It's amazing how much strength a little crisis can mobilize. What's the story?"

"I guess she's been mad at you for a long time."

"Why?"

"She feels like she has been on the outside looking in all her life."

"I thought so," sighed Mae, "but that was a choice she made a long time ago."

"Maybe, but she's hurting bad now. She needs to make a connection with you while she can."

Tears hung on Mae's lashes. Keith took her hand in one of his and, with the other, wiped them away.

"I need that too," she whispered. "I've wanted it for so long. But how are we going to do something we've never been able to do before?"

"It won't be as hard as you think, babe."

"Really?"

"Nope. We're going to get a start on it tomorrow."

"How?"

"Mae, how would you feel about having Sarah Louise take care of you in the mornings?"

The hand in his grew tense.

"Easy, babe. I'm not going to let you get hurt. I don't mean tomorrow morning, I mean in a few days, after I've had the chance to teach her what to do and how to do it."

"If she did, would that mean you wouldn't be coming anymore?"

"No way. Where else can I get the kind of breakfast I get here? And in the presence of two gorgeous females?"

"Is she willing to let you teach her?"

"She says she is. We've already set a time. And by the way, she's going to come on over a little later, after lunch probably. Are you okay with that?"

Mae nodded.

"I've got to get going now. I still have to sleep sometime today."

Mae pulled him down so that his darkly stubbled cheek rested on hers and put her thin arms around him. "Thank you," she whispered. Then she kissed him.

As she waited for Sarah Louise to come, Mae wondered if anything would have been different had Sarah Louise lived as far away from Shelton as Karen or Terry. Maybe, she thought.

Maybe Sarah Louise would have crossed Mae's name off her list of people to take care of. At the very least, she wouldn't have been so immediately available to do things for Mae that Mae could very well do for herself. But managing her mother's life in any and every way possible was an obsession with Sarah Louise.

It came down to a battle of wills. Sarah Louise was serene in the certainty that her viewpoint on any and every subject was the one correct viewpoint. She was very young when this stubborn need to convince everyone that her way was right began to manifest itself, and the person she challenged most often was her mother.

"I don't know how I ever got a daughter like Sarah," Mae commented one day to her mother, Lenore. "We can't agree on anything. She doesn't like the way I do my hair; she thinks I'm a lousy cook . . ."

"Well?" remarked Lenore with raised eyebrows.

"Okay, I don't like to cook, but is that a crime?"

"No."

"The thing that gets me is that even when I do start a nice meal, Sarah is right there giving orders and criticizing. Then I blow up, and she gives me her 'Oh *Mother*' look. My only salvation is to get out of the kitchen altogether. Of course, then I'm a total failure, as far as she's concerned." Mae sighed heavily. "There's no way out."

"Why do you think she does that?"

"It's her dad," said Mae grimly. "She has this thing about her dad."

What had once been a comfortable division of labor (Fritz taking over with Sarah Louise when Karen was born) had developed into a contest that first amused and then terrified Mae. Sarah Louise was her daddy's girl—she resented any indication that there was a woman in her daddy's life who was more important than she was. When she grew old enough to understand that Mae was first in her father's life, she began a campaign to prove that Mae wasn't worthy of that position.

Mae had never been in the habit of greeting Fritz at the door when he came home from work. Usually she just called out to him from her position in front of the stove, where she was preparing dinner.

Sarah Louise began welcoming her father at the door with exaggerated solicitation. She began doing her father's shirts, which Mae had never been able to starch and press to Fritz's satisfaction. She began putting an extra polish on Mae's passable housekeeping and never failed to point out to Fritz that she was the one who had done it, while her mother was out in the hammock reading a book.

She also began reading everything her father wrote in the editor's column of the *Journal* and made a great show of commenting on it during dinner. She made fun of Mae's thirst for knowledge ("What good does it do her, anyway?

She never leaves Shelton.") and criticized her frank way of speaking and her sometimes risqué jokes. Sarah's behavior didn't do much for a good mother/daughter relationship.

Mae was able to survive all of that with some equanimity, mostly due to the sympathetic support of her husband, but she was furious when she found out that Sarah Louise was going around explaining her to anyone who would listen. Sarah seemed obsessed with the necessity of making a respectable woman out of 'crazy Mae.'

She was still doing it, years after her father's death.

Fritz had died at a relatively young age. He was fifty-seven when stricken by a heart attack while sitting at his desk in the *Shelton Journal* office. It was over quickly—he was gone before the ambulance arrived.

Mae had been looking forward to spending many years in comfortable companionship with the man she had married thirty-seven years previously. She had never even considered that such a thing could happen, for Fritz had seemed the epitome of health. She was completely devastated, and in the aftermath she allowed Sarah Louise to run interference. It saved her the emotional strain and seemed to be her daughter's way of coping with the situation.

Sarah Louise continued in that mode long after the difficult first months were past, doing her mother's wash, coming in to clean once a week, and organizing little get-togethers meant to pry her mother out of the house. And explaining her mother's behavior.

Mae had needed none of these services. She had always had an extraordinarily rich inner life, and her abiding curiosity in the world around her had not diminished. Aside from the irritations incident to advancing age, such as stiff joints, lack of stamina, and increased weight, she had been pleased with her life.

Sarah Louise—my social director, house-cleaner, and apologist, Mae thought now as she waited for her daughter to come. It's not much in the way of a mother/daughter relationship, and I'm not sure we can change anything at this late date.

The tension of waiting made it impossible for Mae to rest as she usually did in the afternoon.

"Why don't you just call and find out when she's coming?" suggested Edith.

"Because I don't want to talk to her over the phone."

"I'll go in the back bedroom when she comes. I seem to be spending a lot of time there."

"I'm sorry about that. I don't suppose you thought you were signing up for 'The Continuing Story of Mae Thomlinson' when you agreed to move in."

"No. But it has kept things lively around here, you have to admit that."

Sarah Louise finally came, pausing hesitantly in the doorway before approaching her mother's bedside. Her hair was disheveled, her eyes were puffy, and her nose was red and raw from crying.

"I'm sorry," she said in a choked voice.

"For what?"

"For everything. For being such a rotten daughter. No wonder you liked being with Karen more than me."

"You aren't a 'rotten daughter.'"

"I sure haven't been a very good one."

"And I haven't been the best of mothers, either."

"I didn't let you—"

"Sarah, don't get on a guilt trip. Exaggerating whatever problems we've had won't help any."

"I guess not. But I am sorry. I don't know why I said all those things. I wish you would pretend it never happened."

"What good would that do? You said them because that was how you felt. There must be some truth to it."

"A little, maybe."

"Sarah, do you know I love you?" asked Mae.

When Sarah finally answered, her voice was thick with emotion. "I know it, but I don't think I feel it."

"You've never let me hug you, really hug you, for as long as I remember," said Mae, the hunger strong within her. "I've wanted to for so many years. Will you let me now?"

Sarah Louise began to cry, and she gingerly moved into the circle of her mother's arms.

187

19

"Is tomorrow all right?" Sarah Louise asked her mother.

"Yes," said Mae, but the hesitation was obvious.

"I can do it, Mom. I've learned a whole lot more in the last few days than just how to give a sick person a bath. I guess I've got this thing about touching and being touched. But Keith's helping me out, and Edith's given me all her books to read. I've even driven over to Powell for a short course on the hospice program. This is really important to me. It's like the last chance I have . . ."

"We'll do just fine," said Mae, touched by her daughter's earnest need.

Nevertheless, Mae was frightened at the prospect of having Sarah Louise bathe her, not only because of her tender skin, but also because the two of them had rarely communicated through touch. To Mae's relief though, Keith also came the next morning.

"I thought I'd tag along and watch my best pupil in action," he said to mother and daughter, who were both visibly nervous. Then to Sarah Louise he added, "Don't worry. You've really learned well."

"How is she at foot rubs?" Mae asked mischievously.

"Pretty good, as long as you don't ask her for one on Sundays." After he helped Sarah Louise assemble what she needed, he said, "Well, you're on. I'm going to sit over here where I'm out of your way."

A flash of fear crossed her face. "I don't know—"

"You'll do just fine, dear," said Mae, and Keith nodded his encouragement.

Mae held her breath as Sarah Louise moved the covers to expose part of her mother's body. At the sight of the emaciated limbs, so thin in contrast to the grotesquely swollen stomach, Sarah's face took on a pinched look.

Mae had to close her eyes—though she knew how her body looked, Sarah's reaction had made her acutely aware at that moment of how ugly she looked. When she finally felt courageous enough to open her eyes again, the look of disgust had been replaced by compassion. And as Sarah began her task, her face reflected her complete concentration.

Mae's fear that Sarah Louise might not be gentle enough was quickly laid to rest. Her daughter's hands were uncertain but always tender and careful. When the bath was finished, Mae said in a voice trembling with pride and love, "You did a fine job, dear."

"Couldn't have done it better myself," Keith commented.

"Thank you—for everything," Sarah Louise said to him. Mae was no less surprised than he was when Sarah Louise hugged him.

After he left, Sarah said, "I've learned a lot from your friend, Mother. And not just how to give you a bath."

"He is a good teacher, isn't he?"

"Yes. Did I tell you he's going to help Mark with his Eagle Scout project? Ron and I have been trying to get Mark to do it for years. You know how it is. If a kid doesn't get his Eagle before he's fourteen, he most likely won't get it at all. Well, Keith suggested to Mark that he teach first aid to fourth and fifth graders. Then he helped Mark fill out the papers to submit to the Scout board of review for approval. Mark just found out that he can go ahead with it."

"That's wonderful!"

"I can't tell you how pleased I am. All the talking Ron and I did got us nowhere."

"Sometimes it takes someone other than parents to teach a child."

Sarah Louise saw the glint of humor in her mother's eyes, and she smiled ruefully. "Sometimes it does."

After that, Sarah Louise came every morning about

seven o'clock and waited quietly until Mae awoke. In the morning stillness, they would greet each other in soft voices or spend a moment holding hands. Then, when Mae indicated she was ready for her bath, Sarah Louise would bring in the basin of warm water and the cloth, and with careful, unhurried motions, bathe her mother.

Because Mae's skin was so fragile, Sarah Louise gave her mother a full bath only every third or fourth day, alternating with what Keith called a "PTA" bath. Mae, whose emaciated muscles were tense the first few times, soon regretted her lack of faith and trust in her daughter.

However, despite the fact that Sarah Louise's skill and ability to nurture through touch were developing rapidly, Mae was still uncomfortable. Searching for the reason, she realized that, while she had not minded someone else caring for her physical needs, this flip-flop of the parent/child role was disconcerting. She was now the helpless one, with full consciousness of her incapacity. Mae took another step toward peaceful resolution when she accepted that as also being part of the process.

The time shared by mother and daughter became the most important part of the day. Sarah Louise's strong fingers were gentle on Mae's delicate skin, and Mae felt a current of physical comfort flow between them at the point of contact. "It feels so good," she would comment.

"For me too," Sarah Louise would reply.

Often Sarah Louise would finish what had become for her a sacramental task by putting her arms around Mae. At such times, Mae thought her daughter's face was more beautiful than it had ever been.

As a new mother, Mae had come to know and love her other babies through stroking, bathing, cuddling, and kissing them; they in turn had come to know and love her through her touch. That bonding process had not taken place between Mae and Sarah Louise at the time of Sarah's birth. Now, as Mae's death approached, they were learning to love one another through touch.

Karen, who had come in response to a call from Sarah Louise, was moved to tears as she watched her sister perform the loving task.

"Would you like to?" Sarah Louise offered Karen the washcloth.

"No," said Karen, shaking her head. "I just want to watch."

Later she said, "Something's happened between you two, hasn't it? I can tell just by the way you look at each other."

Sarah and Mae smiled at the same time, and Sarah bent to embrace her mother.

"Hey, don't leave me out," Karen protested, and joined the circle.

One day while Karen was still there, the two of them approached their mother's bed.

"What is this?" asked Mae. "An official delegation? A posse? You look mighty grim."

Karen looked at Sarah Louise.

"Well," began Sarah, as firmly as she could with her childish voice, "I learned in the hospice program that it's best to be real frank about things, and I, well, is there something you want . . . "

"For my funeral? Yes. As a matter of fact, there is. I want the ward choir to sing."

"That goes without saying. But is there some song in particular that you'd like?" Sarah Louise asked, pencil poised.

"I do have something particular in mind, but it's not a song."

"What?"

"The *German Requiem* by Brahms. The whole thing."

Karen laughed right out loud, and Mae chortled as Sarah Louise's face dropped.

"You don't want that," protested Sarah Louise. "You're just saying that to get me going."

"Oh, but I do. I don't suppose I can have it though, unless we import the Tabernacle Choir."

"We could always ask," said Karen.

"Oh, for heaven's sake. We can't ask for that, and you know it. Who wants to sit for two hours and listen to nothing but the choir? Besides, it's not very personal. Usually we—"

Sarah Louise stopped as Mae waved a warning finger. "If you're really interested in hearing what I want, then don't interpret what I say or try to change my mind."

"Sorry," Sarah Louise said, chagrined.

"I'm going to be 'crazy Mae' to the end, you know. In any case, I happen to know that the ward choir is practicing a song from the *Requiem*. And if I can't have the whole thing, one song will do."

"Which one?"

"'How Lovely Is Thy Dwelling Place.'"

"That'll be beautiful, Mom," commented Karen.

"Is that from the *Requiem?*" asked Sarah Louise. "I didn't know. Well, as long as they're practicing it anyway—" A sudden suspicion stopped her in midthought. "Mother, you haven't been talking to the choir director, have you?"

"What, me?"

"You sneak," laughed Karen.

"I don't believe it!" Sarah Louise put down the pencil and paper.

"But I haven't, and that's the truth. 'Course I might have mentioned it to Melody when she was visiting once."

"How much of this have you already got planned?" asked Karen.

"Nothing else, except . . . "

Sarah Louise sighed.

"Except I'd like Keith to have some part in it."

"Mom—" began Sarah Louise, then she stopped. "I'm sorry. I do seem to be having a hard time letting you be you. What would like him to do?"

"I don't know, but something more than just using his muscles."

"Are you sure? He isn't family, and besides, not everyone can just stand up and say something in that . . . situation."

"He will. I've hinted to him that I want him to talk. He can explain what these past months have meant better than anyone else."

"Maybe you're right. Okay, anything else?"

"I'd like Howard to play 'Whispering Hope' at the funeral—and afterward I want bluegrass."

Both girls laughed. "You're incorrigible," said Karen.

"Probably. I'd like Brent to give the family prayer and Ron to read the obituary, and if you would, I'd like you two to give tributes."

"Mom, what about Terry?"

"Have Terry dedicate the grave."

"It won't seem like much to him."

"I'm sorry about that, but I don't want him to give a tribute. I'm a real person, Karen, not the paragon of virtue he would make me out to be."

When they had finished the planning, Sarah Louise sighed with satisfaction. "Well, that's taken care of," she said. "Is there anything else you'd like us to do?"

"Find a home for my trees. And give me some time alone with Karen."

Sarah Louise stood up awkwardly. "There're plenty of things I need to be doing at home . . ."

"Sarah. There's enough love in me for both of you; don't you know that yet?" Mae held out her arms, and Sarah Louise bent to receive her mother's kiss. Then, to Mae's great satisfaction, Sarah hugged her sister as well. In that moment, Mae knew that her two daughters had crossed over the barriers that had kept them from trust and intimacy for so many years.

After Sarah Louise's departure, Mae motioned to the bonsai in the greenhouse. "Take your pick," she said to Karen, but Karen didn't move.

"Go ahead," encouraged Mae gently.

"It's too much like saying good-bye," said Karen, beginning to weep.

"Yes. Because that's what it is."

Then Mae began speaking softly, saying all that she wanted to say. It was the first of many such private sessions with the ones she loved.

Not all of those sessions were satisfying, for even in the face of the obvious, there were those who didn't want to say the final words. Her brother Howard, for one, and for another, Sarah Louise, who, having just found her mother, was unwilling to contemplate her loss. And, surprisingly, Edith. "We don't need any fancy farewell scene," she said tersely. "We've always been honest with one another; we've never held back how we felt. We don't need to make any formal statement now."

It was much the same with Brent, whose sympathy, empathy, and honesty had been a support from the first. He never understood Mae's intent the day they talked in private—that visit had seemed no different to him than any of the other private times they had had together. Mae realized it was so because he had never hedged, or tried to ignore, her steadily worsening condition. Nor had either of them been reticent about acknowledging the feelings they had for each other. The realization of his constancy made their final moments together especially precious to her.

Ron had understood her purpose. His acceptance of her need to know that all loose threads had been tied allowed her to say exactly what she wanted to. She was able to tell him how she had admired his strength in staying with and loving Sarah Louise, and how she appreciated his way of handling the M and Ms. At the end of their time together, Mae's kiss was both a benediction and a blessing.

Unexpectedly, Keith was the one who was most upset when she spoke to him. Before she had gotten half a sentence out of her mouth, he laid his head upon the covers beside her and began to weep.

"Why, Keith," she said, astonished. "Don't cry."

The covers muffled the words he spoke so Mae couldn't understand him. "What is it?" she asked tenderly, stroking his unruly curls.

"I love you, do you know that?" he asked without lifting his head.

"Yes. And I love you. You are more a son to me than my own son."

When he was able to speak he said, "I don't know how to tell you what you mean to me."

"I thought you were doing fine already, dear."

He raised his head. "It was karma that brought us together. Mine and yours. I needed to know something you could teach me—"

"And I needed to have you with me during this time,"

she finished for him. "Keith, are you going to be all right after . . ."

He smiled. "I know how I want to live the rest of my life now, and I've gotten quite fond of Shelton. I've made a few friends among the reprobates of the community. No, don't look worried. Things are going much better for me. The nurses on my shift now think I'm okay. I'm doing a lot in scouting, and I get along well with the teacher you introduced me to. He's taking me hunting this fall."

"You be careful," said Mae.

"Yes, Ma'am," he said, like a dutiful child.

The planning of the funeral and the private sessions weren't the only indication of how close the end was. Mae had been giving away little pieces of her life for the last few months. Some of her books on Wyoming history went to Howard; her gardening books she gave to different friends; her church books (filled with comments in the margins) were all marked with the names of her children and grandchildren. Many of the cups and saucers from her collection she gave to friends when they visited; others went in the boxes of things she had sorted out for her children. The gifts she had received from friends and relatives over the years she returned to the givers; and odd arrowheads, fossils, and geodes were presented to neighborhood children.

Those moments were poignant but not painful. On the contrary, Mae was reveling in a wonderful feeling of order and accomplishment as one possession after another left the little white house. Her sense of self was not diminished as the shelves grew empty; in fact, it grew stronger, for she realized that it was not dependent upon things.

Giving away her plants was something else.

She gave away the first one on impulse. Little Samantha, despite her mother's injunction, came with a handful of flowers one afternoon when the stoplight on the front door showed green. They weren't flowers, actually; they were weeds. Small blossoms crowned the straggly stalks, but the bouquet was beautiful, nonetheless. As she accepted the gift, Mae said, "And I have something for you. You may choose a plant to take home."

"Oh!" said Samantha, astonished and thrilled. "D-does it matter which?"

"Except for the bonsai, any plant you pick is yours."

"I l-like that one with the fuzzy l-leaves," the girl said shyly.

"Which one? Oh, that's a violet. Her name's Milly."

"Do they all have n-names?"

"Yes. Every living thing needs to have its own name, but it doesn't matter if you call Milly something different."

"It's a nice name. I'll k-keep it."

That, more than anything else was what prompted Mae to announce to Keith the next morning, "We're getting closer, aren't we?"

His eyes glistened, but he said steadily, "Yes."

"Am I doing okay?"

"You're a champion."

"There's just one thing that worries me . . ."

"What's that?"

"My trees. I'm going to give the last two indoor bonsai to Sarah Louise's oldest children, Mark and Melody. But the others . . ."

"There must be somebody."

"Yes, but who? I thought of giving them to Edith, but sooner or later she'd have the same problem I've got. Then I thought of the city—if Lovell can be the Rose City, why couldn't Shelton be the Bonsai City? But bonsai aren't like roses; there's not anyone else in Shelton who cares about them but me."

"How about the University of Wyoming. They have a horticulture department—maybe they'd take them."

"They would, if I left them enough money to establish the Mae B. Thomlinson Memorial Bonsai Garden. But what if there's nobody in the department who cares. I want them to go to someone who cares."

"I could take them."

Her eyes misted. "Thank you, Keith, but where would you put them? Apartments don't come with yards, do they? We'll have to come up with something else."

But that very day, Mae's worry about her bonsai was dispelled by a telephone call from Karen, who had gone back to Minneapolis a few days earlier.

"I know who you can give your bonsai to, Mother," she said excitedly.

"Who?"

"His name's Kevin Oshima. He lives on St. Mary's Point on the St. Croix River, and he's an expert in bonsai. He's probably the only specialist in the pure art of bonsai in the whole country, and if not that, he's for sure the youngest."

"Oh."

"What's the matter? I thought you'd be excited about this."

"If he's an expert, he won't want my bonsai."

"Oh, yes he will. I talked to him about you and told him how you got started. He said it didn't matter if your trees weren't the most well-trained. He said, 'The preservation of the tree is the most important thing. If the tree is preserved, it will get better.' How about that!"

"How did you get to know him?" Mae's voice was once more animated.

"You know how I like to go out to the University of Minnesota's arboretum when I'm feeling down. Well, the other day when I was out there, he was giving a talk on bonsai in the auditorium. You wouldn't believe this, Mom, but he actually has some bonsai that Japanese in other internment camps started. When their children inherited the bonsai, they didn't know what to do with them, so they sent them to Kevin. He's studied with some of the last old masters in Japan and has bonsai trained by them in his garden too. Yours will be in good company."

"It seems like a long way to ship them. They might not make it."

"You don't need to worry about shipping them, Mom. Kevin's collected bonsai from remote places all around the world, and he's gotten them safely home. He gave me instructions. I have them all written down, and I'll mail them to you tomorrow."

In the pause following Karen's words, she could hear her mother weeping.

"It's going to be okay, Mom," she said in a choked voice.

"I know. It's just that this means so much to me."

"It means a lot to me too. Kevin's garden isn't that far away from me, you know. I can go visit your bonsai whenever I want." Karen could barely articulate the next words, "It'll be like visiting you."

When she hung up the phone, Mae realized that the last unfinished task had been taken care of. "Now I can go," she said to herself. "Now it's time."

But it wasn't that easy. The next days went by as had the previous days—the only difference was an internal one. Mae was not trying to hold on anymore; the world around her was no longer pertinent. Thus, she didn't open her eyes when the doorbell rang one day.

It was Bobby of the green hair—she could tell by the voice as she lay with her eyes closed, feigning sleep.

"I didn't know," he said, his manly voice betraying his emotions. "I've been at my cousin's in Tucson since school got out. Now it's too late, I guess."

"Too late for what?" Sarah Louise asked gently.

"Her glider. I wanted to make her one, but I didn't think I had time, so I brought over ours. I don't suppose she'll ever sit in it, now."

Mae had begun shutting out everything around her, but the sound of Bobby's voice reached deeply and roused her. "Sit in what?" she asked, trying to push herself up.

"Let me help you," said Sarah Louise. Putting her arm behind her mother, she slowly raised Mae up. "See, Mom, Bobby's here. He's brought you a present."

"My glider," said Mae firmly.

Bobby nodded. "I would have brought it sooner, but I had to visit my dumb cousin in Tucson. I'm sorry. Maybe I shouldn't have brought it at all."

Mae's grip tightened on Sarah Louise's hand. "I want to sit in that glider!" she said.

"Oh, I don't think—" began Sarah, but the strength of Mae's fingers brought her to an abrupt halt. "Bobby, you hold the door open. Edith, come in here, we need you."

Edith rushed into the room, expecting the worst.

"Help me," Sarah Louise commanded, her wispy voice

198

taking on strength and authority. "We're going to take Mother out to sit in her glider."

The two women maneuvered Mae out of her bed and into her bathrobe. Then, in a slow and solemn promenade, they all but carried her out into the front yard, where the glider sat under the biggest of the trees as if it had always belonged there. They eased her onto the redwood seat of the glider, then Sarah Louise motioned to Bobby.

"Go ahead; sit by her."

Bobby sat down on one side of Mae, and Sarah Louise sat on the other, bookending Mae into an upright position.

"I wanted you to have this," Bobby said, fighting against tears, "because you were my favorite teacher. I bet you didn't know that, but you were. And you're the only one who still treats me like a person instead of a pile of—you know what," he finished lamely.

"You're a good boy," murmured Mae, clutching at his sleeve. "Best boy I ever had in class. You remember that. You don't need this," she said, waving a bony finger at his hair. "You don't have to try so hard to be special."

Bobby began crying, and long after Edith and Sarah Louise had taken Mae back to her bed, he was still sitting on the glider.

It was the last time she left her bed, and as the days went by, she talked less and laughed less too. She ate virtually nothing, except the 'malt,' and she slept away a good part of each day. She realized she was withdrawing from the world around her, severing all the binding ties. While she was grateful to have been granted time to do that, she was exasperated because it was taking so long.

The process of withdrawal was noticed by all and misinterpreted by most. Mae was aware that visitors were often offended by the fact that she didn't seem to be pleased when they came, but she was too weary to care. She was no longer 'crazy Mae'; she was a dying woman.

"This part of me is as real as the other," she complained. "If they were willing to take me as I was before, why can't they take me as I am now?"

"They don't know it's part of the process, dear," said Edith.

"Well, why doesn't somebody tell them?" she asked querulously.

"I will if you want me to, but I think it would be better if you did."

"I can't. Someone else is going to have to fight this part of the battle for me."

"I still think you should be the one to tell the M and Ms."

Mae fretted, but she knew Edith was right. She had to speak to her dear grandchildren, who filed in, only to stand confused and miserable at her bedside. Gone was the ruffled bedcap, gone were the funny accent and the rented movies. And the plants were going, too, leaving the room with a naked look, as if the owner were in the process of moving.

The next day, Mae requested the presence of all the children at two in the afternoon. After they arrived, Edith switched the stoplight to red.

"Come here, my darling children," Mae commanded with a firmness achieved at great cost. One at a time, they approached the bed to get a kiss and hug from their grandmother. It wasn't really much of a hug; they put their arms awkwardly around her thin shoulders as she reached for them with weak hands.

"Now, there's something I want you to do," she said in a strong voice. "I want you to take down that cardboard contraption." She pointed at the bow that was still affixed to the foot of her bed, the bow that for weeks had been plowing onward through the seas toward the East.

"But why?" protested Michael.

"Because, dear, this voyage can't go on forever. Even Caspian finally reached a point where he could go no further. Then, only one person from the *Dawn Treader* was allowed to proceed to the ends of the earth. Remember who it was?"

Of course they remembered. They had finished reading *The Voyage of the Dawn Treader* aloud in that very room not so long ago.

"Reepicheep, the mouse," said Michael, who had begun to cry noisily. He was joined by the older M and Ms, who knew what she was going to say. Anticipation made the next words easier to hear, yet at the same time, harder.

"We've come to the end of our voyage, children," said Mae, and her sorrow was so great she could barely speak. "For weeks now, our own little *Dawn Treader* has gone straight into the morning sun, day after day. And now, we have reached the point beyond which the *Dawn Treader* can't go."

"But Gram—" protested Morgan.

"Only one person can go on to the Utter East, my sweet, sweet children, and that person is me. Very soon, I must go on without you, and you must return to your own world."

"Do you have to?" asked little Matt, who was crying with the kind of abandon and disregard for appearances that only the very young possess.

"Yes. It seems terrible right now, I know, but it will be as great an adventure for me as it must have been for Reepicheep. Only it's hard for me. It takes all of my energy, and I don't have any left to have fun with you anymore."

"We don't care!" said Michael.

"I know you don't, dear," said Mae gently. "I just want you to understand what is going to be happening. From now until I go, you will find me pretty dull company. I'll sleep a lot of the time; sometimes I won't even know you've come. And even when I do, I probably won't talk much; in fact, this is my last big speech."

Mae grinned suddenly at her two oldest grandchildren. "How was it? For a last big speech, I mean."

"I think you're going to have to work some more on it," said Melody. "You can't go until you've got it perfect."

Thus the hospital bed shed its *Dawn Treader* disguise. When Brent came that evening, its absence was the first thing he noticed. He stopped abruptly in the doorway, an odd expression on his face.

"What's wrong?" asked Mae.

"Your boat-thing. It's gone."

"Yes. I had the kids take it down."

After a long silence he said, "So you don't go in for dramatic scenes anymore?"

"No," she whispered, remembering. "It's curtain time."

That was the last time Mae met life straight on.

20

The next day, Edith changed the stoplight to red; she never changed it back again.

The room Mae occupied was no longer a living room. On the table stood various medications, disposable syringes, a bottle of special massage oil, a jar of moisturizer, and an emesis basin. Crushed ice in a plastic pitcher and Mae's personal soap and towels were on the bottom shelf of the table. Next to it was a plastic-lined trash can, and a portable commode stood where the wing back had been.

Her emaciated body lay on a bed especially made up with a spongy "egg carton" cushion between the mattress and the bottom sheet to help protect her fleshless body from developing bedsores. Under her heels, where the pressure could most easily turn the skin from red to white to ulcered in a matter of hours, was a square of lambskin. Mae no longer actually wore her nightgowns—Edith had slit them up the back because the seam there could also damage her skin.

The daily routine was simple: Mae lay passively as Sarah Louise bathed her with warm water to which a little oil was added, taking time to put moisturizer on her face, hands, and feet. The massage with the specially formulated oil came next, and then Sarah would help her brush her teeth—sometimes even doing the actual brushing—and her hair. She took less food every day, but when she did take food, it was only the Ensure "malt." She rarely drank anything except the liquid morphine she took every two or three hours. When her mouth was too dry, she asked for ice chips. When she needed to use the commode, someone had to help her. She didn't always make it. The diapers were now a reality. She was unable to do anything for herself, and it didn't matter to her anymore.

"Why is it taking so long?" she asked Keith one day.

"I don't know, babe. You're just too tough, I guess."

So the days dragged on and on, each with a terrible external sameness, made even more so by the fact that her focus was entirely inward. Her consciousness of her physical self had diminished, except when she was ravaged by pain. It was as if her essential self were withdrawing bit by bit from her extremities in preparation for the final departure.

Those who watched and waited with her were few: Sarah Louise and Ron, Brent Weinberg, her brother Howard and his wife, her sister Susan (whose visit had come too late), her bishop, and Keith. They watched and waited in silence, except when they spoke in subdued tones to one another or when Howard, unable to articulate his sorrow, played plaintive tunes on his violin.

Dr. Melton, who checked in now and then, approved of the way Keith was orchestrating things in the little house on Cook Street. He never stayed very long when he came, however—there was little he could do.

For Mae, there was no easy way out; neither was there any way to hurry the process. It progressed at its own pace, inexorably but slowly. Soon, Mae had to have a pillow between her knees even when lying on her back, and she had to be rotated every two hours. She ingested virtually nothing, and no one forced food or drink upon her.

"Have I eaten today?" she asked one evening.

"No," said Edith. "Do you want something?"

Mae shook her head.

Another evening, Edith asked, "What would you like me to tell you about? Do you want to know what's happening in Washington, or in Hollywood, or right here in good old Shelton? What would interest you the most?"

"There's nothing that interests me."

"But there must be!"

"Not anymore."

When Terry called that evening, Edith asked Mae if she wanted to talk to him. Mae shook her head, her shrunken lips pressed tightly together. She did speak briefly to Karen, who called a little later, but when Karen asked if she could come out again, Mae was firm. "We've said everything we needed to say, haven't we?"

"Yes."

"Then don't come."

The first time she stopped breathing for an inordinately long time before resuming respiration, Edith panicked and called Keith, although Mae tried to assure her that she was all right.

Keith came immediately and went straight to Mae's bedside. After checking her vital signs, he smoothed her hair and smiled encouragingly, "You gave me a scare."

"I told Edith not to call you."

"She did the right thing. Now you just rest. Edith and I need to have a talk."

He led Edith into the kitchen and lowered his voice, but Mae could still hear him say, "I should have warned you about those pauses in breathing. They're called 'chain stoking.' They happen toward the end."

"But what should I do if she stops breathing again?"

Just let me stop! thought Mae, the words so loud in her ears she thought for a moment she had said them out loud. But Keith answered Edith's question with no sign that he had heard anything, "Call me or Dr. Melton. Whatever you do, don't call 911. Mae wouldn't want any heroic measures taken to prolong her life."

You're right about that, Mae thought. This is hard, harder than I imagined it would be. And enough is enough.

She thought about that often as the days dragged on and pain became the only reality. She still visualized her safe place; in fact, she lived in it most of the time. But it wasn't enough, for added to the pain caused by the rampantly growing tumors was the burning, excruciating pain that was the result of liver failure. No matter how careful Sarah Louise and Edith were to give the medication at the proper time, it was no guarantee against the pain, which could pounce out from some dark corner when least expected, causing Mae to weep and groan. Although she had once promised herself that she would not cry out no matter how bad the pain got, she was beyond caring who heard her or how it might affect them.

Again, Keith was the one who found a way to help. Sitting at her bedside, he would regulate his breathing to match Mae's, then he would gradually lengthen it out in an effort to smooth out her jerky, shallow inhalations. They would enter a meditative state as they breathed in and out together, and the breaths would lift Mae over the brakers and out to a smooth, less painful wave.

The first time Edith saw them in this state, she gasped.

"Don't do that again!" she cried. "You don't know how much it frightened me to see you like that. If I hadn't heard your breathing, I would have thought . . ."

"I'm sorry we startled you," said Keith.

"Don't stop," whispered Mae through dry lips. "It helps."

"The pain's real bad, isn't it," said Edith gently, touching Mae's gaunt cheek.

"It . . . it's *pushing* me. Sometimes I think it's a midwife . . . if I could just find the way out, it would birth me into another world."

But pain was an unhurried midwife—it took another whole week. By that time, the morphine dosage was so strong and Mae's inward focus was so consistent that she was rarely aware of the room around her or the people in it. Pain alone forced her to the surface. Yet on the last Friday of August, a little more than five months after she slipped and fell in her own bathroom, she opened her eyes to a room that was in surprisingly clear focus. And the first thing she saw was her greenhouse full of plants.

For a moment, she thought that the plant-laden table was only a dream; then she thought that her illness must have been a dream. She rose and walked over to the greenhouse—at least it seemed to her that she did. Then she saw her hand lying motionless by her side. She had not moved at all.

She looked back to the greenhouse—it was still there and

was still full of plants. She couldn't understand it, because she remembered having given them all away, except the bonsai, which were to stay until after she was gone. It bothered her, and without realizing it, she began to whimper.

"Mother, what is it?" asked Sarah Louise.

"The plants . . . where did they . . . come from?"

"I brought them over today," Sarah replied.

"I can't . . . take care . . ."

"I know. You don't have to, dear. They're mine."

The question in Mae's mind surfaced in her eyes. Sarah Louise answered it. "Melody helped me pick them out, and she's going to teach me how to take care of them. I had to get some, Mom. Your greenhouse looked too empty with nothing but the bonsai."

"Did I give . . . Karen . . . bonsai?"

"Yes, you did. She took it home with her."

Mae closed her eyes. A little while later she asked, "Terry?"

"Terry didn't take his, remember?"

"Keith. Give to . . . Keith."

"Are you sure you want me to?"

Mae nodded; the movement was so small as to be almost imperceptible. Without moving her head, she turned her eyes toward the bonsai.

Sarah Louise noticed where her glance was focused and said, "They are lovely, aren't they? You know, I've been watching them a lot lately. I never understood before why you thought they were so special, but they do grow on a person. They're each so *real*. I mean, each one of them sort of *demands* that you prune it a certain way. Or am I imagining things?"

"No." Mae thought she said the word, but she couldn't be certain.

"Like this one. It's been a while since you've worked on it, and it's getting straggly. Would you believe even I can tell where it needs to be clipped and where it needs to fill out?"

Sarah Louise walked over to the table on which the bonsai were sitting. Mae watched her as she turned one of them slowly around. "See, it's grown a little too bushy here, don't you think?"

Mae squinted her eyes as she tried to see the plant Sarah Louise was referring to. It didn't do any good. Everything was again becoming fuzzy and indistinct, and her field of vision was narrowing, as if the room were growing suddenly, unaccountably dark—a darkness that moved in from the periphery, leaving the indistinct image of Sarah Louise encircled by the remaining light. The glint of light on metal caught Mae's eyes—she saw her daughter pick up the small clippers and begin snipping, first tentatively, then with greater confidence.

Watching, Mae Thomlinson smiled.

It was an inner smile that almost, but not quite, reached her lips.